Th[...] seemed to
b[...] shaking

Momentarily losing control of the jetpacks, the men struggled to stay away from the walls as the tunnel started to break apart, wide cracks lancing along the interior making countless bricks fall free.

Desperately dodging out of the way, Cinco flew too low and scraped a boot heel across the floor, then Bolan went sideways to carom off the shuddering wall, sparks spraying off the housing as it rubbed the shattering bricks.

Suddenly a bright light filled the tunnel, and Bolan saw a monstrous fireball billowing toward them like the exhaust charge of a firing cannon.

"Fly or die!" he yelled, twisting the controls to the max.

Don Pendleton's Mack Bolan®

Oblivion Pact

A GOLD EAGLE BOOK FROM
W❂RLDWIDE®

TORONTO • NEW YORK • LONDON
AMSTERDAM • PARIS • SYDNEY • HAMBURG
STOCKHOLM • ATHENS • TOKYO • MILAN
MADRID • WARSAW • BUDAPEST • AUCKLAND

Recycling programs
for this product may
not exist in your area.

First edition September 2012

ISBN-13: 978-0-373-61555-1

Special thanks and acknowledgment to
Nick Pollotta for his contribution to this work.

OBLIVION PACT

Printed in U.S.A.

Our single most important challenge is to help establish a social order in which the freedom of the individual will truly mean the freedom of the individual. We must construct that people-centred society of freedom in such a manner that it guarantees the political liberties and the human rights of all our citizens.

—*Nelson Mandela*
May 25, 1994

We all face challenges, sometimes just to survive. Unfortunately it seems there is always someone, some group, who thinks they have the right to take what is ours. Over my dead body.

—*Mack Bolan*

PROLOGUE

Cancun, Mexico

Death watched from high above.

It was a scorching tropical night, the heat unforgiving in spite of a cool breeze coming off the ocean. A thumping techno beat filled the air with a palpable presence, the lyrics indistinct over the laughter of the drunken college students cavorting on the white sandy beach.

Standing on the balcony of his penthouse suite, Dalton Greene looked down on the raucous party with the impersonal gaze of a surgeon preparing to cut a tumor from the body of a patient.

"Enjoy yourselves while it lasts," Greene whispered, checking the load of the 10 mm Falcon pistol before tucking the weapon into its shoulder holster.

Neither handsome nor ugly, Greene was simply plain with an ordinary, easily forgettable face and nondescript features. Except for one. The man was huge, not fat, although he would have disagreed on that point, but genuinely enormous, well over seven feet tall and as broad as a gorilla.

Most people the billionaire did business with called him The Jolly Greene Giant, but never to his face. The one person who had been foolish enough to do that disappeared the next day, and was found a year later.

From what the New York coroner could ascertain, the man had been tortured, then allowed to heal, and tortured again, over and over, for weeks, until his head was smashed.

Whether the horrid story was true or not, the billionaire had done his best to circulate it worldwide, and the tale certainly fitted Dalton Greene's profile. He never got angry or upset, only even, and somehow he always managed to make a profit. Even from death.

"They call it spring break, right?" Greene asked over a shoulder, dispassionately watching the dozens of campfires blazing along the beach.

Hundreds of college students reveled in drunken celebration, singing to the techno beat, the combination creating a low growl.

"Yes, sir, spring break," Samantha LoMonaco answered, carefully loading a 12-gauge Neostead shotgun.

The lights were off in the palatial suite, making it easier for them to discreetly observe the party below. A dozen other people were in the suite, all of them checking a weapon, or adjusting the straps on military body armor.

"Ridiculous. A break from what?" Greene demanded. "The strenuous task of sitting in a comfortable chair in an air-conditioned room reading books?"

Working the pump-action on the Neostead, LoMonaco shrugged. "Americans are a ridiculous people, sir."

Easing a clip into an F88 assault rifle, a bearded man scowled. "I thought you came from America, Ms. LoMonaco?" he asked in a thick accent.

"I'm Australian now," LoMonaco stated with an air of pride. "Just like the rest of you."

A diminutive brunette with a full luscious figure,

Samantha "The Hammer" LoMonaco was a stunningly beautiful woman with lovely dark eyes and a smile so sweet that she often managed to talk her way out of traffic tickets and past security checkpoints.

Her long hair was tied in a ponytail to keep it from her face, and more importantly out of the breech of her weapon. Her nails were cut short, almost to the quick, to make it easier to reload her weapon.

She was also covered with tattoos. Although born in America, she had been raised in the slums of west Canberra, and at a very early age had started getting a tattoo for each confirmed kill.

The first killing had been done in the dark alley behind a bar where a drunken man was trying to assault her friend. LoMonaco grabbed a loose brick and pounded him to death. The next day her friend took LoMonaco to a tattoo parlor and paid for both of them to get matching stars on their wrists so they could always remember that night. As news of the incident spread, LoMonaco was quickly dubbed with the nickname The Hammer because of her assault with the brick.

Then another friend asked for her help with an abusive boyfriend, and LoMonaco earned a second tattoo, then a third, fourth, fifth.... Soon, she learned the terrible truth: blood was like whiskey. After enough of it had flowed, you didn't want the river ever to stop.

These days, LoMonaco carried a Gerber combat knife sheathed at the small of her back where it couldn't be easily seen. A boxy Glock 18 machine pistol was holstered at her side, and in her wallet was a fake credit card that contained a ceramic razor blade undetectable through airport security.

Officially, LoMonaco was registered as a profes-

sional bodyguard, and thus was allowed to carry fire-
arms in places where other people couldn't. In reality,
she was an assassin, a hired killer for Dalton Greene.

"Mr. Greene, the truck has arrived!" announced
David Thomas, adjusting the pipe in his mouth. Still
in the long process of trying to quit smoking, the man
was chewing on a briarwood pipe these days to help
control his urges.

Rolling out of the dunes, an electric flatbed truck
was trundling along the beach. The driver stopped at
each bonfire to drop off a plastic cooler, and briefly
speak to whomever was in charge.

As he drove away into the darkness, the eager college students dragged the coolers out of the light and
into the darkness. Minutes later, swarms of people descended on the area, many of them still talking on their
cell phones. In rapid order, the party escalated to a new
level of debauchery, as the students reeled about smoking what looked like homemade cigarettes. Their laughter became disjointed, and soon items of clothing started
coming off, which was a short procedure as most of
the students were wearing only bathing suits and flip-
flop sandals.

"Is that marijuana?" Thomas asked curiously, clipping a grenade to his belt. Dashingly handsome, the
man was an expert hacker, and always carried an Australian army combat laptop slung at his side.

"I ordered zooters," LoMonaco replied.

He scowled. "What's that?"

"Marijuana soaked in formaldehyde."

Thomas was stunned. "Isn't embalming fluid poi-
sonous?"

"Extremely." She laughed. "But first you get incredibly high."

"How much did you get?" Greene asked, raising an arm to shoulder height. He flexed his hand and a small .44 derringer slapped into his palm, then back out of sight.

"Five kilos."

Greene frowned. "Do we really need that much?"

"Probably not," LoMonaco said with a shrug. "But I assumed it would be better to have too much than too little.

"Agreed. Failure isn't an option," Greene said, then he turned and shouted the phrase. "Failure isn't an option!" Inside the darkened suite, the men and women of Operation Daylight repeated the words over and over as if it was a battle chant.

"Where are the whores?" Thomas asked, walking over to the balcony.

"They'll be here soon," Greene replied, strapping on body armor. It was as supersized as himself, but fitted perfectly, molded to his specific contours.

"And here they come," Victor Layne stated gruffly.

Unlike his giant employer, Victor Layne was fat, and didn't give a damn. His incredible physical strength was infamous from Adelaide to Christmas Island.

A few moments later, six more electric trucks rolled out of the dunes, each carrying dozens of shopworn but still mildly attractive women in skimpy bikinis or loose summer dresses. As the ocean breeze lifted the hem on one, it was clear that the woman wore nothing underneath but tan lines.

Taking LoMonaco by the arm, Greene pulled her

aside. "Samantha, are all the supplies ready at Compose?" he asked quietly.

She nodded. "All set, sir."

"Excellent," Greene said with a brief smile, then he turned. "Victor, what did you tell the colleges about the party?"

"That I was an alumni and just wanted to help the kids celebrate the big win."

"What big win?" Thomas asked.

Layne shrugged. "Who cares?"

"Alumnus," LoMonaco corrected, walking onto the balcony with the Neostead resting on a shoulder. "*Alumni* means several, *alumus* is the male singular."

Layne scowled. "You're kidding. *Alumnus?*"

"God's truth."

"Then God is an idiot," Layne snorted, walking back into the darkness.

Down on the beach, the party was starting to get out of control as naked people began running about, and numerous students were having sex on the beach. Mostly it was couples, but sometimes there were three people involved.

"Bah, sex on the beach," Thomas muttered in frank disapproval.

"It's sort of romantic," LoMonaco countered. "Even for these drunken fools."

"But the sand gets everywhere. And I do mean everywhere!"

"So you shower afterward," Layne contributed. "Let's let them enjoy what little time they have remaining."

Just then, they heard the crackling of explosions,

and suddenly rockets soared high into the night sky to explode into colorful blossoms.

"Fireworks," Greene grunted, sliding on clear surgical gloves. "Nice touch."

"Thanks," Layne said "I thought it might stimulate a faster response from the local PD."

Softly, in the distance police sirens howled. Soon flashing lights appeared along the coastal highway.

"How many?" Greene demanded, grabbing the banister with both hands, and squeezing tight. "How many did they send?"

"Six, eight…ten cars!" LoMonaco reported, dialing for enhancement on a US Army–issue monocular. Computer-operated, the device took the ambient light of the stars, blocked out the bonfires, and delivered a perfectly clear black-and-white image of the beachfront debauchery.

"Excellent," Greene exhaled, sliding on a ski mask. "Okay, time to go to work, people."

"Daylight!" Thomas shouted, brandishing a Colt revolver.

"Daylight!" the armed people in the suite repeated, and surged out of the room.

In the hallway, a young couple gasped at the sight of the armed mob pouring from the suite.

"Go to your room," Greene commanded, cradling an F88 assault rifle. "This has nothing to do with you!"

The man nodded and dragged the terrified young woman inside with him, and slammed the door shut.

"Why leave them alive?" Thomas snarled, hefting an Atchisson autoshotgun.

"We do not harm our own kind," Greene stated, just as the elevator opened.

Inside the cage were three Latina maids dressed in clean white uniforms, and carrying the various tools of their trades.

Firing from the hip, Greene, Layne and LoMonaco ruthlessly slaughtered the dark-skinned women in a hail of gunfire.

Leaving the bodies where they fell, Greene and Daylight moved through the luxury hotel, wounding any Caucasian they encountered, but ruthlessly executing everybody else.

In the lobby, one of the terrorists drew a bead on the desk clerk, but LoMonaco stayed his hand.

"One of us," she whispered.

Exiting the building, Greene and his people paused to reload, then moved out, heading directly for the main access road to the secluded beach, and their scheduled meeting with the Mexican police.

CHAPTER ONE

Columbus, Ohio

Firing from the hip, Mack Bolan, aka The Executioner, took out both of the liveried guards, the discharge from the silenced 9 mm Beretta no louder than a hard cough.

As the dead men crumpled to the ground, Bolan moved in fast, smashing both of their handheld radios. Then he put a squirt of fast-acting glue onto the slides of their automatic pistols. If anybody found the corpses, they'd spend precious minutes trying to get the jimmied weapons to work again, and that was all the soldier needed now, just a few more minutes to get the job done.

The search for Eric "Mad Dog" Kegan had been long and hard. The gunrunner shed identities the way most other people did socks, and he always left behind a trail of bodies, most of them innocent bystanders who saw his face. But that reign of bloodshed would end here and now. If only Bolan moved fast enough.

Dressed for full urban combat, The Executioner was wearing a loose trench coat, and soft fedora. Underneath he wore a military blacksuit, Threat-Level-Four body armor, an old canvas web harness rigged with a wide assortment of weapons and tools of war and dark combat sneakers. They didn't offer the full protection of combat boots, but made less noise.

Easing through the dark Bolan paused just before reentering the sunlight. Across the street was a small building nestled amid leafy trees and shrubs. He could see brick walls and a house set far back from the road. White stucco, the structure was two stories tall, probably a shoe store or something similar in the past, big picture windows on either side of a nice wooden door. The shutters on the second story were closed, with a small red-and-white For Rent sign in the left window that was partially obscured by streaked dust. Old, dirty, valueless, abandoned and forgotten, the store was just part of the neighborhood—there, but never truly noticed.

Crossing the busy street, Bolan attempted to look through the window, but couldn't see anything. The pebbled glass was tinted a deep blue. Nice. Only a foot away, Kegan would have total privacy to conduct his business.

Easing into the greenery, Bolan checked for traps and hidden alarms, but found the area clear. The interior of the building would contain an advanced security system, but to maintain his cover, Kegan had to relay upon plain, ordinary locks outside so as not to draw any suspicion on the place.

Studying the building, Bolan wondered if the second floor was an apartment. This was an older neighborhood and lots of stores used to have living space above them in order to save money.

Going to the door, Bolan tried the handle but it was locked. Reaching under his windbreaker, he unearthed a keywire gun and shot the lock full of stiff wire, then turned the gun. The lock disengaged with a subtle click.

Wiggling the device free, Bolan tucked it away and drew his Beretta 93R machine pistol before sliding inside the dark building. Using a small can of pressurized talcum powder, Bolan filled the air with a swirling dust cloud to check for laser beams. But the powder revealed nothing, and he continued onward, staying alert for hidden video cameras and trip wires. This was home for Kegan and it was guaranteed to be a major hard site. He simply hadn't found any security devices yet, which made Bolan slightly nervous. You never heard the bullet that got you. He had to stay alert, watch for everything and live another day. That was all any soldier could hope for in war.

And that's all this was, a covert war for the streets of America, Bolan noted. On one side were Kegan and his kind, cannibals in thousand-dollar suits, and on the other side was civilization. Long ago, Bolan had decided that he wasn't Animal Man's judge, or jury, but his executioner. The soldier wasn't here to enforce the law, but to dispense justice, hard and absolute. Street justice. Red law.

Kicking some torn manila folders out of his way, Bolan crossed the littered floor and stood amid the piles of destruction. There was no other way to describe the office area but totally trashed.

Pictures were smashed on the walls, the empty frames hanging from bent nails. The file-cabinet drawers had been removed and cast aside, sofa cushions ripped apart, the stuffing scattered about randomly, and assorted papers were everywhere. Somebody had been very serious about searching this room. An amateur, but dead serious.

However, just because a room had been searched, Bolan noted privately, didn't mean that anything had been found.

The next room was an office, just as bedraggled as the waiting room but now empty shell casings from a dozen different weapons lay scattered about, telling Bolan how things had gone down. Four people had entered through the sitting room, each armed with automatic pistols, and one with a shotgun. Three others had opened fire from the staircase using M16 assault rifles, and something that left bullet holes but didn't eject brass. The fire pattern was too tight for a bolt action...a caseless rifle? Impressive. The weapons sounded like a zipper in operation, and threw out lead faster than anything but a motorized Gatling gun. A caseless assault rifle was a serious threat. Bolan would have to keep a sharp watch out for— He froze.

Lancing through the swirling cloud of talcum powder was a scintillating red beam, thinner than a human hair, almost invisible. Dropping low, Bolan eased under the laser and carefully rose on the other side, his heart pounding. Touch the beam of light, and all hell would have broken loose, probably in the manner of a dozen Claymore mines plastered inside the wall. Close, but no cigar.

Going to the window, Bolan saw the real-estate sign. At the bottom was the monthly rent, a phone number and the name of the management company. Out of curiosity, Bolan tried the number, and wasn't surprised to get only a busy signal, then voice mail, but the box was full. That was all anybody would ever get, a busy signal. Kegan lived in a building advertised as for rent. Clever. That would have stopped most investigations, but Bolan had sources everywhere, most of them whispers and hints. Add a few together, and suddenly a pattern became visible. A soft probe, followed by a hard probe, and when the target was confirmed, a full blitz with guns blazing. But he wasn't there yet, this was just the soft probe.

Making sure the door was locked, Bolan did a quick sweep of the place and found nothing more interesting than a couple of thousand in cash and a kilo of marijuana. He took the cash.

"Thanks, Mad Dog," Bolan whispered, tucking the wad of bills into an empty pouch on his gunbelt reserved for just that purpose.

Bolan really didn't have an accurate count of how many millions he had stolen from the Mafia, terrorist organizations and organized crime in general, but their bloody profits had purchased a lot of hard justice rammed back down their throats. If that wasn't karma, then Bolan had no idea what the proper definition was.

The last room on the ground floor was an office, all brass and leather, and smelling of death. A man lay behind the sofa in a position it was impossible to achieve while alive, and a woman was draped over the desk. Her tattoos identified her as an assassin for the Colombian drug cartel.

Pitting rival gangs against each other was an old trick in his book, and one that worked extremely well most of the time. Not always, but often enough. Bolan knew that it had been a gamble to tell Kegan's enemies where the gunrunner could be located. But he hadn't read them as foolish enough to drive up to the building and unload a couple of rocket launchers through the front windows. Kegan's former customers, cheated of their goods, and often betrayed to the police for the reward, wanted hands-on revenge, up close and very personal. If they had succeeded, so much the better. But at the very least, they had diverted Kegan and his people, giving Bolan a precious few minutes to try to find Kegan's next identity and permanently end his reign of terror.

Alongside the corpse was a cheap pressboard computer desk, the PC smashed to pieces, the hard drive gone. Damn. That could have been useful. Not that Kegan would keep anything major on the drive, but there could have been hints and subtle clues. Sometimes Bolan felt as though he was fighting ghosts in the dark.

All the way across the office was a huge dark wooden desk sporting a stained brass plaque with the name *Edward Carter.* A common enough moniker to sound real, and close enough to his real name so that Erik Kegan wouldn't make a fatal slip. In spite of being a bloodthirsty monster, Kegan wasn't a fool.

On the wall behind the colossal desk was the usual assortment of impressive diplomas, testimonial letters from satisfied clients, mostly major corporations, and quite a few newspaper clippings showing Edward Carter with the mayor, and other noteworthy folks, with everybody smiling at the cameras. All fake of course, but the pictures did show Kegan himself.

Built like a bull gorilla, Eric Kegan still had the winning smile of a politician selling used cars, slicker than a snake in oil. The only tell was his eyes. The face could smile, the mouth laugh, but the eyes stayed the same, cold and dead, like the eyes of a shark.

It was strange that a man forever in hiding would allow himself to be photographed, especially by a newspaper. Anonymity was paramount for his line of business—selling death wholesale. Maybe Kegan just liked having his picture taken. Bolan shrugged. People were often contradictory.

Lifting the slashed leather chair from the floor, Bolan checked the sides for hidden controls but found nothing. Sitting in the chair, he twisted back and forth a few times, listening for a squeak, but hearing only the rustle of his clothing.

The desk itself was huge, a monstrous slab of cherrywood, topped with green leather and edged with shiny brass studs. It was clearly an antique from a bygone age and had to weigh a ton.

Going around, Bolan checked the front and sure enough saw a line of holes in the wood from three different pistols, but none of the lead had achieved full penetration. Even his furniture was bulletproof. That was when he caught a whiff of something in the air other than the talcum powder and blood. Perfume from the woman? No, what assassin would do a job wearing perfume to reveal her presence in the dark? It might be a man's cologne, brandy-cut tobacco mixed with the faint aroma of homogenized oil.

He checked the top right-hand drawer and there was a cleaning kit for a gun. Plus a spare magazine and a box of ammo for a 10 mm Colt Magnum pistol—semisteel jacketed hollow-point rounds. Serious ammo. Those tens hit like sledgehammers and punched holes through everything short of Threat-Level-Five body armor.

Wearing only Level Four at the moment, that gave Bolan pause. Then he moved on. Kegan had to be stopped. End of discussion.

Closing the drawer, the soldier looked over the office again and tried to reconstruct in his mind how it got this way. Everything had been smashed or slashed open, even the books on the shelves. The plastic fern in the corner had been removed from its wicker pot and wood chips were scattered everywhere. Looking for something small and flexible... Documents, perhaps?

There were three doors lining the interior wall. Wading through the mounds of trash, Bolan went to the first and found that it opened onto a short hallway with stairs going up and another door to the left that had to lead to the basement.

The stairs didn't creak as he'd expected, which was a good sign of proper maintenance. At the top, Bolan reached a blank wall with picture-used-to-be-here stains and a short hallway. Just to the left was a modern kitchen, obviously a recent addition, with a small breakfast area.

The kitchen table was in pieces, the steel tube chairs disassembled. Same as downstairs, the kitchen had been thoroughly searched, corn flakes littering the floor, bag of sugar busted wide open. Bolan studied the sugar for patterns in the granulated surface but found none. Whatever was hidden hadn't been found here.

Rummaging through a drawer Bolan found a can opener and wasted precious minutes opening a couple of soup cans from the bottom cupboard. He had once encountered drug lords who smuggled messages to each other hidden inside sealed cans of soup. Simply open the bottom, insert your item, then weld the bottom back on. It had worked for years before the DEA got wise, then they did nothing to stop the transfer of information, merely opened the cans, copied the messages then sealed them up again.

Moving upstairs, Bolan moved onward, keeping an ear out for a car arriving or a knock downstairs. A neighbor might have seen him enter and called the police. But this was Columbus where everybody minded his or her own business and quietly got killed without disturbing the people next door. An open doorway led to what remained of a living room, couch flipped over, cushions slit open, the covers removed from the electrical outlets, pictures off the wall, even the television set had been kicked in and the cover removed. After the assassins had been chased away by Kegan and his crew, somebody else had entered the building, and done a thorough job of searching the place from top to bottom. Smart move, and the perps were certainly thorough enough, he'd give them that.

The curtains were off the windows, and the blinds torn down, the weighted bottoms cracked apart. Impressive. Bolan never would have thought of hiding anything inside the bottoms of venetian blinds. He was starting to get the feeling that whatever Kegan had hidden had to have been found and was long gone. But he still had to double check. Just the chance of stopping Kegan was worth the effort.

Down the hall was a bathroom with grout dust covering the fixtures. Somebody had run a knife along the wall tiles to look for fresh work over a secret panel. They really were good! Bolan filed that trick away to use himself sometime in the future.

The bedroom looked like a hurricane had hit a rag factory. Nothing was intact. Feathers swirled about his shoes from pillows gone to heaven. The northern wall was a single expanse of closets with a bare top shelf. Bolan probed for a panel leading to a crawl space or attic, but found nothing except dust and deceased spiders.

The light-switch panels had been yanked off the walls, exposed wires dangling dangerously loose, and the carpet was torn up in several spots. A rush of adrenaline was building within Bolan. Time was short, the numbers falling, and he wondered if there was any place they hadn't looked.

Going to his personal favorite spot to stash important things, Bolan lifted the ceramic lid off the toilet tank and looked inside. Nothing there but water, the usual mechanical works and a drained sanitizer cylinder. The pros who'd hit this place would never have missed an area so obvious as the toilet tank. But had they searched everything?

Tucking away the Beretta, Bolan pulled a knife. Grabbing hold of the copper support rod to hold it steady, he slid the blade along the slightly slimy rubber. The knife slipped once and cut him, but no blood welled from the wound. Just a surface scratch. Bolan proceeded more slowly, switching to a fillet blade and sawing through the resilient material, rather than trying to slice it apart like a ripe melon. The slick bulb wasn't cooperative, but he finally got through, and a clear corner triangle of a plastic bag jutted into view.

Forcing the blade along the side of the bulb, Bolan widened the cut until it was big enough for him to grab and pull it apart. There lay a clear plastic bag filled with maybe a dozen film negatives. Going to the sink, he wiped the bag off on a dingy towel bearing the name *Sheraton.* The bastard had millions in a Swiss bank, but stole hotel towels?

Opening the sandwich bag, Bolan lifted out the negatives, only touching them by the edges, and held a strip to a flashlight. They were negatives of a passport, birth certificate, college diploma, dental and general medical records for a Shawn MacTeague of Glasgow, Scotland. The man in the photos was Kegan. Bolan knew that the man spent years building a perfect identify and with these gone, Kegan would have no place left to run. He'd be forced to make a stand and fight, which was exactly what Bolan wanted.

Slipping the bag full of negatives into a pocket, Bolan paused to text a brief message to a friend in Washington: Kegan was Shawn MacTeague, Glasgow.

Done and done. Now if Bolan was killed, Hal Brognola at the Justice Department would make sure somebody else finished the job. Mostly Bolan worked alone, but every now and then he did find it convenient to have backup, and he could trust Brognola with his life. He had many times before.

Giving the apartment a fast once-over, Bolan checked a few more locations where small items could be found, then eased down the stairs. Mission accomplished!

Bolan was halfway down the stairs when he heard the front door crash open, and people stomping into the building, working the arming bolts on automatic weapons.

CHAPTER TWO

"Kill everybody you see!" a man growled, his voice nearly inhuman in its violent rage.

Nice to meet you, Eric, Bolan thought sarcastically, pulling the safety ring on an antipersonnel grenade. Then he released the handle and flipped the sphere down the stairs. It hit the landing hard and bounced around the corner. Instantly, Bolan surged into action, running for the living room.

"What in the...run!" a man screamed, the blast cutting off the startled cry.

The entire building seemed to shake from the force of the fiery blast, windows shattering on the ground level, and a couple of alarms cutting loose with deafening sirens.

So much for hiding in the shadows, Bolan noted, diving through the cracked window. Welcome to the light, Eric!

Daggers of glass cut into the trench coat, but the body armor underneath protected Bolan from any serious damage, and he landed sprawling in the fork of an oak tree, startling a small squirrel.

"Better run, amigo," Bolan whispered, sliding down the tree to land in a crouch, both of his weapons drawn and at the ready.

Lights began to appear in all of the nearby houses,

people roused by the explosion, and a couple of big men carrying M16 assault rifles appeared from around the front of the building.

Bolan and the gunners opened fired in unison. They missed, he didn't, and they fell away into forever, their chattering weapons strafing the open night sky.

As much as Bolan wanted to walk around to the front and take out Kegan right now, there were too many civilians in the area to risk a gun battle. He felt sure that had been part of the man's defense strategy, and the soldier couldn't fault the bastard for coming out with a winning plan. People dressed in pajamas and slippers, armed only with flashlights, were starting across the street, and shuffling this way. In spite of that, Bolan still hesitated and took a step forward, then he saw a couple of kids appear, and a pregnant woman. Time to go.

Whirling, Bolan took off at a sprint and hit the back fence at a full run. He easily scaled it and paused, with one leg in sight until he heard somebody curse. Then he dropped over, just as a hole appeared in the old wood, spraying out splinters from the thunderous passage of a big-bore round.

Aiming at the sky, Bolan answered back with two shots from the Beretta, then took off again, jumping over an inflatable pool and dodging patio furniture. A glass door slid aside and out waddled an enormously fat woman cradling a double-barrel shotgun and wearing a fierce expression.

"Trying to rob me again, motherfucker!" she snarled, discharging both barrels.

Moving fast, Bolan got out of the way in time, and only a few of the lead pellets hammered him across the back of his armor. Christ, this was a nightmare!

He had civilians coming out of the woodwork! Had to move this fight to something more secluded before innocent lives were lost.

Skirting a huge Cadillac, Bolan heard scampering claws and flipped his gun in the air to grab the Beretta by the hot barrel. A split second later, a huge Doberman charged into view, and Bolan neatly clubbed the animal unconscious with a single blow to the skull just behind the ears. The dog dropped with a sigh, and the soldier continued running, almost becoming entangled with a tricycle, and hopping over a low hedge.

Reaching the relative freedom of the street, he shot out the light on the corner, and quickly dropped the partially used magazine to slam in a fresh one. Suddenly, a car appeared at the end of the street. The headlights were off, and Bolan could see the dim silhouettes of men holding long objects out the open windows.

Dropping into a crouch, Bolan switched the Beretta to 3-round-burst mode, and emptied the entire magazine into the front of the vehicle. The stuttering barrage smashed both headlights and took out a tire, then the hood flipped up as the radiator exploded into a hissing geyser of steam.

"Get that son of a bitch!" Kegan screamed from inside the car, and the darkness became alive with the bright flashes of automatic gunfire.

Already running low and fast, Bolan took cover behind a Ford Pinto just as the first hail of lead arrived. The car rocked from the arrival of the military rounds, more glass shattering, then there came the strong smell of spilled gasoline.

Springing along the row of parked cars, Bolan heard the car ignite into a fireball as more house windows started lighting up, dogs began to bark from everywhere, and in the distance there came the long, drawn-out howl of a police siren.

Not pausing for an instant, Bolan pulled out a flash-bang grenade, armed the device and flipped it over a shoulder. He heard the doors slam shut on the crippled car and men cursing, then the grenade detonated. Designed to incapacitate an enemy, not kill, the stun grenade banished the night with a magnesium-fueled flash ten times brighter than the sun, along with a bone-jarring boom.

As Bolan dove behind a mailbox, he dimly heard the other men weeping and cursing, their weapons wildly discharging as leaves fell from the trees from the passage of the bullets.

One more corner, and Bolan saw a huge BMW motorcycle parked at the next corner. It was sleek and shiny and looked like polished speed. The front wheel of the BMW was covered with a bright yellow locking clamp, the infamous Denver Boot. A single kick disengaged the fake plastic clamp, and Bolan climbed onto the bike, twisting the ignition.

The big engine softly came into life. The only visible signs of operation were the dashboard indicators starting to glow softly, and the shaking of the muffler exhaust. One of the main attributes of the Beamer bike was that it used a transmission instead of a chain. That reduced the noise level significantly. Add a few modifications to the muffler, and the BMW become a purring mechanized ghost, barely discernable from a yard away.

"Fuck, fire, he's got a bike!" a man snarled, an M16 cutting loose with a long burst.

Several of the 5.56 mm hardball rounds ricocheted

off the dark pavement as Bolan lurched away, missing the man by the thickness of a prayer. Accelerating as he braked, the soldier took the corner fast and low, throwing out a leg to keep from toppling over. The friction nearly tore the combat sneaker off his foot, but he made it out of sight intact, then he slowed to a crawl, the huge engine barely ticking over.

Lost in the sounds of people, dogs and police, Bolan couldn't hear any pursuit, so he fired a couple of more rounds into the air to give them a lock on his position. Bolan knew this was a dangerous game, but he wouldn't kill civilians, even by accident.

A few moments later, something large and dark appeared at the far end of the road, then the halogen headlights crashed on, fully illuminating both man and bike. For a moment, Bolan realized that he might have overplayed his hand. That was a military Hummer!

As the huge vehicle surged forward with a full-throated roar of controlled power, Bolan twisted the throttle and silently streaked away. This was going to be close....

Just then, a police car flashed through an intersection, the light bar flashing and siren howling.

Knowing the local PD was no match for the kind of firepower carried by Kegan and his street soldiers, Bolan angled away from the police and took off down a side street, then popped a wheelie to get over a high curb and started through a weedy field.

The Hummer stayed right on his tail, the military vehicle taking the curb with barely a jounce.

Hanging on to the handlebars with all of his might, Bolan plowed through the weeds and cut across a Little League baseball field. As soon as he reached bare earth, he fishtailed the bike to throw up a cloud of dirt, then swung around the concession stand and came out the other side with his second handgun ready.

As the bright headlights of the Hummer appeared within the swirling cloud, Bolan used both hands to aim and fire the massive .50-caliber Desert Eagle. The big-bore rounds slammed into the engine, and it whoofed into flames.

The vehicle streaked past Bolan, the men inside screaming and cursing and fighting to get out of the burning vehicle. One dove to the ground and hit hard, his bones audibly cracking from the impact. As he rolled along, more bones snapped, then he slammed headfirst into the dugout, and stopped moving or making any noise.

Shooting out a tire on the Hummer, Bolan helped the driver bring the big car to a ragged halt. Then he switched weapons and raked the smoky darkness with the Beretta, the stream of 9 mm Parabellum rounds invoking a series of painful cries, and then deep silence.

Kicking down the stand, Bolan reloaded, then warily approached the burning car, his every combat sense on the alert. Unless Kegan had hired fools, the men were either dead, or only playing possum to lure him in closer. But either way, he had to see Kegan's lifeless corpse before allowing this matter to end.

Bolan was only a few yards away when the Hummer unexpectedly detonated, the blast illuminating the entire ball field and throwing him backward. The breath was knocked out of him as he hit the ground, then the soldier rolled over and came up with both guns primed, searching for targets. But there was only the smoking ruin of the Hummer strewn across half the ball field, bits and pieces of sizzling flesh lying scattered about in grisly display.

For a long moment, Bolan watched for any signs that Kegan or one of his people had survived the stentorian explosion, then reluctantly holstered his weapons and walked stiffly back to the bike. He had to consider this mission a failure. Kegan might be dead, or he might not. Not even a team of forensic scientists would be able to tell for sure from that level of fiery destruction. Once more, Kegan the Unkillable had escaped.

Climbing back onto the BMW motorcycle, Bolan revved the engine and checked for any damage from shrapnel, then drove away into the night, heading for the main road out of town. His trench coat had a dozen holes in it, but it still served the basic purpose of hiding the majority of his weapons. If his radar-detector pinpointed any cops, he would simply swing off to the berm and get behind the bike, pretending to fix the engine until they were gone.

Worst-case scenario, Bolan would use the FBI commission booklet he had stashed in the luggage compartment of the bike. It was real enough for the locals, just not good enough to stand up to the scrutiny of the FBI, or any of the other Alphabet Agencies.

Cutting through a quiet shopping mall, Bolan took an on-ramp onto the elevated 465 beltway, and rode in somber contemplation until reaching the exit for the Columbus International Airport.

Throttling down the engine, he swept down the off-ramp, when there came a distant flash of light and a fiery dart streaked out of the night to impact on the ramp. A roiling blast shattered the concrete, and Bolan went flying. Soaring through the air, he forced himself to relax in an effort to not break his bones, and bit down on a sleeve. As little as it was, the cushioning effect might save his teeth. But no matter how he looked at it, this was going to be a bad crash.

In a jarring thud, Bolan landed in the swampy marshland around the airport, the splash of mud jutting yards high. An unknown length of time passed, then the soldier jerked awake, a hand clawing for the Beretta. It was gone, but the Desert Eagle was still at his side.

Weakly standing, Bolan wobbled as he desperately attempted to remember what had just happened. Clearly, there had been some sort of explosion, but what had detonated, he had no idea. Everything was a blur of chaotic images in his head. Then he saw the crumbling exit ramp, the burning motorcycle and everything came rushing back with the speed and ferocity of an express train. The ramp had been a trap!

Obviously, Kegan hadn't been killed in the Hummer. Bolan had no idea how that was possible, but now the gunrunner and his troops were in hot pursuit. Having seen the horrors Kegan did to enemies to make them talk, Bolan decided he wouldn't let these animals capture him alive. Everybody could be broken given enough time. Everybody. That was just the hard reality of life. A soldier simply had to decide what was more important, a few more minutes of life, or dying with dignity. And hopefully taking a couple of the bastards with you straight to hell! he thought.

Suddenly, there was a flash of bright light on top of the elevated roadway, and a fiery dart lanced across the field to slam into the smashed motorcycle. The explosion threw chunks of burning bike far and wide.

Diving to the side, Bolan rolled through the reeking

mud trying to get far away from his point of arrival, then started crawling deeper into the gooey marsh until he reached scummy water. Pausing to catch his breath, Bolan felt his ribs grind and wondered if he had a full break. The body armor had saved his life, but now it was deadweight, and he reluctantly cut it free.

Moving with speed, he holstered the Desert Eagle and did a quick check for any further damage, then dug out the small medical kit behind his back. Thankfully it was still intact, and Bolan shot himself full of painkillers, just enough to dull the pain without impairing his judgment. Then wrapped duct tape around his muddy chest. For about the next hour, he'd feel fine, then all bets were off.

Struggling to recall the details of the airport, Bolan glanced at the starry sky to get his bearings, then headed due north, away from the airport. That would be another trap.

Finding a culvert, Bolan sloshed through the dirty water, disturbing countless frogs and huge clouds of buzzing insects. He may have been stung once or twice, but the painkillers were doing their job, and he felt nothing. There was only a sort of throbbing in his limbs from the combination of drugs coursing through his veins.

The culvert fed into the Ohio River, but bypassing that, Bolan continued northward until he encountered an old abandoned cement factory. It was quite possibly one of the worst locations he had ever found for making a last stand, but the huge feeder towers made an excellent landmark. Now he turned sharply west, wading through fields of debris and garbage, rats constantly underfoot, until he spotted a small squat building set alongside the river.

As Bolan stumbled for the ancient factory, there came unbidden into his mind the adage: *to achieve success plan for failure.* He thought that was Ben Franklin, but couldn't be sure at the moment. However, it was absolutely true. Bolan laid out a plan for battle with extreme care, and no matter how perfect it seemed, he always memorized an escape route. On the roof of the cement factory was a duffel bag full of food, medical supplies, weapons and a cell phone. Everything he needed to keep breathing, and to call for an immediate evac. Just a few more yards, is all, he thought, almost there...

The boom of a long-range sniper rifle echoed across the landscape, and Bolan felt something hot briefly tug on his wet shirt. Damn, that was close! From the sound he could tell it was a .50-caliber rifle, and those were very bad news. Even the worst one he knew about still had a range of a quarter mile, and the best easily tripled that. As long as he was outside, he was in range for the hidden sniper. Only one answer to that problem.

Redoubling his efforts, Bolan sprinted across the field, zigzagging randomly to throw off the sniper's aim. The big rifle boomed twice more, but hit nothing.

Reaching the rear fire door to the factory, Bolan checked the wax seal he had placed on the lintel. It was intact, meaning that nobody had gained entrance to the factory since his last visit, or at least, not through this door.

As Bolan forced open the metal door, he struggled to remember if there were other doors, but the information eluded him. Closing the fire door, the soldier threw the heavy bolt he had installed only that afternoon, then turned and started directly for the stairs to the second level. There was an access ladder up there, and—

In a thunderclap of ripping steel, the fire door exploded off its hinges.

Taking refuge behind a concrete pillar, Bolan watched as the door rattled about the rows of hulking machinery until finally coming to a rest in a pool of moonlight streaming in through a skylight. The fire door was deeply dented in the middle, the hinges and deadbolt only tattered remains of twisted metal. Unfortunately, that meant the sniper was a professional. He had a variety of bullets for the big-bore weapon, including blunt-nosed rounds perfect for smashing open doors or knocking down brick walls.

Changing direction, Bolan lumbered to the elevated control room. The office was dark, the air thick with dust, but the talcum powder he had spread across the floor was undisturbed. Going to a fuse box, he quickly screwed in a couple of the old-fashioned fuses, then threw the main switch.

None of the overhead lights came on, that would have been suicide, but about half of the cement machinery squealed into operation; stampers loudly banging, degreasers hissing steam, and a long snaking conveyor belt squealing in protest at its decades-long slumber being so rudely disturbed.

Easing open the door, Bolan slid out on his belly and crawled directly under a large piece of machinery. The air down there smelled of grease, rust, dust and petrified mouse droppings. Staying perfectly still, Bolan waited until somebody came into view. From this angle he couldn't see his face, so the instant he had a good view of the sniper's feet he fired the Desert Eagle.

The man's shoe exploded into tattered leather, and he screamed, falling to the dirty floor and grabbing his mutilated foot with both hands in an effort to staunch the blood.

Moving to another dark machine, Bolan fired fast three times at a support leg. The booming .50-caliber rounds from the Desert Eagle ricocheted off the steel, and the man cried out, then went silent.

One down, and an unknown number to go, Bolan noted with little satisfaction. He had been ambushed like a rank amateur! But the soldier tried to move past that. This wasn't the time nor the place for recriminations. Stay cool, stay sharp, kill on sight, live another day.

Rising slowly upward in the shadowy darkness between two hulking machines of unknown purpose, Bolan tried to move again as he studied the rattling, clanking factory. Smoke was rising from one of the distant machines, and he had no idea if that was just years of accumulated dust burning off the hot metal, or if the factory was on fire. Then he went stiff at a soft mewling noise, followed by crying.

Remaining still, he tried to track the noise when the source came into view. Tied to the conveyor belt was a woman dressed in dirty rags. She was struggling to get free, but clearly making no progress.

His only guess was that Kegan had grabbed some homeless person and dragged them along as a bargaining chip. Only now her status had abruptly changed to bait. Bolan had no idea where the convoluted belt went, or how Kegan had gained access, but since this was a cement factory, the chance of it ending at a pile of feather pillows was roughly zero to the power of ten.

"Surrender, feeb! Only I can save her!" Kegan boasted, firing short bursts from his weapon about randomly.

Bolan said nothing. Feeb? So he thought Bolan was an FBI agent, eh? Interesting.

Just then, a light flickered into life on the distant ceiling. Aiming and firing in a single motion, Bolan blew out the fluorescent tube, then darted back under the machine before the rain of glass shards arrived.

"Oh, you're fast!" Kegan yelled from somewhere, the words echoing among the machines. "But I've got ten guys and you're all alone!" He paused as if waiting for a response. When none came, he continued, "How about a deal? Tell me who you work for, and I'll let you leave, alive and unharmed!"

Bullshit, he'd be shot on sight, Bolan knew, but that wasn't the Executioner's main concern at the moment. The woman on the belt was slowly heading away, and Bolan had to get close, even though he knew in advance it was a trap. But he couldn't allow a noncombatant to die in his place.

Searching around on the filthy floor with a bare hand, Bolan found a couple of large bolts that had worked their way free from the machines. Holstering the Desert Eagle, Bolan pulled out his last grenade, yanked out the pin, then dropped one of the bolts, and threw the other.

"Grenade!" a man bellowed, and Bolan heard the sound of people running.

Releasing the handle on the grenade, he now threw it ahead of them, then scrambled onto the conveyor belt and started sprinting.

As he ducked under a steam pipe, the grenade violently exploded. A chemical thunderclap of brilliant light filled the entire factory, and Bolan heard several men shout in pain and surprise, their voices fading away into eternity.

When the conveyor belt took an unexpected dip, Bolan nearly lost his footing, and he dropped flat to hold on to the tattered leather strip with both hands. Some of the staples holding the belt together were coming loose, and he got cut and slashed, but the punctures were only flesh wounds and he ignored them.

Suddenly, the whimpering increased, and there she was, only a yard away, moving in the opposite direction. The blasted belt had reversed course somewhere! Diving forward, Bolan grabbed an overhead pipe and felt it start to give as he swung forward. It broke free just as he let go, and Bolan landed on the conveyor belt just as the pipe loudly crashed to the floor, closely followed by a rain of assorted metallic debris.

Instantly, gunfire strobed the darkness, hot lead ricocheting off the machines at that location. But Bolan was already far away, and steadily accelerating. Going to the prisoner, the soldier punched her in the temple to expertly knock her unconscious and stop the crying. He felt sure she'd rather have a throbbing headache, and live, than die.

Running his hands over her body, he was surprised to find her so healthy and well-fed. Suspicious, he drew a knife and slashed away her clothing until she was down to her bra and panties. That was when he found a slim Remington .32 pistol taped under a breast. She was a fake!

Pocketing the gun, Bolan eased off the rumbling leather belt and back into the darkness.

Moving away from the sporadic gunfire, the soldier headed back to the second floor, and started up the ladder for the roof. Whoever the woman was, he felt no pity or remorse. Obviously she worked for Kegan and deserved whatever kind of cruel justice was offered by the grinding gears of the ancient rattling machine.

Reaching the skylight, Bolan checked to make sure the wax seals were still in place, then pushed open the now-lubricated hinges and stepped into a cool refreshing breeze. Heading directly for the emergency pack, Bolan sent off the signal for an emergency evac, took a few grenades, and the spare Beretta, then went back to the open skylight.

Below there was only darkness and the rumbling machines. Then a woman screamed in mortal agony, the cries becoming high-pitched as the machines took on a lower tone. The conveyor belt stopped, but the screaming continued.

Pulling the pin on an antipersonnel grenade, Bolan tossed it in that direction. Before it even landed, he pulled the pin on three Willy Peter grenades and tossed them about the interior of the factory—then he moved back fast.

At the first blast the female's screaming thankfully ceased as the spray of shrapnel zinged about madly off the walls and machines. Two more voices shrieked, then the incendiary grenades ignited, and the entire factory flashed as an inferno of incandescent chemicals spread outward, blanketing everything they touched with deadly white phosphorous.

As a hellish blaze began to swiftly grow, a side door

burst open and out staggered a coughing man. Immediately, Bolan recognized him as Kegan. Drawing and aiming the Beretta in a single move, the soldier emptied the machine pistol in prolonged bursts. The hail of 9 mm hollowpoint rounds slammed Kegan to the ground, ripping into the man until he collapsed to the roof.

"Debt paid in full," Bolan growled, reloading the Beretta.

The roof was starting to get warm under his feet, and Bolan was considering a jump toward a pool of stagnant water when a deep throb sounded in the starry night sky. Bolan looked up to see a Bell Huey helicopter heading his way.

"Taxi!" he shouted with a wave, then put two fingers into his mouth and sharply whistled.

Swinging about, the helicopter landed a couple of yards away, and Bolan yanked open the side hatch to half step, half fall into the passenger seat.

"Tough day at the office, Sarge?" Jack Grimaldi asked, smiling behind his visor.

"Nothing special," Bolan replied, buckling a seat belt around his bloody clothing.

Laughing in reply, the Stony Man pilot pulled back on the control yoke, and the helicopter lifted off the roof of the burning factory. It disappeared into the night only moments before the local fire department arrived, closely followed by a brace of ambulances and a heavily armed SWAT team.

CHAPTER THREE

Mexico

A long conga line of police cars drove along the mountainous road, their lights flashing, but the sirens oddly silent.

The backbone of the USA–Mexico combined anti-drug effort, Firebase Azules, was a heavily fortified Mexican military base situated on top of a low hill that gave it a commanding view of the surrounding valley and the distant mountains. Concrete K-rails surrounded the entire base to deter suicide bombers from driving a truck loaded with explosive onto the base. Past the rails was a hurricane fence made completely out of barbed wire and topped with deadly coils of concertina wire, the endless coils of razor blades glittering in the early morning sunlight.

Grim soldiers stood in concrete guard towers, smoking, drinking coffee or polishing their M16 assault rifles. Security cameras constantly swept the perimeter, radar scanned the air and sonar probed the nearby river.

The United States of America and Mexico had signed a mutually beneficial treaty many years ago: the US supplied Mexico with military ordnance to help the nation's endless fight against the drug lords that kept coming up from South America. The best of the best went to Azules.

Only recently, a submarine had been stopped off the Atlantic coast, and 180 million dollars' worth of cocaine had been found. The crew was in jail, the cocaine destroyed at a special incinerator and the Mexican navy got a slightly used diesel submarine. All things considered, a pretty good day for the Federal Border Patrol.

Slowing down at the maze of K-rails, the police cars proceeded slowly over the expanse of speed bumps and hidden land mines. Stopping a short distance from a fortified guard kiosk, Dalton Greene turned off the engine of the stolen police car, and climbed outside. The billionaire was now wearing the regulation uniform of the Mexico police, including sidearms, sunglasses and wristwatch. A spray tan had darkened his skin to something more appropriate to a Caucasian living below the Rio Grande. The only subtle difference was the Threat-Level-Five body armor he wore under the uniform.

"Good morning, Lieutenant!" Greene hailed in flawless Spanish. "Is the base commander available?"

"Perhaps I can help you with something?" the officer asked, pushing back his cap.

The soldier was armed with a .45 Colt automatic pistol, while his partner inside the kiosk was cradling an M16 assault rifle with an old-fashioned M203 grenade launcher attached underneath. On top of the kiosk, a small radar dish never stopped spinning in its endless search for incoming enemy planes.

"No, sorry, I need to see the base commander," Greene repeated, trying to sound apologetic.

Warily, the guard looked over the men and women in the eight police cars. Aside from the fact that they were all Caucasians, he wasn't suspicious in the least. Mexico did things differently than most countries, not better or worse, just different, so while this seemed like a lot of police to send to a military base for any reason, it wasn't unusual. More than likely somebody important was arriving at the base, and they were here to escort him to someplace else, like Mexico City for example.

"You have papers?" the lieutenant asked at last.

Greene grinned. "Of course!" He passed over a clipboard stuffed with documents.

The officer gave the sheaf of expertly forged papers only a cursory glance, then nodded to the soldiers inside the kiosk. One of them threw a switch, and the steel barricade that blocked entry onto the base slowly descended into the ground with the sound of working hydraulic pumps.

When the way was clear, Greene took back the forged documents, got back behind the wheel.

Driving onto the base, the members of Daylight smiled and nodded at the hundreds of soldiers going about their daily routines. Some were policing a grassy field, marching in formation, hauling away garbage, or yawning and scratching while standing in line at the galley. The smells wafting from the numerous air vents of the cinder-block structure were tantalizing.

"Any chance we could grab a bite?" a terrorist asked, leaning forward in his seat.

"Can't see why not," a driver said with a dismissive shrug. "But only afterward, I mean. You know…"

"Yeah, sure. No problem, mate."

Parking directly in front of the base commander's office, Greene got out once more, noticing that the other police cars were dutifully parking at strategic points around the sprawling base: the fuel depot, barracks, galley, armory.

Sauntering inside alone, Greene introduced himself to the young corporal at the reception desk, and was briskly escorted into the private office of General Juan Dias.

"A pleasure to meet you, sir!" Greene said, giving a crisp salute.

"At ease, Captain." The general returned the salute, then offered a hand. They shook. "Way out here on the front line Azules is nowhere near as formal as back in the capital."

"Good to know." Greene smiled, gesturing at a chair.

The general nodded, and the billionaire took a seat. "I'm sure that you can guess why I'm here."

"Some VIP is arriving unannounced at our airfield, and you're here to escort them back to the capital."

"Exactly, sir! Your reputation precedes you, sir."

"Thanks. Now stop blowing smoke up my ass and tell me why you're really here?"

Greene shrugged. "Honestly, we're just here for the VIP. Some congressman from the United States wants to get a reputation for being tough on drugs. Same old, same old."

"Fair enough, then. Cigar?"

"Thank you!" Greene lit a match, and let all of the sulfur burn off before applying the flame to the tobacco. "Magnificent!"

"Of course! Only the best here. We don't share the crazy American's trade embargo with our brothers in Cuba."

"Obviously!" Greene sighed, savoring the thick rich smoke.

"So tell me about your latest kill?" Greene questioned.

Removing his own cigar, the general laughed. "You heard about that, eh? It was our biggest haul ever in drugs and hardware. Nineteen tons of heroin, and six more helicopters. Six!" Turning slightly at an angle, Dias looked out the window at the airfield. "This gives me a combined total of nine helicopters, eighteen assorted gunships and one submarine."

"No! Really?"

"Honest to God. Plus more Hummers, trucks and APCs than I can remember."

"Wow. You are a credit to our nation, sir," Greene said, gesturing with his cigar.

General Dias shrugged. "It is my job." But his tone said something different.

Glancing about as if to make sure they were alone in the office, Greene pulled a small black box from his pocket. "Now, this is something you may find very interesting," he said, working the controls. A light flashed green on the box, then changed to red.

"What is it?" Dias asked, puffing away contentedly. "Some new form of radar jammer?"

"Oh, no, sir, something much more simple than that," Greene replied, pressing the light.

Instantly, the box burst open and something lanced across the desk to wrap around the general's neck.

"This is my own invention," Greene boasted. "A new form of limpet mine designed to take out a moving torpedo. Watch what happens next, eh?"

Fighting to breathe, Dias clawed for the alarm switch on the intercom. But the linked segments of metal around his neck rapidly tightened until blood began to ooze out from underneath, and he dropped to the desk, his face purple, his eyes bulging.

"The more advanced version has explosive charges included," Greene said, puffing contentedly on the cigar. "But I need this to be done quietly. Sorry about that."

Shuddering, the general rolled over and went still. A moment later, there was a soft crack as his spine was crushed.

Saluting the general for a job well done, Greene went to the window. He smiled at the sight of the police cars parked at different locations across the military base, his people standing in a cluster on the grassy field reserved for drills and marches.

Here we go, he thought.

Changing the settings on the transmitter, Greene waited until the red light turned white, then he pressed it again and ducked.

The entire base rocked to the hammering concussion of all eight police cars exploding, their cargoes of dynamite and plastic explosives combining into a devil's brew of annihilation. To the few survivors, the cars had seemed to simply vanish in a deafening fireball, the blast spreading out to flatten buildings, and send hundreds of soldiers flying high into the air in tattered pieces.

Even before the blast completely died away, the members of Daylight removed their earplugs and surged into action. Using their police revolvers to gun down any unharmed soldiers, the terrorists quickly reached the armory and upgraded to M16 assault rifles, M203 grenade launchers, Armbrust rocket launchers and flamethrowers.

Now the terrorists did a fast sweep of the burning base, ruthlessly exterminating anybody found alive. Some of the soldiers tried to fight back, others ran and a few begged for mercy, but it made no difference. The white supremacists of Daylight removed the Mexican soldiers with brutal efficiency.

Striding out of the main office, Greene headed for the airfield firing his 10 mm Falcon Magnum at several scurrying military officers. The unarmed men died bloody, still trying to escape. An older sergeant managed to get his pistol out, and Greene coldly emptied the entire magazine into the man, the 10 mm Magnum rounds blowing gaping holes.

Still smoking the cigar, Greene sauntered onto the tarmac and paused to reload. Several of his people were already at the airfield, the only section of the base that hadn't been damaged in any way by the booby trapped police cars.

"Report!" Greene demanded, around the cigar.

"The executions are done," Layne reported, easing a fresh clip into his exhausted weapon. The Barrett XM-25 rifle was a recent acquisition and fired 25 mm shells. At short range, the shells punched through the chest of a man, and at long range the chemical warhead detonated with enough force to blow the victim to hamburger.

"Perhaps, perhaps not," Greene muttered, holstering the revolver. "Miss LoMonaco, if you were hiding from an invasion force such as ours, where would you go?"

Scratching the treble-clef tattoo on the inside of her wrist, the woman paused in thought. "Grease pit in the garage with a car parked on top," LoMonaco said at last.

"Or inside the water tank on top of the roof, or inside an oven in the galley kitchen."

Pleased at the quick response, Greene smiled. "Take twenty men and check those locations. We need to be sure there are no survivors."

"Not a problem," LoMonaco said, resting the warm barrel of the Neostead shotgun on a shoulder and starting forward.

"Alpha Team, follow LoMonaco!" Layne bellowed, and a squad of armed men surged after the diminutive beauty.

The garage proved to be empty, as did the water tank, and the ovens. But checking the freezer, LoMonaco found a suspiciously large pile of frozen beef in the corner. "Surrender or die!" she yelled, working the pump action on the weapon.

"Please, I surrender!" a young private replied, scrambling into view with both hands raised. "Please, don't shoot, I'm just the cook!"

Amused, LoMonaco burst into laughter. "Sorry, but I saw that movie." She blew the head off the cringing teenager.

Heading back to the airfield, LoMonaco had a strange smile on her face, and her eyes sparkled with excitement. The other members of Daylight noticed that, but said nothing, deciding that discretion was the better part of keeping lead out of their heads.

"All clear, Mr. Greene," LoMonaco reported, pulling a fat Cuban cigar from a pocket and applying the flame from a butane lighter to the tip.

"Excellent! Thank you, Samantha," Greene said, and went to join the others on the busy tarmac. "How is it going, Victor?"

With one boot resting on a crate of air-to-air missiles, Layne looked up from a clipboard. "Perfectly, sir! We now have eight Apache gunships, fully fueled and armed. Plus four Cobras and ten Black Hawks."

"Are all the Blackhawks transports?" Greene asked as a man handed him an M249 Minimi machine gun.

"No, sir. Five are transport, four are being packed with spare fuel and munitions, and one is a mobile medical bay."

"Any radar defusers?"

"Yes, sir. Plus radio jammers."

"Excellent," Greene said around his cigar. "Most excellent. My compliments, Victor!"

"It was your plan, sir," the man said with a shrug. "By the way, how did the limpet function?"

"Perfectly!"

Somewhere across the base, a man screamed, an assault rifle chattered, and a burning building started to collapse in ragged stages, thick black clouds of smoke rising high into the morning sky.

"Now what about all of those F-14 jetfighters?" LoMonaco asked, brushing back a loose strand of hair. The action left a streak of blood across her face.

"Nobody in Daylight can fly a jet aside from the two of us. They only know helicopters," Greene growled. "Besides, a jet would only get in the way of the next mission. Low and slow is the key, not death-from-above as the Americans like to boast."

"Such a shame." LoMonaco sighed, looking longingly at the nearby hangar, a sleek F-14 Tomcat sitting in the entranceway fueled and ready to go.

Unexpectedly, a bright flash erupted from the roof of the base library, and a fiery dart lanced across the decimated base to slam directly into the Tomcat. The multimillion-dollar jetfighter thunderously exploded inside the hangar, the spreading fireball set off the next jetfighter and the next. The entire airfield was hammered by a long series of strident detonations that continued for an obscene length of time.

When the last roiling blast finally dissipated, Greene rose from the tarmac to scowl in open hatred at the smoking ruin of the hangar. All of the planes were gone, totally destroyed, the smoldering rubble spread out for as far as he could see.

"What the fuck was that?" Layne loudly demanded, working his jaw to try to clear his ringing ears.

"Sir, does this base have a bomb shelter, or some sort of hidden panic room, whatever the military calls them these days?" LoMonaco growled, brushing debris off her police uniform.

"If so, it didn't appear in any of the floorplans I stole!" Greene snarled, slowly pulling a long sliver of steel from his bloody arm. "Okay, Layne, your turn. Kill them!"

"On it!" the man yelled, starting forward at a full run. "Thomas, Hannigan, Stone, Ferguson! Follow me, boys! It's showtime!"

Spreading out so that they wouldn't offer the hidden Mexican soldiers a group target, the terrorists raced across the base, darting from building to building, bushes to cars, never fully exposing themselves.

"Okay, LoMonaco," Greene started, then stopped.

Buckling on a flamethrower, the woman ignited the pre-burner, then sent out a hissing lance of flame and started setting fire to anything between the library and the all-important helicopters.

As a wall of fire rose high, the billionaire nodded in approval. LoMonaco was hiding the machines from any further attacks! Smart girl. The Mexicans might still shoot more rockets, but, unable to aim properly, it would be a total gamble on their part.

Suddenly, a great commotion came from the base garage, and the metal doors were battered open as a pair of Bradley Fighting Vehicles surged into view. The squat machines charged at the library, rolling over debris, rubble and corpses. Smashing aside parked cars, the vehicles cut loose with 7.62 mm chain guns, arcs of spent brass flying away, then the 25 mm rapid-fire cannons roared into operation, the streams of high-explosive shells chewing a path of destruction across the marble face of the building. Windows shattered, doors disintegrated and hundreds of burning books were blown out of the library to flutter away like dying birds.

There was a flash on the roof, and a rocket streaked down to explode in the street only feet away from one of the Bradleys, then another from the first floor flashed right past the second one to continue onward and disappear into the distant mountains.

Slamming headfirst into the side of the burning building, the Bradley crashed through the brick wall and men briefly screamed, their cries barely discernable over the blazing chain guns. Then the second Bradley slammed through the opposite wall, and the whole library visibly shook, loose bricks tumbling off the cracking walls.

Revving their big Detroit engines to full power, the pair of Bradleys smashed through the interior walls in irregular patterns, crashing through offices, computers and lavatories, crushing a dozen scurrying soldiers.

Smashing out the other side of the sagging building, the armored hulls of the Bradleys were covered with plaster dust, blood, paperbacks.

Stopping only a few yards from each other, the Bradleys unleashed their 25 mm rapid-fires again, tearing holes in the weakened walls and blasting apart support columns.

The roaring conflagration inside the library blocked most of what was happening, but everybody on the base could hear the groan of the structure as it finally succumbed to the brutal attack. A wall broke free to fall across the street, scattering loose bricks for several blocks. The roof bowed, another wall cracked open wide and the entire building collapsed into itself, throwing out a thick gray cloud of concrete dust.

Still firing, the crews of the Bradleys sent in waves of 25 mm shells, pounding the library nonstop, grimly determined to permanently end the threat of the soldiers inside the hidden bomb shelter. Tons of loose masonry tumbled into the basement, along with broken slabs of concrete, and endless piles of hardback books. Soon the basement was an inferno of fiery chaos, the roiling clouds of dense smoke rising high into the sky to form the classic mushroom pattern of any intensely hot ground fire.

Pulling back a safe distance, the Bradleys stopped and the triumphant crews climbed out to start walking back to the airfield with Layne in the lead.

"It looks like we nuked the base," LoMonaco chuckled, easing off the straps of the flamethrower to set the empty canisters on the sidewalk.

"Pretty damn near," Greene said in agreement, slinging the Minimi machine gun across his chest. "All right, let's do a sweep and recover any of our people who died. Bring the bodies along, and we'll bury them at sea."

"Razor up, people! Get those birds hot!" LoMonaco added through cupped hands. "We need to be airborne in fifteen minutes!"

As a clean-up squad got busy with body bags, a small man wearing thick glasses stumbled out of a prefab hut. "Mr. Greene, sir! I found the Gladiator!" the technician shouted happily, triumphantly holding up a control box.

"About damn time," LoMonaco muttered with a disgusted expression. "Is it a newer model?"

"No, sir. But it's still fully functional."

"Good work, Langstrom!" Greene shouted, giving a thumbs up. "Take everything! We can use it in the Triangle."

"Don't forget spare batteries!" Layne added over a shoulder, already heading for a Black Hawk.

A few minutes later, everybody had a seat in a helicopter, and the stolen armada gracefully lifted off the tarmac in a whirlwind of smoky exhaust and acrid smoke from the countless small fires.

Quickly rising high, the helicopters angled away from the obliterated base and followed a whitewater river to disappear into the nearby mountains, heading due north toward the United States.

CHAPTER FOUR

Bethesda, Maryland

The dark sedan pulled into the parking lot of the Ambassador Hotel and took the first spot available among the limousines and imported sports cars.

As the door opened, a middle-aged man got out and started walking briskly toward the outside swimming pool. He wasn't quite running—that would have drawn unwanted attention—but the man certainly wasn't out for a casual stroll, either.

Hal Brognola was a bulldog of a man, still physically fit even though middle age had added a light sprinkling of gray to his dark hair and a bit of paunch to his midsection. Brognola was also the person in charge of the Sensitive Operations Group, a clandestine antiterrorist organization based at Stony Man Farm, Virginia. He handled a lot of black-bag operations, ferreting out the secret enemies of freedom, and bringing them to a hard and swift brand of justice.

Mack Bolan had helped put the Stony Man teams together and at one time had had a hand in running the program, but these days Bolan had an arm's length relationship with the big Fed. He'd take on a mission if it was mutually beneficial. He rarely turned one down.

The hotel's swimming pool was particularly busy

on such a warm day, families splashing about, bored teenagers texting, a cadre of diplomats and attachés at the bar already knocking back shots of straight vodka in a futile effort to hide their early morning consumption of alcohol.

Mixed in with the others were quite a few strikingly beautiful women in skimpy bathing suits. Relaxing on chaise longues, the ladies were slowly oiling their perfect skin, obviously enjoying the admiring looks they garnered.

Slowing his brisk pace on the wet concrete, Brognola smiled at several of the older women. Then one of them smiled back, and shifted on her longue to make room for a guest. Pausing for only a moment, Brognola nodded in thanks for the offer, then touched the plain gold wedding ring on his finger and moved on. A man could appreciate a gorgeous sunrise without trying to take it home.

The damp air was redolent with the aroma of pool chlorine and coconut-scented suntan lotion, the dulcet smells of summer, and Brognola breathed it in deeply, briefly invoking memories of his younger, more carefree, days, days before he'd joined the police force and eventually entered government service.

Times past, youth gone, but sweeter still for the missing or however the poem went, Brognola thought he couldn't recall the last time he'd read a book for the fun of it. His life was purely work, with little time for family and friends anymore. Just another sacrifice for the greater good.

A velvet rope closed off a private section of the swimming area, but Brognola walked in as if he owned the place. A frowning lifeguard started his way, but the big Fed simply flashed his Justice Department credentials, and the man turned and went back to his business watching over the assorted swimmers. This was Washington, and everybody knew not to bother a member of the Alphabet Gang at anything they did.

Stretched on a cushioned table, Mack Bolan was getting a vigorous massage from an elderly Chinese woman, his face set into an emotionless mask of control as her strong hands kneaded his bruised skin to reach the hard muscles underneath.

"Does this story have a happy ending?" Brognola joked.

Looking up, Bolan grinned at his old friend. "Better not say that again, or Mrs. Feinstein will kick your ass."

Brognola arched an eyebrow at the Jewish name, then shrugged. After he had learned that back in the sixties the mayor of Dublin had been a rabbi, he'd stopped trying to pigeonhole anybody and simply took people as they came.

"Wu, my last name is Wu," the woman said in lightly accented English. "My old friend is trying once more to be funny."

"Trying?"

"No wonder so many people shoot you," Mrs. Wu snorted, drying her hands on a towel. "You wouldn't know a joke if it bit your ass." With that, she slapped him on the said area, then turned and walked away, humming a tune.

"You have the strangest friends," Brognola said with a chuckle.

Sitting up, Bolan stretched and flexed his arms, the muscles visibly moving under the skin. "A strange few," he said. "There's no better massage therapist than

Cindy. She's a black belt in kung fu, and can kill just as easily as heal with those old hands."

Brognola paused, then realized it wasn't a joke. "Cindy Wu? Like in the Dr. Seuss books?"

"I think that was Cindy Lu, and she prefers to be called Cynthia."

Bolan slid off the table and pulled on a robe. "Walk with me."

Moving away from the busy pool, the men entered a hedge maze and soon found a more secluded area. There was a table with two chairs, a pile of sandwiches and a pitcher of iced coffee.

"So what's up?" Bolan asked.

"Sorry about this. I know you just got back, but I've got one of those feelings," Brognola said, pouring himself a glass of the iced coffee.

"What happened?" Bolan asked, all of the humor gone from his voice and demeanor.

Laying a briefcase on the table, Brognola pressed a thumb to the glowing biometric lock. He felt a brief tingle as an electronic sensor confirmed that it was living flesh pressed against the contact plate, then it read his fingerprint, compared it to those on file. The case disarmed the self-destruct charge, then unlocked.

"Roughly twenty-four hours ago some people disguised as the Mexican police destroyed a Mexican military base in the Azules Mountains," Brognola said, opening the case. Inside was a US Army laptop.

"They attacked the base?"

"*Destroyed* is the correct word." Flipping up the screen, Brognola tapped a button, and the monitor flickered into life. "These shots were recovered from a dozen smashed cell phones, and the one security camera that the terrorists didn't find and smash."

"Terrorist is a big leap from thieves," Bolan said, his full attention centered on the disjointed images: running shoes, a rain of spent shells, fire and destruction everywhere. A soldier firing his handgun from the ground, then instantly torn apart by converging streams of bullets from several different directions.

"Are those M16 assault rifles?" Bolan asked, furrowing his brow.

"F88," Brognola corrected him. "Standard issue for the Australian military. They use the same ammo that we do, but it cycles a little bit slower than an American version."

"That's what caught my attention," Bolan said, playing the images again.

Brognola was impressed. Bolan heard the difference in the middle of a firefight? "Now, they didn't take the payroll in the commander's safe, or even the loose cash in the register at the officer's club. They did take a hundred kilos of pure heroin that was waiting to be incinerated, but ignored an even larger amount of crystal meth."

Bolan gave a low whistle. That made no sense since the meth would be worth twice, maybe three times, more than the heroin. Everything seemed to point to the thieves being be narcoterrorists, but again, why leave behind the crystal meth? Why in the world would anybody need that much heroin?

"How do you know they're not really the police, the drugs are purely misdirection, and in fact this was some kind of a political junta?" Bolan asked pointedly.

"No way they're blue," Brognola stated. "The fat guy

is way too big. The woman is too short. The Mexicans have a minimum height requirement for female officers, and there is no record for anybody over seven feet tall ever working for the Mexican police."

"Fair enough. Okay, what did they take?"

"Mostly heavy weapons, rocket launchers, Stinger missiles, radar defusers, VX nerve gas, and every working gunship on the base. Nineteen to be exact."

"What types?"

"Mostly Apache and Cobra, but also a couple of armed Black Hawks. Not state-of-the-art, but all in perfect working condition, and armed to the teeth."

"Maybe they plan on selling the helicopters. The Apaches alone would fetch a small fortune in certain parts of the world."

"I wish it was true." Brognola frowned. "However, they also took a Black Hawk medical unit."

"Any blood missing from the base hospital?"

"According to the records, about a hundred units of blood plasma, and ten more of AB positive."

"But nothing else?"

"Just the usual medical supplies, sutures, bandages, forceps and such."

"AB positive is a pretty rare blood type," Bolan said slowly.

"Yes, it is," Brognola said. "So I ran that through the Interpol database, along with the general descriptions of the three people armed with unusual weapons."

Bolan understood. Most of the thieves were carrying an F-8S. Anyone carrying a different weapon would be either a specialist, who might have a crime record, or else he or she was the person in charge.

"Now, the fat guy has an XM-25 grenade rifle,"

Brognola said flipping through the shots to find the ones he wanted, then freezing them. "The woman has a Neostead shotgun, while the giant is carrying an F88 assault rifle...but has a Falcon automatic pistol in his shoulder holster. Everybody else is carrying a police-issue Glock."

"What did you find?" Bolan asked, suddenly interested.

"Again nothing," Brognola admitted honestly, taking a sandwich. "The President thinks I'm overreacting. But he's a politician, and I'm a street cop."

"Correction. The top cop for the nation."

"Just a cop all the same. Half of this job is going with a gut instinct, and I've got a bad one on this thing, Striker," Brognola said with a grimace. "There was just something hinky about these three, so I ran their descriptions through the entire government database. That brought up something."

He took a bite of the sandwich, chewed and swallowed. "The giant appears to be Dalton Greene, the Australian billionaire, which makes the other two his bodyguards, Victor Layne and Samantha LoMonaco."

"How hard is that intel?"

"Weak, only around fifty percent accurate."

"*Weak* is a nice way to put it."

"Accepted. Then I read that Greene and his bodyguards all died in a fiery car crash last week, the bodies burned beyond recognition."

As the pictures on the screen stopped, Bolan sat back in his chair. "Chalk up another win for the gut instinct," he said slowly. "This reeks to high heaven."

Dalton Greene had been on Bolan's radar for quite

a while. There was nothing specific, just a lot of little indicators that the Aussie billionaire was dirty.

"How did they take the base?" Bolan asked.

Brognola shrugged. "Forensics isn't sure yet, but I think they staged a riot in Cancun yesterday, then ambushed the police and stole their cars."

"You *think?*"

"None of the police officers who responded to the call have been found yet. The attack zone was swept clean. Literally swept clean, like it was a zen rock garden."

"Which means the cops are most likely shark food at the bottom of the Gulf of Mexico."

"Probably."

This was an interesting puzzle, Bolan realized. Greene was rich enough to buy the number of stolen helicopters, plus the weapons, on the black market. So why would he go to all the trouble to steal them? Merely to hide his identity, or was there something darker at play, some twist that he couldn't quite see yet?

Reaching out, he tapped a button to start the flow of chaotic images once more. By now, Bolan was starting to get a bad feeling in his own gut. Ruthless, patient, cool and bloodthirsty. These were hard boys with a game plan. That always spelled big trouble.

"It looks like I'm going to Mexico...."

CHAPTER FIVE

Mexico City, Mexico

The air was cool and crisp inside the Alhambra Night Club, scrubbed and sterilized by a host of machines designed to remove any trace of pollution from the bustling metropolis just outside the front door.

A sparkling disco ball on the ceiling filled the room with artificial starlight, and a live band on the stage softly played classical love songs. Young couples danced on the floor and old married couples looked on from their tables, holding hands and smiling in fond memory. Everybody was well-dressed, suits and ties for the gentlemen, flowing dresses with wrist corsages for the ladies.

Standing outside the club was a pair of former bank guards whose only job was to keep out anybody deemed unsuitable, no matter how much money they were offered as a bribe, or what amazing sexual favors were promised in exchange for a quick peek inside. Unfortunately, no security system was perfect.

With a lopsided smile, the drunk woman leaned closer. "I lo-love big men," she slurred, a plump breast nearly falling out of her black satin dress.

Saying nothing in reply, Special Agent Willard Cinco moved one chair away at the hotel bar.

She followed along.

"I sa-said that I love big, muscular, men," she whispered, attempting a sexy smile and failing utterly. "Don't you like me?"

"I like you fine, sweetheart, but I'm married and my wife is the jealous type." He flashed her an apologetic smile, stood and walked away without another word.

Going to a table, Cinco waved down a passing waitress and ordered another scotch and soda. Maria smiled in reply showing dimples, then walked away with a definite swaying of the hips, but slowly, to let him admire the view.

Six feet tall, and as almost as wide, the hulking Mexican intelligence agent liked to joke that he was built like a bull, and easily twice as smart. But that was just one of his many lies. An expert in cryptography, countersurveillance and high explosives, Willard "The Bull" Cinco was one of the top agents at Centro de Investigatión y Seguridad Nacional de Mexico—CISEN, Mexico's intelligence agency.

The television behind the bar was showing a football game, what the crazy Americans called soccer for some unknown reason, and Cinco heard the overly excited announcers talking about how one team's defense was murdering the opposition, what a slaughter it was going to be this night, somebody wearing guts for garters, and how the blood would flow! Sipping his drink, the CISEN agent didn't know whether to laugh, or cry.

Reaching into a pocket, Cinco pulled out a universal remote and shifted to the weather channel. Nobody in the club seemed to notice, or care. He liked the Weather Channel, it was oddly soothing, almost hypnotic.

Folding a stick of chewing gum into his mouth to help fight off the urge for a cigarette, Cinco chewed in peaceful silence for a while, and wasn't terribly surprised when Maria delivered his drink accompanied by a free bowl of cheesy crackers, and a slip of paper bearing the name Rosetta and a local phone number. Exercising restraint, Cinco snacked on the first and burned the other in the ashtray, his impatience growing by the minute. His personal network of informants was rarely wrong about such things, but this time Cinco was starting to think that—

She walked into the nightclub as if she owned the place. Tall, slim and deliciously dark with raven-black hair and a wide generous smile, the woman was dressed in a designer gown that couldn't have been any more formfitting if it had been sprayed onto her flawless skin. Diamonds sparkled from her fingers, circled both wrists and her neck. Her shoes showed toes, the nails painted the same color as her fingernail polish, and her long hair was swept forward across her face to help hide the jagged rope scar on her neck where she had been hung and hideously tortured by the formerly corrupt spy agency. Helping the federal army to bring it down hard, Lucia Cortez had been generously rewarded by Mexico by not being arrested for stealing millions of dollars from the secret coffers of the agency. Soon, Cortez had a string of restaurants, hotels, gas stations and nightclubs across the nation and happily fed CISEN any juicy gossip her employees heard in passing.

"Good evening, Bull," Cortez said, sitting down at his table. Smiling, she placed a cigarette between her lips and waited.

Removing it, Cinco crushed the tube in one hand and sprinkled the remains into the ashtray.

Her dark eyes flashed with surprise, then Cortez laughed and relaxed in the cushioned leather chair. "You never change," she said, reaching out to playfully ruffle his hair. "When the worms come to eat you in the grave, you'll arrest them for trespassing."

"My coffin, my rules." Cinco smiled, then recoiled as the woman jerked backward in the chair, a small black hole appearing in the middle of her forehead. As blood began to trickle from the bullet wound, Cinco was hit twice in the back with something very hard.

Flipping over the table, he dove to the floor and came up with his Magnum pistol blasting. Standing near the fire exit was a man holding a silenced rifle, preparing to fire again. But the heavy slugs from the .357 Magnum slammed him against the fire door so hard his head audibly cracked on the metal, and he tumbled to the floor, gushing blood.

Panic filled the nightclub at the sound of the gunshots, and people started rushing about in a blind panic, screaming and shouting.

Ignoring the civilians, Cinco knelt by Cortez, and saw that it was too late to do anything. Her face was ashen, the pulse in their throat weak, and her skin already felt cold and lifeless.

"Lucia," he whispered putting a lifetime of emotion into the name.

"Ca-Cancun…" she whispered in reply, the words almost lost in the general commotion of the rioting nightclub. She trembled once, then went still forever.

Laying her head gently on the floor, Cinco rose to his

full height and proceeded directly out the fire exit. He passed by the killer without a second glance. He knew the man, Hector Martin, a contract killer from Quarez, who never asked why, merely who and how much? He had done a lot of work for the Sandanistas back in the bad old days, and Cinco knew that there was nothing new he could learn from the corpse. Martin cost a lot, so that meant whoever had had Cortez killed was very wealthy, and had good intel about the criminal underworld. That wasn't much to go on, but he had to start somewhere.

The back alley was hot, humid and dank, ripe with the smell of rotting garbage. Feeling like a machine set on autopilot, Cinco strode through the reeking darkness, his fist clenched around the pistol, his heart pounding as he desperately sought somebody to kill in revenge for the senseless slaughter of his old friend. But the alley was clear, and the parking lot was total chaos, any possible clues destroyed by the mob of frightened civilians running for their lives.

Standing alone for what seemed a long time, Cinco slowly holstered the weapon, then went to his car and got inside. Opening the glove box, he pawed through the collection of maps until he found one that showed how to get to the Cancun Peninsula.

International Waters, Gulf of Mexico

THE *ALLENDALE* ROSE and fell on the easy swells of the open water. There were no nets hanging from the tall cranes of the converted fishing boat, and the cold bay had long ago been made into a sort of dormitory with rows of bunk beds.

Sitting in a canvas chair, a blind man was softly strumming an old guitar, while his family and friends gathered around. Nearby, on several hibachis filled with hot coals, hamburgers and sausages loudly sizzled and gave off the most amazingly delicious mixture of smells.

"What are you going to play, Grandpa?" a young man asked, twisting off the cap from a frosty bottle of beer.

"What would you like to hear?" Jefferson LaSalle asked, then paused to tilt his head.

"Something wrong, sir?" a young woman asked, glancing around at the empty sea and sky.

Dropping the guitar, Jefferson felt cold adrenaline flood his body as he flashed back decades ago to the hated Vietnam war. Dear God almighty, he knew that noise all too well. It was the very sound that had robbed him of his sight and killed his best two friends at the exact same moment.

Lunging forward, the old vet grabbed the first child he could reach and strained with all of his might as he flung the little girl over the side of the *Allendale* and into the ocean.

"Grandpa!" a woman screamed. "Have you gone mad!"

But before he could answer something dark streaked past the boat leaving behind a long contrail of smoke.

"That's a rocket!" A young boy laughed, starting to applaud.

Reaching for the noise, Jefferson grabbed the boy and dove sideways over the gunwale holding the child tight to his chest.

"What in the world is going on here?" a fat man demanded, setting down his beer. "Has the old man gone loony?"

High overhead, the dark shape was spiraling about in the growing twilight, swinging this way, and that, to finally start directly for the fishing boat.

With a growing feeling of dread, a woman grabbed her two children and dove over the side of the vessel. Dropping a book, a thin man began throwing small children overboard as fast as he could, then everybody scrambled to get off the deck, fueled more by family loyalty than fear.

The last man clumsily dove over the stern to belly flop loudly in the salty water a split second before the stealth missile slammed into the boat. The wooden hull shattered into pieces as it came out the other side, and then exploded, the ancient wood just barely offering enough resistance to trigger the warhead.

The chemical hellstorm filled the area, illuminated the ocean for miles, the blast smashing the *Allendale* into kindling and slamming the assorted swimmers deep underwater. But only a few moments later they bobbed to the surface again, coughing and spitting, treading water furiously.

"Grandpa, how...how did you know?" a man asked, his hair plastered flat onto his head.

But the old man merely shook his head in reply, already starting the arduous journey back to shore. There were no sharks, or barracudas in the area, so with some luck his family would reach the shore alive. However, he couldn't say the same thing for whomever that swarm of military gunships was after. God help them all, he thought, the poor bastards.

Cape Canaveral, Florida

WHENEVER NASA HAD A ROCKET on the launch pad, they guarded it with a staggering display of physical defenses. A dozen Navy warships encircled the launch facility, and the sky overhead was full of Air Force jet-fighters, chasing away the curious and ready to strike with lethal force any more determined advance. Navy submarines patrolled the deep waters, radar filled the sky, sonar probed the sea, and NORAD satellites watched everything from high in orbit. The cost of this military "ring of steel" was staggering, but deemed well worth it.

At any other time of the year, NASA and the sprawling launch facility used only standard security protocols established for any government facility in an effort to save the taxpayers some money. That was deemed prudent and cost-effective by the politicians, scientists and anybody who wasn't trained in military tactics or security.

Following a modified version of the old Japanese plan of attack on Pearl Harbor, the forces of Daylight swept in from the west, maintaining tight formation, flying below the radar, and destroying any vessel they encountered in the open water. A dozen assorted boats were sunk with long-range heatseekers to remove any chance of advance warning to NASA. The Apaches were the fastest craft, so they hung back in the rear, and let the slower Cobras take the lead, with the armed Black Hawks maintaining a cluster formation in the middle, especially the one medical Black Hawk. That was assigned as their command ship, and contained Dalton Greene.

Bent over a table covered with maps and satellite photographs, the Australian billionaire was directing the mission using the one form of communication that couldn't be effectively blocked—a Gertrude.

Everybody in the civilized world knew how submarines used a sonar "ping" to locate obstructions underwater. Fewer people had any idea that sonar would be modified into a form of underwater transmitter that somewhere along the way had gotten the odd nickname of Gertrude, original source unknown.

It broadcast a powerful pulse into the water, one that everybody and anybody within range could hear, which rendered it useless for general combat. There had been numerous attempts to scramble the pulses that never seemed to work because of countless technical difficulties. Encoded underwater transmissions weren't possible, only general broadcasts, which the Navy strongly disliked. Even in times of peace, one submarine commander chatting with another could reveal far too much valuable information to non-Navy listeners. So the practice was strongly discouraged. When the commanders wanted to talk, they would "ping" each other, then rise to the surface and use more conventional forms of communications.

However, Greene had spent years laying plans for these attacks. The initial sortie on NASA was crucial, and after spending millions on experiments, his scientists had finally managed to shift the operational frequency of a Gertrude into the ultrasonic range, where nobody could hear it but dogs. And since one hundred percent of all airplanes, even seaplanes, didn't have sonar receivers, nobody else in the air could even receive the transmission, much less understand. The failed form of underwater communications had proved highly successful in the lab. But only between helicopters in close-quarter combat. Airplanes and jetfighters simply made too much noise.

Those were the first obstacles to overcome today.

A self-made millionaire, Dalton Greene had been born in South Africa. When the white regime fell and Nelson Mandela took over, a disgusted Greene fled to Australia.

But now, swarms of immigrants were flooding into his adopted homeland, and Greene knew that soon it would became a nation of mongrels—just like South Africa. In a desperate effort to stop the influx of immigrants, Greene decided to liquidate his vast financial holdings and save Australia from the unwanted invasion in the only way possible—by starting a new world war.

Radiating a broad spectrum of radio, radar and cellular telephone jammers, the armada of stolen helicopters separated into groups. The forces of Daylight attacked from five directions, with Greene steadily issuing commands over the modified Gertrude.

Coming in from the west, the first salvo of missiles from Alpha Wing was sent arching over the horizon long before the American space base even came into view. The guided missiles matched the terrain below to the maps in their computers, and dove for the kill.

At the first indication of jamming, the local Air Force base assigned to protect NASA scrambled a full wing of Hornets, and the jets were just taxiing along the runway when the missiles arrived to slam into the tarmac and unleash a tidal wave of napalm.

The jetfighters were drenched by the sticky compound, and dripping flame. The pilots first tried to extinguish the hellish blaze by going faster, but that only seemed to feed the fire, making it hotter, the fuselage of the Hornets starting to soften in spots, the temperature gauges registering off the dial. With no other choice, the pilots decided to eject—only to realize that they were dangerously close to the civilian territory: homes, schools and hospitals.

Trapped between duty and honor, the grim Air Force pilots made the hard choice, and directed their melting jetfighters toward the open sea. Not one of them made it there.

Only moments later, the SAM bunkers assigned to protect the space facility cut loose with multiple salvos. But, designed to stop incoming missiles and enemy planes, the heatseekers went completely out of control at the wall of napalm, and streaked down to crash into the burning tarmac, removing any possibility of additional jetfighters attempting to take off.

"This is Zed Commander. Take out the helicopter hangar and fuel depot!" Greene commanded, moving small figures across the map. "Bravo Wing, go-go-go!"

Flashing across Coco Beach, Bravo Wing easily located the city power station and took it out with a single concentrated salvo. Then, following the high-tension powerlines, they systematically destroyed each substation encountered until the electric grid for Florida collapsed and half of the state went dark.

Right on cue, dozens of computer hackers across the

world began flooding the internet with conflicting message about what was happening, blocking any possible attempt by the National Guard or the police to coordinate local defenses using bleep transmissions, or even email. Pretending to be trapped victims, the hackers claimed there were Cuban warships hitting Miami harbor, al-Qaeda overwhelming Tallahassee, and suicide bombers killing everybody at all of the larger amusement parks.

Unable to tell the real information from the false, the police were forced to simply wait until they knew what was actually happening. Which was exactly what Greene had wanted in the first place.

Using the chemical sensors in the Apache gunships, Charlie Wing easily located the exhaust fumes from a large petroleum refinery, and took out the main storage tanks with a salvo of 35 mm rockets, and then a single air-to-ground missile. Ripped wide open by the devastating combination attack, the colossal storage tanks burst, and ignited into gargantuan fireballs that registered as a nuclear explosion on the Keyhole and WatchDog satellites in orbit.

Following the coastline, David Wing easily found the main NASA facility, and spread out to hammer the base with multiple salvos of rockets and missiles. The multiple explosions formed a wall of fireballs before the Daylight gunships, and they charged straight through with their machine guns firing. Civilian cars were ripped apart under the barrage, windows shattering, hoods flying up and the older models burst into flames. People were scurrying everywhere, shouting, praying, cursing and firing handguns at the armored gunships. Ruthlessly, the Daylight pilots gunned down everybody.

Unexpectedly, a single antiaircraft rocket zoomed up from the ground, and a Black Hawk was blown out of the sky, flaming debris and bodies raining back down across the base.

A thousand people on the ground began to cheer, until all of the remaining gunships cut loose with everything they had. Rockets, missiles, bombs and chain guns strafed the base, detonating massive storage tanks of liquid hydrogen. The stentorian explosion shook the entire base as if a volcano had erupted. The noise was almost beyond description, and a mob of screaming people were blown away like dry autumn leaves.

Caught in the initial blast, the armored gunships were buffeted about, several of them taking damage, and two Apaches coming so close to each other that their spinning blades threw off sparks at the fleeting touch. But the Daylight armada survived, and did the same thing again to another underground storage tank of liquid oxygen. Prepared this time, they were hardly bothered by the hellish detonation, and continued their Draconian rampage across the base, delivering swift and unremitting death in every way possible.

Protected by the expanding ring of bloody chaos, David Wing landed on the unprotected roof of the NASA administration building. Pouring out of the helicopters, the terrorists stormed down the stairwell, executing anybody they encountered. Smashing into a lab, they gunned down the terrified scientists and blew open a safe. Inside were neat rows of electric components nestled in the soft gray foam normally used for transporting high explosives.

Gingerly loading the devices onto hand trucks, the terrorists returned to the roof, loaded them onto the waiting Black Hawk and immediately departed.

"Time?" Layne asked, slamming the hatch shut.

"Four minutes twenty-two seconds," Greene replied, clicking a stopwatch. "One full minute ahead of schedule."

"Told you I could," Layne boasted proudly, dropping into a jump seat.

"Indeed, you did." LoMonaco chuckled. "Well done."

"We're not out of this yet," Greene stated. "This is Zed Commander. Tango Niner. Repeat, Tango Niner."

Instantly, all of the Daylight helicopters ceased their attacks and headed out to sea until the curvature of the Earth took them out of the sight, then they banked hard and dropped low, skimming across the waves as they streaked due south.

A few seconds later, rented fishing tugs moored at Daytona Beach, Tampa and Miami released thousands of Mylar balloons filled with helium. Carried aloft by the sea wind, they swiftly spread across the entire state, completely scrambling any attempt by the military to track the escaping terrorists.

"How much did all of this cost us, sir?" LoMonaco asked.

"Roughly a hundred million dollars," Greene replied, still working on the maps.

"And the components we stole couldn't be made for much less than that amount?"

"Not for any amount," he corrected sitting back in

his chair. "These are prototypes of a new boron-plasma enginette."

Bandaging a wound on his arm, Layne scowled. "A... What was that word again?"

"Enginette," Greene replied slowly. "It is a kind of miniature engine with no moving parts."

"And this will help us start the war?" LoMonaco asked skeptically.

"Start the war?" Greene laughed, lifting up one of the boron enginettes for closer examination. "This will bring about the end of this uncivilized world." A smile slowly spread across his ruddy face.

CHAPTER SIX

Mexico

"Flight 75, you are cleared to descend and use runway four," a voice crackled over the ceiling speaker. "Repeat, runway four. Flight 75, do you copy?"

"Roger, tower. Runway four. Seventy-five, willco," former Air Force Captain Levi Sorenson repeated, easing the steering yoke forward, and feathering the propellers to slow their speed. The huge engines eased their sustained roar and changed pitch as the captain angled downward, and pulled back on the throttles.

Gracefully descending from the rainy sky, the huge C-130 Hercules transport lightly touched down on the slick landing strip of the civilian airport, and rolled to a stop in front of a private hangar at the extreme edge of the field.

Mack Bolan nodded his thanks to the pilot, a blacksuit who had rotated into Stony Man Farm, then disembarked.

For this mission, Bolan was carrying credit cards, driver's license, passport and other documents that identified him as George Adams, a geologist for a major petroleum company. Adams was just one of the many aliases he used in his line of work, and the documents,

provided by Aaron Kurtzman at Stony Man Farm, were
first-rate.

Killing the engines, Sorenson set the brakes and
called the tower to arrange for the plane to be refueled
and prepared for an immediate departure. The man had
no idea where he might be going next, but it never hurt
to be prepared to leave at a moment's notice. All the
blacksuit pilot knew was that when Striker decided it
was time to go, it was time to go.

ACCORDING TO HAL BROGNOLA, the area around the destroyed Azules military base had been effectively sealed
by the Mexican air force, the sky jammed full of jetfighters and helicopter gunships, the ground covered
with a full battalion of soldiers and a dozen Abrams
tanks, all of them grimly looking for somebody to attack as revenge for the slaughter of so many of their
brothers-in-arms.

Bolan knew that going anywhere near that hot zone
would probably buy him a pine coffin, and so he elected
to start the mission by investigating the death of the police officers at Cancun. If it proved necessary, he would
drive to the Azules base, and obtain the reports from
the military forensics teams. But first, Bolan wanted to
know more about the slaughter of the police officers.

It was common knowledge that the Mexican police
conducted a rather cavalier attitude toward partying
college students. The flood of money they brought into
the local economy was the lifeblood of the isolated resort community. Yet somehow, this particular celebration had gotten so raucous and out of control that they
had been forced to make an appearance.

While still in Mexico, the rattled American students

had nothing to say about the matter. But once they were back home, all of the gory details were posted on various social-media sites. The party had been starting to wind down when somebody delivered an assortment of recreational drugs: weed, zoomers, ecstasy, as well as the ever-popular cocaine. In short order, the party flared back to life, rapidly escalating to a full-fledged orgy. After receiving hundreds of complaints from the row of hotels along the public beach, the police had finally decided to try to calm things down. But they had been ambushed on the main access road and had never reached the beach alive.

To Bolan it was obvious that whomever was behind the slaughter had delivered the drugs to turn the students into the bait of a deadly trap. That gave him somewhere to start the hunt, somewhere the police couldn't safely venture—the Broken Coyote.

Bolan left the flight deck of the Hercules, climbed down a set of aluminum stairs to the cargo deck, and started the lengthy procedure of releasing the cushioned iron clamps and spiderweb of canvas straps that held an old battered delivery RV tightly in place.

Actually brand-new, the vehicle was artistically coated in several locations with antirust primer, and Bolan himself had used a sledge hammer to put a couple of small dents into the reinforced bumpers. Both of the front seats were heavily coated with duct tape, and there was a hole in the dashboard where a radio-CD player would usually have been located. Appearing old and dilapidated, the recreational vehicle seemed just about ready to crumble apart from decades of abuse.

In reality, the chassis of the vehicle was sheathed in multiple layers of advanced ceramic armor, the windows were made of bulletproof plastic, the military-grade tires sealed any puncture all by themselves, and the colossal V12 power plant had been transplanted directly from a LAV-25 armored personnel carrier.

For all intents and purposes, the RV was an urban tank. The rear compartment was a mobile command post packed with state-of-the-art surveillance equipment, a satellite uplink, several computers, shortwave radio, radar jammers, medical supplies and a small arsenal of weapons. Plus, the RV itself was armed with hidden machine guns, and the bulky air-conditioner on the roof was actually a disguised missile pod.

Finished freeing the RV, Bolan deactivated its antiintruder systems and climbed inside. Starting up the massive engine, he ran a fast check over the systems while he waited for the vehicle to warm to operational temperatures.

When the needle on the gauge finally reached the mark, Bolan rolled down the rear ramp of the Hercules and drove out of the cargo plane, hitting the rainy tarmac with a hard jounce. The wiper blades came on automatically as Bolan waited for the ramp to cycle closed and lock. Shifting into gear, he started for the access road leading from the airport, then due west for the infamous Broken Coyote. The soldier left the airport unchallenged. The C-130 had been expected and a favor repaid to Hal Brognola.

A small cantina located somewhere deep in the Yucatán desert, the Broken Coyote was generally considered by most law-enforcement officials to be the nerve center for all major smuggling in eastern Mexico and the southwestern United States. Although that was purely hearsay and had never been proven in court.

"Not yet, anyway," Bolan muttered, taking out his smartphone and establishing a piggyback relay to the federal data archives.

As the information began to stream in, he linked it to the latest updates on the forensic discoveries by the police. Correlating the data from the two sources, Bolan slowly started to define the attackers. Roughly a hundred strong, they mostly wore civilian shoes, and used an odd mixture of military weapons. That seemed to mark them as merely heavily armed amateurs, except that the brass casings of their spent ammunition didn't have a manufacturer's stamp.

Bolan frowned at that. All commercial ammunition carried the trademark of the manufacturer, unless it was made for an intelligence agency. No CIA wet team wanted to do a job in Prague, and announce to the world that it was them by the brass they left behind. Mossad, MI-6, FSB, Red Star, CIA, NSA, ANSI—every intelligence agency had a private source of untraceable ammunition.

Heading off the main road and into the desert, Bolan impatiently waited for the mass spectrometer results from the crime lab in the capital. It was nearly midnight before he got them. The casings contained a better grade of copper than Russia's or China's, but a lower grade of tin than the United Kingdom's, Germany's, or France's… Bingo, there was a match!

"Australia?" Bolan said out loud. Why would the Aussies attack Mexico? They didn't have any known terrorist groups operating Down Under, and some small part of Bolan wondered if that was about to change. Australian terrorists. It really was becoming a strange new world.

Even constantly checking the dashboard GPS, and the aerial maps, it still took Bolan several hours to find the crooked arroyo that held his target for this night.

Located halfway inside a cave, the Broken Coyote was made of concrete blocks edged with brick support columns. The door was covered with slat armor, the window shutters were made of rusty steel and the roof was covered with coils of razor wire.

Turning off the headlights to hide his approach, Bolan grunted at the sight. Cantina his ass. The Broken Coyote was a hardsite, and looked more than capable of withstanding any conceivable raid by the Mexican authorities.

Standing on either side of the front door was a pair of guards cradling Atchisson autoshotguns, and the gravel parking lot was packed with Jeeps, Hummers, 4x4 trucks, horses and dozens of motorcycles.

Correction, several dozen motorcycles, but the rest were choppers, Bolan amended. A chopper was basically a standard motorcycle with the front end removed, and replaced with an extended frame and tire. The conversion made long-distance driving on a highway very comfortable. However, a chopper couldn't maneuver worth a damn in rough country.

A city-based motorcycle gang and a local one operating out of the same location? That smacked of a much larger organization than he had originally estimated. Not good news.

There was no sign that the local gang owned a Mad Max. Those had been causing a lot of trouble lately for the border guards of both countries. However, Bolan felt sure that the Amsterdam missile pod on top of the RV could handle whatever kind of homemade tank the locals might have been able to cobble together at a junkyard.

Bolan ghosted past the Broken Coyote to park the RV behind some boulders. Draping the vehicle with a camouflage tarpaulin, he armed the security system.

Nodding to the guards flanking the door, Bolan boldly walked inside and was immediately hit by a palpable rush of smoke, heat, laughter, sweaty leather and the nearly overpowering smell of stale beer.

Inside, the cantina was old and dirty, the stucco walls almost black from the decades of accumulated cigarette smoke. The brick floor was covered with crunchy peanut shells, and if there was a ceiling it was impossible to see it in the smoky gloom. A long bar edged with neon sat to the right, and a stage to the left where a rock band was belting out a classic while a pair of topless women nimbly spun around chrome-plated poles. Two more guards sat on chairs near the bar, both with Neostead shotguns laying across their laps. The double magazines of the Neostead gave you a choice of using double-O buckshot, which would blow a man in two, or using a stun bag to put him down hard, but still alive.

The customers were a dirty lot, generally unshaven men with scars, but there were a few heavily tattooed women mixed in among the crowd. At first glance, Bolan was unsure if the burly women were hookers, customers or dates, and after a second glance he was even less sure.

Everybody sported tattoos, and most wore combat boots, denim pants and leather biker jackets. The only exceptions were a handful of men in white-linen business suits and couple of muscle-bound women in tank tops that showed a lot of sloping cleavage and their massively overdeveloped biceps, triceps and deltoids.

Absolutely everybody was armed, the checkered grips of revolvers and automatic pistols jutting from boots, belts and, in a few cases, shoulder holsters. Obviously those were the big-city boys who had arrived in the 4x4 trucks.

Heading for the bar, Bolan maneuvered his way through the maze of tables, the peanut shells on the dirty floor crunching under every footstep. A lot of people watched him pass with complete indifference, but a few studied him intently as if detecting trouble coming their way. However, the man wasn't overly concerned by the scrutiny. A stranger in the Coyote was either lost or an undercover cop or on business. It was only natural for the crowd to try to find out which he was before making a move.

"Hey, gringo!" a bald man snarled, starting to rise from a chair a knife in his hand.

Without pausing, Bolan slammed an elbow into his face. Bloody teeth went flying, and the man crumpled to the floor with a low groan.

The band kept playing, but all conversation in the cantina paused for a moment, then went back to normal, and the unconscious man's friends dragged him outside.

Taking a seat at the counter, Bolan flashed two fingers, and the bartender brought over a partly full glass and a bottle of mescal. Taking a sniff, Bolan poured the contents of the glass on the floor. "I ordered a drink, not your mother's piss," he growled.

Everybody at the bar laughed, and the bartender shrugged, then brought over a sealed bottle of tequila. He offered it without comment, and Bolan nodded. As the bartender went back to filling pitchers of beer, the soldier used a pocketknife to cut away the seal and pour himself three fingers. In here, trust was even more rare than mercy.

As the rock group finished the song, there was a smattering of applause, and they left the stage to be replaced with the steady thumping of bass music from the wall speakers. Moving to the beat, a busty teenager dressed as a cowgirl spun onto the stage to dramatically stop in the exact center of a bright spotlight. Then she ripped open the star-spangled vest to proudly reveal her amazingly firm breasts decorated with twinkling electronic nipple rings.

Energetically applauding this time, the crowd voiced its approval as the dancer shrugged off the vest, then everything else except a g-string and started moving across the stage in perfect time to the beat of the music.

In spite of himself, Bolan was impressed. The woman obviously had real talent, and he wondered what she was doing in a dump like this. Then she paused in the bright lights with both arms raised and he saw the needle tracks up both arms. Mystery solved.

Coming out of the back room, a burly man in loose clothing stopped at the sight of Bolan sitting at the counter, then hurried over.

"Whatcha want here, gringo?" he demanded in a guttural tone. His thumbs were tucked behind an Alamo belt buckle, only a few inches away from a British-made Webley .445 revolver.

Taking his time, Bolan raised the glass to his mouth, but only let the liquor wet his lips.

"Well?" the man demanded even louder, advancing a step.

Everybody nearby moved backward a little, preparing to leave the combat zone.

"And who the fuck are you, mate?" Bolan said, trying his best to sound Australian.

"Me? I'm Julio Quarez, and I own the Coyote!" the man stated, jerking a thumb at himself. "Now who the fuck are you?"

"John Smith," Bolan drawled. "And unfortunately for you, mate, my employer was seriously unimpressed with the quality of the merchandise you delivered."

A minute passed, then another, with nobody watching the dancer anymore. All eyes were riveted on Bolan and Quarez.

"That's bullshit," Quarez muttered uneasily, raising both hands. "My people delivered exactly what your boss requested!"

"Did they now?" Bolan whispered, glancing sideways. When there was no reply, he slid off the stool and faced the other man. Both of his arms were hanging casually at his sides, and both the Beretta and Desert Eagle were in full sight.

Trying to generate a smile, Quarez then nervously frowned. "Maybe we better take this into the back room," he suggested, turning and moving fast.

Bolan followed the man down a short hallway and into a back room. So far so good. His hunch had been right. This was the supplier of hookers and drugs at the Cancun beach party. Now, if he could only get a name, he'd be halfway to putting the son of a bitch into the dirt.

Inside the storage room were shelves of empty beer pitchers, assorted bottles of liquor, barrels of sawdust, bags of peanuts, jars of pickled onions and all of the sundry items needed to operate any bar. There was also another door. This one was made of burnished steel and had a combination dial in the middle.

Spinning the dial, Quarez rotated in the combination, then braced himself to pull open the heavy door. Bolan could see that it was almost a foot thick, and supported by a single hinge that extended along the entire side. Stepping over the raised threshold, he noted some minor scoring along the edge of the door, burn marks that had been scratched off.

"You've had some trouble with thieves, I see," Bolan commented.

Quarez shrugged. "Nothing serious."

"They couldn't get through?"

"Nobody can. We stole that door from a bank vault in Bolivia! You'd need a tank to blast a hole in that, amigo."

The next room was spotlessly clean, with no sign of dust or disorder. The air was flat and tasteless, like that in a hospital or laboratory, and for good reason. In every corner was a humming air purifier, and a dehumidifier sat on a shelf above a small sink, a drainage hose steadily dribbling into the drain.

Lining the walls were racks of weapons of every description, war, nationality and age.

At the far end of the room, several pallets were stacked with plastic bags containing a wide spectrum of materials: white and golden powders, leafy greenery, tiny pills and small vials of an amber fluid.

As the armored door slowly closed by itself, Bolan looked for anybody else in sight, but they were alone.

"So what was wrong with the drugs?" Quarez demanded, taking a folding chair. "The grass was Colombian, the best on the market! The coke was pure quill, never been stepped on, and the ice was made by my cousin, Gomez. Good stuff. Fuck you up bad for a week!"

"The quality of the crystal meth wasn't the problem," Bolan said slowly, straightening the cuff on his pants.

"Was it the whores?" Quarez asked skeptically. "That short bitch that works for your boss asked for hot sluts in bikinis, and that was what we delivered! If he rode one and now needs a doctor, that's his problem, eh? Not mine."

"I suggest you show my employer some proper respect," Bolan growled, a hand going dangerously near the Beretta.

"Fine." Quarez sighed. "So what the fuck was wrong with the whores I sent to Mr. Greene?"

Maintaining a neutral expression, Bolan filed away the name but didn't get any hits. It was too common. There were too many Greenes in the world, probably just as many as Smith and Adam. He needed a first name, or a description... Suddenly, he felt the name click into place, and a rush of images filled his mind. F88 assault rifles, Australia...Greene...whores....

Bolan grimaced. Dalton Greene, the billionaire?

There was no KKK or Nazi Party Down Under, but Greene was running a close second with some White Supremacist group called Sunshine, or Daylight, something like that. Greene had been implicated in a dozen murders and even in several lynchings of Chinese prostitutes, but he had never been successfully prosecuted. Like most billionaires, he was protected by an army of lawyers who didn't care what their client did, only how much they were paid, and when necessary, the people testifying against Greene would mysteriously disappear the night before the trial.

"Jesus, you don't work for Greene!" Quarez said in growing horror, as if those particular words had been arranged in that order before. "Who are... What... *Intruso, intruso!*"

Instantly, an alarm began to ring, men began shouting in another room. The combination dial on the locked door began to spin rapidly....

CHAPTER SEVEN

The Cayman Islands

The azure water of the Gulf of Mexico was clean and clear, a gentle breeze was blowing from the south, and the sky was full of puffy white clouds that offered no chance of rain to spoil the perfect morning.

The water surrounding the Greater Cayman Island was full of stately yachts, windjammers, catamarans, lumbering fishing trawlers, countless small pleasure crafts and literally hundreds of tourists on personal watercraft cavorting about.

"An entire nation of mongrels," a member of Daylight snorted in disdain, leaning on the safety railing. The man was repulsed, and oddly fascinated by the open display of Caucasians peacefully mixing with the lower races.

"Their day will come," a woman muttered, using an oil rag to clean the breech of her assault rifle.

Just then, a collision warning blared, and even the fools and the drunks hastily got out of the way of the oncoming steel behemoth, *Blackjack*.

Ponderously heading for the coast of the main island, the colossal oil tanker was already starting the long process of slowing down in spite of the fact that there were at least two miles to go before reaching the deep-water harbor. However, fully loaded with one-hundred million gallons of raw crude from Colombia, the *Blackjack* needed both of those miles to slow down from its top speed of only twenty-five knots.

Parked on the deck of the tanker were all of the remaining helicopters from the deadly Florida sortie. The *Blackjack* was nearly twelve hundred feet long, and two hundred feet wide, so there was more than enough room on the top deck. Each of the aircraft was draped with a heavy sheet of canvas as it took on fuel, munitions, and received some fast modifications. The serial numbers were being changed, the radios and Gertrudes altered to new frequencies, and any damaged blades or rotors were being replaced to maintain the gunships in peak fighting condition.

However, all of the radar defusers and radio jammers were operating at full power.

Quietly, without fanfare or ceremony, five bodies heavily wrapped in tarpaulins were slowly lowered over the side of the oil tanker and eased into the crystal-blue water to quickly sink forever into the murky darkness below.

"Ashes to ashes," a crying terrorist whispered. "Dust to dust."

"Shut up and get back to work!" LoMonaco commanded. But there was a surprisingly gentle tone in the harsh words.

Nodding, the man shuffled away to the rest of his cohorts. Trained in combat-survival tactics, the members of Daylight were grabbing catnaps to refresh themselves for the next mission. Each was more dangerous than the last, but each also brought Daylight that much closer to its ultimate goal.

Spread out before the slowing oil tanker, the Cayman Islands were considered a tropical paradise by most people on Earth. The combination of perfect weather and a complete lack of extradition treaties with any other nation made the island nation irresistible. Not too long ago, the Cayman Islands had been rapidly heading for disaster as the local population was too poor to import enough food to stay alive. In desperation, the government decided to offer the world a very special feature in their banking laws, à la Switzerland and Brazil—total immunity.

Soon, the Cayman Islands were flush with capital again. Then they started to receive hundreds of criminals looking to secure a future with their ill-gotten gains.

Numerous scientists and doctors across the world wondered if the Caymans were doing irreparable harm to their gene pool. But since Brazil had done the exact same thing for almost a century, and showed no increase in local-born criminals, the point was considered moot.

On the starboard side of the monstrous tanker, a small wooden launch was being lowered into the water with a gentle splash. As the harness came free, the engine sputtered into action, and it quickly skimmed the waves, heading for shore.

Inside the main cabin of the launch, a dozen members of Daylight were busy helping one man get dressed for the very last time in his life.

"Daniel, this is a great thing that you do," Greene said, tightening the belt around the pale man. "You are helping to preserve the future of the white race."

"Are you sure? Everybody seems so happy…" Daniel Caruthers said, momentarily weakened by doubt.

"What king is not happy?" Layne snorted, checking the batteries. "Slaves do all of the work."

"I suppose," Caruthers muttered. "Now, you promise that my family will be well provided for?"

"A million dollars has already been deposited in a numbered Swiss bank account," Greene said, handing the man a sheet of paper. "Give them those numbers, and they will never be hungry or cold again."

"And you'll help the boys get into a good college?"

Greene nodded. "If that is your wish."

"It is. Thank you."

While the work around him continued, Caruthers called his wife and gave her the bank-account numbers. Then he made her read them back twice just to be certain. Then Caruthers terminated the call in the middle of a conversation. His resolve was starting to weaken, so if this task was to be done, then it had best be soon.

"You're ready," Layne said, stepping back and saluting.

"God bless you all," Caruthers stated, too rattled to return the gesture.

Climbing out of the boat, the man started up the beach and past several pavilions selling soft drinks and flavored ice shavings until he reached the main road.

Back on the launch, Layne watched Caruthers leave with a grim air of finality. "Sir, did you really deposit the money?"

"Of course! He only asked for a million, and I always pay my debts," Greene declared. "Always! No matter what the personal cost."

Hailing a bus, Caruthers rode in silence and got off at the downtown stop.

Compared to a metropolis like Melbourne, the small

coastal city was almost ramshackle. But everybody was clean and well-fed, there were no potholes in the streets and the traffic lights worked, which was something that couldn't be said about Melbourne in the best of times.

Trundling through the crowds, Caruthers headed directly for a large bank situated prominently on a corner and walked inside. The air in the lobby was crisp and clean, and he breathed it in deeply, savoring the feel of it deep in his lungs. He had always enjoyed the cold, and it never really got cold in Australia. Winter was simply a month on the calendar, and he had never even seen snow until he took a vacation in the mountains on his thirty-fifth birthday.

The building was also a stone fortress, the walls thick enough to stop artillery shells, the windows triple sheets of bulletproof plastic. There were video cameras everywhere, and enough armed security personnel to stop any team of conventional bank robbers.

However, there wasn't a security scanner at the door, just some partially exposed wiring where one was scheduled to be installed the following week. Timing was everything.

Walking through the busy lobby, Caruthers went to a desk and filled out a deposit slip, then went to the first available teller. That really wasn't necessary, but he wanted to get as close as possible in case something went wrong.

"Good morning, sir, can I help you?" a pretty woman asked from behind a thick wall of transparent material.

"Sadly, dear lady, this will not be a good morning for either of us," Caruthers said, a sob marring the words as he released the arming trigger of the activator.

The fifty pounds of C-4 plastic explosive strapped to

his body instantly detonated, and the entire lobby of the bank vanished in a thunderclap, the front of the fortified building bulging outward impossibly for a microsecond before shattering into a million pieces and shotgunning across the sleepy island community. Fifty people died at that moment as a thousand windows shattered from the rolling concussion, then more lost their lives in the next second as cars flipped over and tumbled through the morning crowds, crushing pedestrians.

Now the screaming began, mixed with fire alarms and car horns, and a rain of falling glass shards smashing on the bloody sidewalk.

Even as the thick columns of dark smoke started to rise into the sky, a dozen helicopters appeared on the horizon. As the Apaches did a fast sweep around the decimated town, the Black Hawks landed in front of the bank, the wash of the rotating blades extinguishing hundreds of small fires, and making the severed limbs of the ragged corpses move in a ghastly semblance of life.

The hatches slid back on the Black Hawks, and out poured men and women wearing gas masks and full-body armor. But nobody was carrying a first-aid kit, or fire-fighting equipment. Instead, each of them was armed with an F88 assault rifle with a 40 mm grenade launcher attached under the main barrel and a laser pointer on the side. Victor Layne was in the lead, and strapped to his back was a bulky canvas pack bearing the logo of NASA.

The thin red beams cut through the swirling clouds of concrete dust, the rasping of the gas masks making the terrorists sounded like robots with asthma.

Parts of the building were still disintegrating, breaking off and crumbling into pieces, sending out huge clouds of acrid dust from the powdered concrete, a whirlwind of papers swirling in the smoking air.

There was very little inside the bank to show that only a few moments earlier it had been filled with live human beings. Now there were only dark splashes on the cracked marble walls and a scattering of assorted lumps that would be unrecognizable to anybody not a certified crime-scene investigator, or a professional coroner.

Kicking the dead aside, Layne advanced into the bank with a smile. The reinforced wall of bulletproof plastic that sealed off the lobby was on the floor, broken into several large pieces. Success!

The teller's window and front counter no longer existed, and there was a large hole where Caruthers and the pretty woman had been only a minute earlier. Past the counter, the executive offices were broken wide-open. The decorative facade of carved wood and gilded trim had been pulverized, and the raw face of the titanic bank vault was in plain sight. The reinforced expanse of titanium-steel alloy was unmarred by the staggering blast, except for the combination keypad, which was absent, the bent steel rectangle now only containing dangling wires that swayed and spat out sparks when they accidentally touched.

"Fat Man to Zed Commander, we have full penetration," Layne whispered into a throat mike. "Situation is green and go. Repeat, go-go-go!"

Advancing into the rear of the bank, Layne and the other terrorists ignored the vault and proceeded deeper into the trembling building. An iron gate blocked off a hallway, and Layne used the grenade launcher to blow it away with a 40 mm shell.

Just then, one of the terrorists cried out as a slab of marble peeled off the sagging wall to drop, crushing the man flat. The other members of Daylight paused at the terrible sight, then grimly moved on, concentrating on the mission.

An entrance to the back rooms was blocked with rubble and a surprisingly large number of human limbs. Perched on top of a pile of smoldering debris was a battered human head that seemed to stare at Layne in accusation. He shot it between the eyes and kept going.

Using the grenade launchers, Layne and the others smashed their way through the rubbish and debris until they located a relatively undamaged corridor.

According to the blueprints, this should have been blocked off with a set of heavy steel doors. But those had been peeled back by the initial blast and were now embedded into the decorative marble covering the concrete walls. At the far end was a reddish smear containing shoes and smashed MP-5 machine guns that might have been three, or maybe four, security guards, but now it was impossible to tell for certain.

The video cameras were gone, ripped from the walls and sent hurtling away, but their sockets still crackled, showing that this part of the fortified building still had electrical power.

"Watch out for water!" somebody yelled unnecessarily into their throat mike.

Suddenly, an overhead pipe burst and water cascaded down to flow across the sparking wires. Everybody moved fast and got out of the way.

Turning a corner, Layne grinned at the sight of another plastic wall sealing off a hallway. The resilient material was studded with small bits of office shrapnel: pens, pencils, paper clips, chunks of coffee mugs and such. But otherwise it was completely undamaged.

"This is it!" Layne growled, bracing the assault rifle on a hip. "In unison! Three...two...one!"

A dozen of the grenade launchers belched in unison and the bulletproof plastic barrier was hammered from the wall to loudly pancake onto the spotlessly clean floor.

Advancing in formation, the terrorists moved fast through rows of small offices and discovered a small crowd of people clustered inside one, trying to open a bent fire door.

As Layne stopped to aim his assault rifle, the door to an office across the hall slammed open and a bank guard dove out to tackle the man alongside Layne. Punching and cursing, the two men rolled across the floor in a tangle of limbs, then the bank guard rose with the assault rifle tight in his hands.

"Everybody freeze!" he bellowed.

Swinging the F88 that way, Layne fired a single 40 mm shell from the grenade launcher. It streaked past the guard, missing by inches, and went into the office to hit the far wall and violently explode. The blast filled the room and was channeled back out to engulf the bank guard. Blown off his feet, he hit the opposite wall, along with a collection of broken brooms and a bucket.

With a low moan, the guard slid down the wall, leaving behind a long red smear.

Carefully aiming the rifle, Layne put a short burst of 5.56 mm rounds into the guard to end his torment.

"A brave man," Layne said, resting the rifle on a shoulder. "Unlike you yellow bastards!"

Instantly, the rest of Daylight unleashed a full volley

from their assault rifles, spraying the mob of frightened people, their cries and blood filling the air in a hurricane of death and destruction.

When the last person was dead, Layne had started to leave when he heard a sound from inside a washroom. Kicking open the door, he found a beautiful woman lying on the tiled floor, both of her hands holding a towel to a deep gash on her thigh to try to contain the river of life.

"Please, take whatever you wish," she begged, tears on her face. "The secondary vault is over there. Right there!" she indicated the direction with her chin.

"Yes, we know," Layne said coldly, and aimed the rifle. But then he stopped. This was a very big office, which meant that the bitch had to be somebody important.

"Identify yourself!" he bellowed, leveling the rifle.

"Amanda Toulane, chief-information officer," she stated.

A long moment paused with the red dot of the laser on her forehead.

"Sir, she might be useful at the cave," Thomas suggested.

"All right," Layne said, lowering the weapon. "You and you! Bind that wound and take her back alive!"

"You sure about that?" a man asked privately on his throat mike.

"Just do it!"

"Yes, sir!"

"What...what are you taking me back for?" Toulane asked, tilting her head toward the man.

Walking over, a man grabbed a fistful of the crying

woman's long hair, forcing her to look upward. "Are you going to give me trouble?" he asked sweetly.

"No! I... No, I won't!" Toulane gasped.

"Pity." The man chuckled, openly admiring her figure. Then he released his grip and pulled out a medical kit.

Leaving the washroom, Layne turned the corner and smiled at the sight of an iron gate blocking any further progress. Reaching into a pocket, he produced a black coil of linked metal and threw it forward.

Opening in flight, the limpet mine slapped against the door in the gate, the internal electromagnets holding it in place as if it had been welded there. A split second later, the mine detonated, and the door was loudly blown off its hinges to sail away and crash into a wall, knocking down an assortment of pictures.

As the smoke cleared, the terrorists advanced and around the corner Layne paused to smile at the lovely sight of a third plastic wall, this time locked with a small keypad. On the other side was an orderly row of work stations and dozens of softly humming rows of blade servers that constituted the Cray supercomputer.

"Looks like something from a sci-fi movie," Thomas muttered, already hard at work rigging the keypad.

"Actually, this is old technology, from decades ago," Layne corrected him. "The new computers are even larger and much faster."

"Why didn't we take one of them, sir?" a woman asked, working the arming bolt on the F88 to clear a jam from the breech.

"Didn't need it," Layne said with a thin smile. "Never steal more than you need, friend. That way only leads to sloth, followed by mistakes, and then your own death."

"Lean and mean, yes, sir."

"Very wise." Layne laughed, slapping the woman on the shoulder.

"Done!" Thomas announced, stepping back from the keypad.

In response, the round door in the middle of the plastic wall rotated twice to unlock, then swung aside to the low hum of electric motors.

Stepping into the cooler interior of the supercomputer, Layne grinned in triumph. Suddenly the door to a supply closet was thrown open and out came a pair of armed security guards.

Assuming a firing stance, they both cut loose with compact MP-5 machine guns, raking the invaders with a concentrated hellstorm of 9 mm Parabellum rounds. The Daylight terrorists staggered under the furious assault, their shirts ripping apart to reveal the molded body armor underneath.

Rising from behind a steel desk, Thomas triggered a short burst, then fell backward from the incoming rounds. He hit the carpeting hard, half of his face torn away and white bone showing for a brief instant before there was a wellspring of blood, and he started to convulse.

"Dave!" Layne roared, rushing to his side.

Covering his move, the rest of the terrorists rallied their F88 assault rifles, and the bank guards were torn apart by the fusillade of 5.56 mm rounds.

On the floor, Thomas weakly raised his hand as if reaching for something, then dropped the arm and went still. Checking for a pulse, Layne didn't find one, but put a round through his buddy's head just in case. Either way, the electronics specialist was dead. Nobody could have survived that amount of damage even if they got shot in the ER room of a hospital.

Turning, Layne felt the urge to kill well up within him, but he forced it down. This was the one part of the whole mission to save humanity when he dare not kill. Not at first anyway.

Dark shapes were moving behind the misty servers of the humming Cray.

"Here's a problem in logic," Layne shouted. "We need you to operate the Cray. If you refuse to cooperate, then we don't need the Cray and can open fire to kill you."

For a few minutes there was only the soft humming of the huge machine, then three people stepped into view with their hands raised, a man and two women. The man and one of the women were wearing sweaters. The other woman was in some sort of a uniform, and trembling from the cold.

"Who are you?" Layne asked politely.

"Secretary," she managed to say, her teeth chattering.

"Liar, you're the janitor." Layne chuckled, then stitched the woman from knees to nose with the F88 assault rife.

As the body collapsed, the other two people screamed and backed away.

"We're computer techs!" the man said quickly. "Whatever you want, we can do it. No problem!"

"Good to know," Layne drawled, dropping the partially spent magazine to dramatically insert a fresh one. As he worked the arming bolt, the pair flinched, and he knew they wouldn't be any further trouble. Intimidation was an art.

"What do you want, sir?" the woman asked, almost

making the sentence a single word in her rush to get it out.

"Which of you has military training?" Layne asked, trying not to look at the clock on the wall. The numbers were falling and he was not done yet.

"Military training?" the man asked, confused.

Extending the assault rifle, Layne fired off a single round directly alongside his head.

With a cry, the man dropped to his knees, grabbing his ear.

"Let's try this again, shall we?" Layne asked sweetly.

"We don't have the codes to the vault," the woman panted, as if she had just run a mile.

Layne grinned. "Don't need them, don't want them."

"Then what do you want?" the kneeling man asked in a strained voice, a tiny trickle of blood flowing from between his fingers.

Passing away the assault rifle, Layne slid the pack off his back. "I need you to reprogram something for me."

CHAPTER EIGHT

Mexico

Looking around fast, Bolan spotted a bin full of high-explosive grenades, bright orange tape holding the arming levers tightly into position.

Grabbing the bin, he heaved the entire contents across the floor, then ducked out of sight and began to softly hiss.

As the heavy locks disengaged, the vault door cycled open, and a squad of big men rushed through, their hands full of high-caliber death. But then they immediately stopped at the sight of the dozens of grenades strewn across the floor.

A scrawny man in a beard started to speak, then his eyes went wide. "What's hissing... Fuck, boys, one of them is live!"

Instantly, the squad turned to rush back down the passageway, leaving the vault door wide open.

Charging out from cover, Bolan grabbed a couple of grenades and paused just long enough to remove the orange safety tape before pulling the pins, flipping off the spoon, and threw the primed grenades down the passageway. They hit with a clatter and rolled out of sight.

Snatching another pair off the floor, he managed to get them both primed and through the passageway before the first grenade exploded. People wildly screamed a mixture of prayers and obscenities as the blast shook the building, dust raining from above and the racks of weapons rattling like military wind chimes.

Stuffing a couple of spares into his pockets, Bolan waited until the other grenades detonated before charging along the smoky passageway and exiting back into the bar.

Acrid smoke was thick in the air, the floor clear of any trace of sawdust and peanut shells, and a score of tables and chairs were strewn about in broken pieces, along with a couple of extremely dead men still holding automatic weapons.

The nearby stage was empty, the dancers wisely knowing when the show was over. Far across the bar, a huge crowd was struggling to get out the front door, knives flashing and guns barking as the mob turned ugly and began wantonly killing in a futile effort to clear the way.

Tossing an unprimed grenade into the crowd, Bolan headed directly for the counter and scrambled over the top just as a multitude of weapons discharged. The wooden counter visibly shook under the strident hammering, chips and splinters flying out to rattle the liquor bottles on the shelves.

Answering the barrage with a long spray of copper-jacketed rounds from the Beretta machine pistol, Bolan ducked into the back room. He almost collided with a bald man coming out of the next room, an old AK-47 assault rifle tight in his grip.

Cursing in Spanish, the man tried to swing up the assault rifle, but Bolan slapped it aside with the heavy steel barrel of the Desert Eagle, and fired a 3-round burst from the Beretta directly into the other man's face. He fell away, gushing life from his wounds.

Holstering the Beretta, Bolan grabbed the AK-47 and sprayed the next room, the chattering stream of 7.62 mm rounds rattling the pots and pans on the stove and counters of the dirty kitchen. Soup, or maybe stew, went flying, and a tray full of dishes loudly crashed to the floor as several people stumbled out of the shadows, covered with blood.

Turning, Bolan emptied the magazine in a few seconds, ricochets clanging off the stove and grill, a huge cloud of flour exploding into the air as two more men fell into view, their handguns discharging harmlessly into the litter on the floor.

Kicking the debris out of his way, Bolan tossed aside the empty assault rifle and quickly reloaded the Beretta and the Desert Eagle. Angry shouts were coming from the main room of the bar. Bolan was debating tossing another grenade that way when the back door of the kitchen slammed open and in strode three big men, their hands holding automatic pistols.

As they cut loose, Bolan returned fire.

A bullet hummed by his ear, the slug missing by such a small margin that he actually felt the wind of its passage, then another slammed into his chest, dead center above his heart. He grunted at the impact, but his body armor absorbed the brunt of the strike, and he kept firing until the three were down for the forever count, their weapons falling from lifeless, bloody hands.

Holstering both of his weapons, Bolan looked over the dark night, spotting numerous people moving about in the murky distance and among the shadowy cactus. Arming the last two grenades, Bolan threw them far and wide. Then on the count of four, he burst out of the kitchen, sprinting for the RV.

Ignoring any cover, Bolan tried for sheer distance, but had only crossed a few yards before people started shooting at him, puffs of dust rising from the sandy ground. Then the grenades cut loose, the double blast shattering the night and throwing off everybody's aim.

Firing on the run, Bolan took out some lights hanging from poles and got behind a large boulder just as a score of different weapons cut loose, the combined muzzle-flashes strangely illuminating the night. Broken chips fell off the curved edge of the boulder, and Bolan used the precious reprieve to reload his weapons again. He was almost out of ammunition. The soldier knew that he had to reach the RV on this next run, or he would never leave the box canyon alive.

When the hammering barrage slowed, he armed the last stun grenade, flipped it over the boulder and protectively covered his face. As the nonlethal charge cut loose, a thundering boom filled the night, and the darkness vanished from the blindingly bright magnesium charge.

Instantly, Bolan took off at a full run heading straight for the RV. He made absolutely no effort to throw off the aim of any snipers, or sharpshooters, and concentrated purely on crossing the stretch of flat open ground as fast as he possibly could.

Unable to see clearly in his own penumbra, Bolan nearly tripped on some loose rocks, then almost went flying over an unseen prairie-dog burrow. Land mines, barbed wire and pungi sticks he could handle easily. It was the natural chaos of the desert that would cause his demise if Bolan didn't stay sharply focused on expecting the unexpected.

On the horizon, a lone coyote howled at the stars.

As the flare died away, darkness returned, accompanied by random shooting that swung in toward Bolan with surprising speed.

Redoubling his effort, the Executioner dove behind a large cactus just as a hail of bullets arrived to tear it apart, the sharp needles and juicy pulp smacking Bolan as he used the remote control to unlock the RV.

Arching around a boulder, Bolan paused for only a split second to see if the ground around the vehicle was disturbed in any way, then pulled off the tarp, yanked open a door and scrambled inside. As he started to close it, incoming rounds loudly ricocheted off the ceramic armor, slamming the door shut so fast it almost crushed his hand.

Hitting a glowing red button, Bolan locked every door tight, then turned off the lights, started the engine, grabbed the wheel and stomped on the accelerator.

In a roar of barely controlled power, the RV lurched out of hiding, the rear tires kicking up a wide spray of dirt, sand and loose gravel. He had to get back to the highway pronto. For all of the positive attributes of the vehicle, the armor made it very heavy and that would cost him vital maneuverability in the loose sand of the desert. Bolan felt sure that he could outrace any production motorcycle in the world once he had asphalt under his tires, but right now the bikes would have a deadly advantage.

Just then, he heard the sputtering roar of countless motorcycles, and the darkness segmented into slices. To Bolan it seemed as if some of the bikes were separating, heading for the horizon, or the deep desert, but most of them seemed to be coming toward him. On a hunch, he hit the radio, activated the autoscan, and it locked on to the strongest local broadcast.

A chorus of angry voices overlapped one another in total disregard for radio protocol, nor were any codes being used, which was highly unwise in these modern days of satellites and digital recorders. It was difficult to tell for sure, but the general consensus seemed to be that a gringo called Greene had promised a hundred thousand dollars for the head of anybody who came looking for him. The owners of the Coyote were doubling that, and every biker in the bar was promising to get the job done. Some of them were working alone, others were in pairs or groups, but most of them appeared to have joined into a loose pack for this one special job—kill the intruder.

Suddenly, a headlight curved out of the night, the rider firing an Uzi machine pistol with one hand. The 9 mm rounds ricocheted harmlessly off the ceramic-armor chassis of the RV, then the bullets slapped deep into the rear tires. But the vehicle neither slowed nor wavered, the copper-jacketed rounds only producing a brief bubbling as the internal gel sealed the holes almost instantly.

As the motorcycle got closer, Bolan stomped on the brakes, and the machine crashed into the rear of the RV. The driver briefly screamed as the bike crumpled, then Bolan accelerated away, leaving behind a twisted wreck of man and machine.

A group of roaring bikes darted out of the darkness, their headlights off, the riders only blurs in the night. Twisting the steering wheel hard, Bolan sent the

RV crashing through them, two of the bikes going underneath, and three others slamming aside, the riders sent flying.

Yelling a battle cry, a bike zoomed in close to the vehicle, and a man in a sidecar grabbed on to the door handle. Fingering a switch on the steering wheel, Bolan sent a half-million volts cycling through the handle and the man was thrown into the driver. The bike veered away wildly before flipping over and tumbling out of sight.

Unexpectedly, an alarm started softly beeping on the dashboard, and Bolan realized that the RV was being painted with a laser beam! Fishtailing, he tried to throw off the beam, but the unseen gunner kept reacquiring the target. Fingering a control, Bolan sent dark smoke issuing from the rear of the vehicle, but it seemed to have no effect.

Arcing around a stand of cactus, Bolan cursed at the sight of a bike streaking his way, the rider holding the elongated tube of a Stinger missile launcher on a shoulder.

That caught Bolan totally by surprise. The Stinger was designed to take out airplanes, and he honestly had no idea if the SAM could harm his vehicle. On the other hand, he sure as hell didn't want to find out the hard way. Mentally reviewing his options, Bolan decided to throw the dice and let the universe decide if he lived or not. Stomping on the accelerator, he sent the RV hurtling directly toward the startled biker. With any luck, the bizarre tactic might rattle the man enough to make him drop the weapon, and then...

But the biker did the unthinkable and triggered the weapon.

A tight lance of flame shot out, and a wide cone of

red-hot exhaust blasted out the aft end of the launcher. A hurricane of loose sand and rock swept away from the shooter, the maelstrom engulfing a dozen other bikers, ripping men and machines apart, the engines bursting into flames.

Still accelerating toward the incoming rocket, Bolan ran the math in his head and didn't like the results. The Stinger armed its warhead at eight-hundred feet and if that happened, he would probably never see another day. But if he got close enough, the RV would only be hit by a missile traveling at six hundred miles per hour. That gave him a slim chance of survival. Knowing that the side armor of the RV was its strongest point, at the very last moment, Bolan hit the brakes and savagely twisted the wheel to bank to the left.

A split second later, the Stinger slammed into the side of the RV with a deafening crash. For a stunning microsecond of eternity, Bolan knew what it was like to be the clapper inside a ringing church bell—then the RV left the ground and tumbled helplessly along the desert, every loose item inside the vibrating machine flying free.

As the air bag deployed, pinning him in place, Bolan was pelted with loose ammunition, empty clips, spare change, sunglasses, coffee cups, a plethora of assorted debris. Grenades left his pockets to bounce around like tennis balls, smashing the rearview mirror and rebounding off his arm, crashing into the seat directly alongside his head.

Ignoring the pain, Bolan desperately wanted to turn off the engines to try to forestall a possible fire, but the controls were outside his reach, and if he deflated the air bag, he'd go rattling about like everything else. At the very least he'd be knocked unconscious, if he didn't break every major bone in his body. That would leave him alive but helpless and at the mercy of the bikers. That was not going to happen!

Eventually, the rolling RV slowed and came to a rest right-side up. Thankful that the vehicle was bottom-heavy, Bolan drew the Beretta, held his breath and fired. The air bag burst, releasing an acidic cloud of fumes that stung his eyes and nose, but at least he didn't breath in any of the stuff.

Swaying slightly, the soldier needed two attempts to holster the weapon, then fumbled to check the status of the van. Most of the indicators in the dashboard were out, but it seemed as if he had survived relatively un-damaged, aside from a ringing in his ears louder than any artillery he had ever heard.

Rising stiffly from the seat, Bolan needed a few moments to get orientated, then shuffled into the rear compartment. Incredibly, he found it intact, just piled with loose debris. Several assault rifles had burst out of their hidden compartments inside the walls, the re-frigerator had disgorged an assortment of foodstuffs, and there was enough loose brass on the floor to make walking without tripping nearly impossible. But the walls weren't breached, or even seriously dented, al-though Bolan seriously doubted that the alignment of the wheels was still up to the original specifications.

The windshield and side windows were intact, but then he doubted if anything but a LAW rocket could have penetrated the resilient bulletproof plastic. Then he saw that the laptop had smashed to pieces against the ceiling panels. That was inconvenient, but a small price to pay for surviving a direct hit from a Stinger.

The soldier checked himself for any wounds, then looked outside and saw only a flat empty plain that stretched for miles. That was what most likely had saved his life. If the RV had collided with a boulder, or damn near anything else, the vehicle would probably have split open.

Listening to the soothing silence of the windless desert, Bolan couldn't hear the bikes anymore and had started to relax when he suspiciously snapped his fingers. Nothing. He should have known that was going to happen! He was stone-deaf from the initial collision.

Sniffing hard for any trace of gasoline, Bolan got back behind the wheel and tried to tell if the engine was still running. But the dashboard was dead, the sensors scrambled from the brief sojourn sideways. Pressing his thumb to the ignition pad, he turned off the engine, waited for a count of three, then turned it back on again. Outside, the headlights flickered, then the dashboard indicators glowed into life once more.

Buckling on his seat belt, Bolan checked the status of the van. On the surface, everything seemed to be fine. The main radar was down, but the auxiliary was still operational, and the RV wasn't being painted by a laser, or anything else, at the moment. The radio seemed fully operational, but it was rendered useless by his own stunned condition of euphony. Or whatever the hell temporary deafness was called again. The condition happened a lot to new artillery men, and tank crews who forget to use their earplugs. He knew the word, but just couldn't dredge it up right now. Bolan felt sore all over, slightly nauseous and had a colossal headache.

Digging out a medical kit, the soldier injected himself with a NATO Hot Shot, a combination of painkillers and stimulants designed to get anything but a corpse back on its feet and moving again. In about an hour, Bolan would collapse, but by then he would either be long gone, or already dead.

Slowly, the ringing left his ears to be replaced with a cool crystal clarity. He still couldn't hear a thing, but at least he no longer felt like the loser in a ten-car collision.

Cutting away the rest of the air bag, Bolan shifted into gear and grinned as the vehicle started to move sluggishly, then surged forward in a burst of power. Back in business!

Looking around, Bolan wasn't overly surprised to see distant headlights bobbing on the horizon and coming his way. The bikers probably thought he was dead, and were searching for the wreckage to retrieve his body.

"Too slow, boys," Bolan muttered, running a fast computer diagnostic on the van.

All of the defensive and offensive systems were fully operational, except for the roof missile pod, which was missing, and, in a humorous twist, the self-destruct function was disabled.

Snorting a laugh at that, Bolan got the machine guns loaded and ready just as the first of the bikers came over a dune.

Biding his time, Bolan waited until they were closer, then cut loose with both of the forward Remington machine guns, the .308 rounds sweeping death through their ranks. Windshields shattered, tires exploded, men screamed and blood flew high as the bikes and riders were torn to pieces under the hammering barrage.

Lurching the RV into motion, Bolan got moving once

more, backing around in a fast circle, the rear wheels throwing out a huge cloud of dirt and gravel.

As more motorcycles arrived, the riders caught the dust cloud full in the face, and backed off coughing and blinking. But still firing their weapons. Bullets hit everywhere, rocks and cactus mostly, as Bolan raced away, fishtailing the RV to create more dust. The macho fools weren't wearing helmets, and it was always damned hard to hit what you couldn't see.

A peppering hail of rounds ricocheted off the passenger window. Unable to hear the weapon, Bolan had no idea what it was, but the rounds had failed to achieve penetration, and that was good enough for the moment.

A large explosion erupted alongside the van, and a tidal wave of dirt and fire was thrown across the windshield. He recognized the blast as coming from a 40 mm grenade from an M79, or possibly one of the new M320 launchers. The longer shells for the M320 had a slightly different sound. The tires on the RV were bulletproof, but a 40 mm grenade from either launcher could blow them off the rim. Unlike an ordinary van, the RV was built to drive on the reinforced rims for days, but the massive reduction in speed here in the desert would be disastrous. Especially if these men had another Stinger.

Steering with one hand, Bolan punched the button for the onboard map display, and got only the bluescreen of death. Son of a bitch! Not exactly sure where he was located right now, Bolan had no choice but to drive blindly toward his chosen fallback position, a deserted mining town several miles away.

CHAPTER NINE

As the RV raced away, it kept getting hit by sporadic gunfire, but Bolan ignored that and concentrated on finding the abandoned town. Out in the open, the bikes had every advantage, but inside the confines of streets and buildings, the advantage would be his, and hopefully that would make up for his current loss of hearing.

There was no sign of the town for miles, but he did locate the dry river that marked the boundary for the settlement. Angling down onto a dry riverbed, Bolan turned off the headlights for a moment and drew the Beretta and the Desert Eagle, thumbing off the safeties.

A few minutes later, a roaring motorcycle soared across the riverbed to land on the other side. It was closely followed by two more. Then a fourth drove down onto the dried riverbed and started his way. As the headlight swept across the van, Bolan fired a short burst from the forward machine guns. Sizzling white-hot tracers dotted the night. Man and machine tore apart, then the engine burst into flames.

Dripping flame, the bike toppled over, then exploded just as several more bikes appeared along the top of the riverbank. They stopped before going over the edge, and started firing downward at the van, fully illuminated by the burning bike.

Rolling down the window, Bolan cut loose with the

Beretta 93R machine pistol. The bikers were raked by bursts of 9 mm Parabellum rounds, several of them grabbing wounds, but only one falling down.

Withdrawing quickly, Bolan barely closed the window before the riders returned fire, their bullets throwing off sparks as they ricocheted from the armored hood of the van, and zinging off the windshield.

Surging down the sloped bank, the bikers charged the RV, spraying bullets.

Releasing smoke and tear gas, Bolan waited until the coughing riders slowed, then unleashed the forward guns once more. The big-bore combat rounds tore through their leather jackets, blowing out gouts of red life. The riderless bikes veered about wildly, crashing into each other and toppling over, the headlights throwing out a crazy pattern of darkness and light.

Putting a second burst into them, Bolan cursed as the left machine gun jammed, then stopped working altogether. Taking that as his cue to leave, he killed the headlights and angled away from the dying bikers to roll swiftly through the cool night. Long minutes passed as he drove down the riverbed until spotting an Aztec ruin.

The building was nothing special, just a jumbled pile of carved rocks whose original function had been lost in the sea of time. Temple, brothel or counting house, it was impossible to tell. However, not even the patrons of the Coyote disturbed the ancient stones. Not out of respect, of course. They just didn't want hundreds of new reporters swarming through the desert looking for a juicy story on why the Aztec ruins had been desecrated.

Jouncing out of the river, Bolan checked a compass, then briefly had to use the headlights to check for any other ruins in the area, and narrowly avoided going into a sinkhole that would have swallowed the RV whole.

As the miles flew by, the ringing in his ears slowly began to fade. His hearing was starting to return, but Bolan knew that he was still at a serious disadvantage, and had no intention of leaving the RV until he was very far away from this hot zone. Besides, Bolan had what he had come for, a name—Dalton Greene—and he was already starting to recall details about the white supremacist.

He'd been born in Johannesburg, South Africa, father and mother both believed to be the children of escaped Nazi war criminals. Greene had somehow gained control of a small diamond mine, through methods obscured by multiple deaths and numerous fires. When it played out, Greene rapidly acquired several additional mines, most of which proved to be worthless, then he hit a motherlode of blue-white stones and retired from the world richer than Croesus.

Building a mansion almost as elaborate as a palace, Greene forged his own little empire in the rocky desert, and there had been numerous rumors that he was backing an attempt to rekindle the Nazi Party. When Nelson Mandela took over South Africa, Greene had immediately left for Australia.

Why the racist billionaire chose there, Bolan had no idea. Blacks and whites got along fine Down Under. The way Bolan read the man from the files, he guessed it was for personal reasons.

"Okay, Greene, what did you want in Australia?" Bolan asked, pleased that he dimly heard the words.

Suddenly, the mining town appeared on the horizon, mostly just black squares against the starry sky.

But Bolan recognized the sluicing tower and derricks. There hadn't been a chance to stash any supplies there, but then, the RV was self-sufficient. He could comfortably live inside it for a month, and never want for anything but conversation. There was even a DVD player in the back, along with a stack of movies.

Rolling through a field of stubby grass, Bolan grinned as he faintly heard the military tires crunching the dead plants flat. Almost back to normal!

The old town was spread out between a pair of hillocks vaguely resembling old-fashioned loaves of sugar, hence the name SugarLoaf Mine. The buildings were an odd mixture of tan adobe and redbrick, with a network of electrical wiring strung across the rooftops like the web of a mad spider. Most of the windows were intact, but so filthy it was impossible to see through them, but that was a good sign. It meant that nobody had taken over the mine to use as a campsite for smuggling, or… His smile faded at the muffled sound of a motorcycle engine.

Easing to a halt, Bolan strained to discern what direction the bikes were coming from when a store on the corner exploded, throwing dead bodies and broken adobe bricks across the street.

Striding out of the swirling smoke came a large man carrying an M16 assault rifle, with an M203 grenade launcher attached beneath the barrel. A bandolier of old stubby 40 mm grenade shells slung across a shirt so tattered as to clearly show military body armor underneath.

Activating the one remaining machine gun, Bolan was waiting for the stranger to come into range, when bright lights appeared on the destruction and a pack of motorcycles raced into view, the riders firing a wide variety of weapons at the newcomer.

Spraying the ground before the bikers with a chattering barrage from the M16, the big man sent them scattering, then loudly shouted something in Spanish while brandishing a commission booklet.

Bolan couldn't catch the words, but he recognized the booklet, and immediately released the weapon controls. The stranger was an agent for Mexican intelligence! He was probably here for the same reasons as Bolan, to learn more about the attack on the police in Cancun. That seriously complicated things, and Bolan decided to leave and not risk the life of the special agent.

As the howling bikers raced back into view around a corner, Bolan opened fire with the machine gun, and five of them fell, riddled with holes, the bikes skewing off to crash into walls and burst into flames.

Looking for the CISEN agent, Bolan couldn't find him anywhere, and assumed the man had taken cover when a glass window shattered, and the man aimed the M203 at the RV.

Knowing the weakened frame of the windshield might be vulnerable to the 40 mm shell, Bolan started to dive for the floor, when the agent shifted aim and fired. The 40 mm grenade hit the base of a derrick, and the wooden structure came crashing down, spilling the lifeless bodies of several men into the sandy streets, along with a LAW rocket launcher. It bounced off the cracked pavement, then fired, the antitank rocket streaking away to glance off a brick building, before disappearing into the night.

Looking at the agent, Bolan snapped a salute as thanks, and the man nodded, then grimaced, and snapped open the breech of the grenade launcher to yank out the spent round.

Glancing at the rear video monitor, Bolan saw more bikers coming around the hillocks, their Tech 9 machine pistols spitting daggers of flame.

Activating the rear machine gun, the soldier waited until they were in range then cut loose with a prolonged discharge. Riding directly into the hammering stream of bullets, both men and machines were chewed apart.

Halogen lights brightly lit up the street and a Mack truck drove around a corner.

Knowing the onboard Remingtons couldn't do enough damage to that hulking behemoth, Bolan prepared to go EVA, when the agent appeared on a rooftop and fired downward. The 5.56 mm rounds shattered the windshield, then he sent in a 40 mm shell. It exploded inside, and the cab was lifted off the ground by a roiling fireball.

Almost instantly, the rear doors to the trailer slammed open and out rumbled the biggest Mad Max that Bolan had ever seen. The homemade tank was completely covered with riveted steel and surrounded by a slat armor cage. Bolan thought that he saw a louvered metal skirt hidden under multiple axles, and a double row of ties, but couldn't be sure from the brief glance. He identified some of the parts as coming off bank trucks, but there were also pieces taken from diesel locomotives, and at least one armored hatch transplanted whole from a Sherman tank, circa WWII.

More importantly, the main body of the Max was covered with gunports and halogen lights, both of which lurched into operation, the blazing beams sweeping the town to focus on the face of the agent, effectively blinding the man, while the people inside the Mad Max cut loose with hand guns, shotguns and various assault rifles.

As the rain of different caliber bullets chewed apart the landscape all around him, the agent fired the grenade launcher again, and scored a direct hit on the open ground in front of the Max. The explosion obscured the armored vehicle for a moment, and when the smoke cleared the agent was gone.

If the missile pod had still been operational, Bolan could have made short work of the tank. But now he would have to do this the hard way. Scrambling into the rear compartment, the soldier lifted up the couch and withdrew a Carl Gustav. Loading in an antitank rocket, he left by the rear door and hit the ground running.

Bolan knew in advance the slat armor was something new for the smugglers, and a real problem. Invented by the US Marines in Iraq, the soft steel slats would prematurely detonate any incoming missile a good yard away from the tank. Bolan would need at least two missiles, and possibly three, to blow a hole through the slat armor and take out the rolling fortress.

The only known weak spot was from directly above. If the tank had slat armor there... Well, Bolan felt sure that he would think of something else to do. Probably find a working bike, grab the intelligence agent and run for the hills.

He barely reached the corner when the tank cut loose at the RV with everything it had, the halogen beams aimed at the windshield to blind the driver, while the gunners hammered it with small-arms fire. Then there came the rumbling boom of a .50 sniper rifle, and the windshield cracked, but still held in place.

Kicking open a wooden door, Bolan scrambled

through mounds of loose newspapers and countless dirty food containers to reach the stairs. Sprinting to the second floor, he searched for an access to the roof, but there was no staircase or ladder in sight. The exterior ladder had to have simply fallen apart over the intervening years. He would have to find another building.

Risking a fast glance outside, Bolan saw that the Max was steadily advancing on the RV, the people inside still firing away. Removing a small remote control from a pocket, Bolan tapped in a coded command sequence, and the vehicle's headlights came on, then the forward machine gun chattered into life.

The .308 hardball rounds stitched a line across the Max, but failed even to dent the thick homemade armor. Bright sparks flew as the ricochets went everywhere.

The old Sherman hatch clanged open, and a woman rose into view cradling a LAW. She fired, and the anti-tank rocket streaked past the RV, missing it by only inches. Casting away the spent tube, she flipped a middle finger at the vehicle, then ducked back inside.

Bolan was impressed. Not by her marksmanship which was virtually nonexistent, but by the sheer firepower of the smugglers. These people were amazingly well-armed, and he wondered if Greene had paid them in weapons to handle anybody asking about him. That certainly would explain a bunch of ragtag bikers with holes in their pants armed with a state-of-the-art Stinger missile.

Suddenly, something on fire sailed off a rooftop down the street. The bottle crashed on top of the tank, and a thick rush of the burning gasoline spread across the armored vehicle to cover the hatch, and the windshield.

Instantly, the people inside began firing wildly in every direction, a cascade of spent brass tumbling loose from small ventilation holes.

Mentally tipping his hat to the agent, Bolan used the cover to crash out the front door of the building and gain the street. Forcing himself to ignore the countless bullets flying everywhere, he armed the Carl Gustav, aimed and fired.

In a fluttering rush of smoke and flame, the rocket streaked away to slam into an unprotected headlight of the tank. The missile disappeared into the armored vehicle, and Bolan hit the ground just as it erupted into a fireball. Pieces and chunks of riveted armor crashed into the buildings lining the street, the redbricks breaking and the adobe shattering into tiny pieces.

In a sputtering roar, a motorcycle came out of the flickering darkness, the Mexican agent riding with one hand on the controls, and the other holding the M16/M203 combo.

He braked to a halt on the opposite side of the street and beamed a wide smile.

Resting the Carl Gustav on a shoulder, Bolan did the same.

"CIA?" the agent asked over the crackling flames. His English was perfect, and almost entirely without an accent.

"Private!" Bolan answered, which wasn't exactly a lie, but certainly far from the truth. "CISEN?"

The man's grin widened. "Sorry, never heard of them!"

Bolan chuckled.

Just then, something flared brightly inside the burning tank, and both men hit the ground as a blast shook the night, bodies flying high and thick columns of fiery smoke rising up from the roiling fireball. The spare ammunition cooked off, chattering nonstop for several minutes.

"Think these *putas* might have another Max?" the agent asked, opening the breech to reload the M203.

"Not a chance," Bolan stated.

"How do you figure that?"

"Their clothing was too ragged. This must have been the culmination of years of hard work, stealing bits and pieces and smuggling parts across the borders."

"Perhaps," the agent muttered, glancing sideways at the RV parked down the street. "Is that one yours?"

"Borrowed it from a friend at the Coyote."

"A dead friend who can no longer corroborate your story?"

"Amazing! How did you know?"

"Because that's the story I'd tell the police in other countries, too." The man chuckled. Resting the stock of the assault rifle on a hip, he asked a question in Spanish, and Bolan promptly answered.

"Bah, your accent is terrible," the agent muttered, switching back to English again, but this time with a West Texas accent. "This better, Yankee?"

"Your accent is even worse." Bolan snorted, then smiled. "But I can still understand you."

"Oh, I think we understand each other very well, indeed," the agent replied, switching to a Boston accent while easing off the arming bolt and shouldering the weapon.

"No more games?"

"Agreed. I'm Special Agent Willard Cinco of CISEN." He tilted his head waiting for a response.

"Do you have any proof of that?" Bolan asked curiously.

Cinco roared with laughter. "Now who would claim to be that if he wasn't?" he demanded. "Intelligence agents get a lot of girls? People buy us free drinks?"

Us, not *them.* Check. "No, I guess not," Bolan admitted. So this was Billy the Bull, eh?

Bolan had heard a lot about the CISEN operative over the years. Most of the criminals in Mexico feared him more than the Colombian drug lords and the CIA combined. Those others always wanted information and were open to making deals. Cinco only wanted them dead. He was a killing machine, as unstoppable as the newspapers had once claimed Bolan was, but several times he had been hospitalized with critical wounds taken trying to rescue an undercover cop or civilians. An old friend, Carl Lyons, had once referred to Cinco as the Mack Bolan of the south.

"I'm Special Agent Matt Cooper, Homeland Security," Bolan said, extending a hand.

At least that was what the identification papers in his wallet said. The ones that didn't say George Adams.

"So, what do your friends call you, Homeland?"

"Matt," Bolan said. "Does anybody actually call you the Bull?"

"Only the ladies!" Cinco laughed, then stopped and frowned.

Laying the Carl Gustav on the street, Bolan listened carefully. Just barely discernable over the crackling fire of the burning Max, he dimly heard the all-too familiar sound of approaching motorcycles.

Quickly separating, each man headed in a different direction and vanished into the smoky night air.

Moments later, a score of bikes arrived. The riders stared in horror at the sight of the destroyed Max, and tersely whispered among themselves.

From deep within a pool of shadows, Cinco turned on a flashlight and asked a silent question. Turning on his own, Bolan shook his head, then drew a thumb across his throat. Cinco nodded and turned off the light.

Striding into the street, Bolan and Cinco cut loose with their weapons and four of the bikers died on the spot, their voices raised in shock as the fusillade of hot lead tore away their worthless lives.

Ambushed, the rest of the riders wildly fired back in a blind panic, missing everything but the sky. In cold efficiency, Bolan and Cinco finished the bloody job, then calmly reloaded.

"I shot first," Cinco said casually, thumbing a fresh 40 mm shell into the grenade launcher.

"I didn't miss," Bolan replied, easing a magazine into the Desert Eagle.

"Bah, one of your bullets simply got in the way of one of—" In a blur, Cinco raised the M16, aimed at Bolan and fired a burst.

Untouched, Bolan spun with both of his handguns blazing. A mob of men was silently running up the smoky street in their bare feet, their hands clutching automatic weapons or shotguns.

Cinco and Bolan took out the men in front, their blood splashing the others. But as the leaders fell, the rest cut loose. Cinco cursed as he was hit in the shoulder, and Bolan staggered backward as he was hammered twice in the chest, the 12-gauge deer slugs knocking the air from his lungs.

Firing the M203, Cinco put a 40 mm round into

the burning Max behind the bikers, and the blast sent them tumbling. Struggling to breathe, Bolan shattered a nearby window and took cover behind the wooden sill, the Beretta spraying 9 mm death.

Gushing blood, a biker grabbed his throat and fell into the flames, while another man quietly lay down in the gutter and stopped moving as if simply going to sleep.

Screaming insanely, the rest of the bikers hastily scrambled for cover, as Cinco turned and raced down an alley.

Pulling out the remote control, Bolan had the RV empty the ammunition reserves for the forward machine gun, the spray holding down the bikers while he removed the body armor and breathed deeply. The deer slugs had hit him like cannonballs, and he wasn't surprised to see the ceramic chest plates cracked. But the body armor had done its job and bought him a second chance. Fair enough.

As the RV's guns cycled empty, Bolan used both hands to cradle the Desert Eagle, and fired. Caught in the act of triggering an AK-47, a biker was hit in the hip by the .50 manstopper and spun, spraying the other bikers with 7.62 mm rounds. Several of them screamed in pain and dropped from view.

Then the biker with the shotgun fired, and a deer slug hit the standing man in the belly. Blood gushed from his open mouth as he was sent flying backward to slam into an adobe wall. The Kalashnikov continued chattering as he slid to the street, shuddered and went still.

Just then, Cinco appeared on the roof wearing an old-fashioned bulletproof vest and holding a massive

M60 machine gun, a belt of linked ammunition dangling from the side.

Maintaining the cover fire, Bolan was impressed. The agent had stashed spare weapons at strategic locations before the fight even began. He was starting to like the man's style.

With no expression, Cinco raked the chaotic street below, the old Army machine gun chugging flame. Half a dozen of the bikers died on the spot, and the rest started running. As he tracked them, Bolan got a dark suspicion and looked in the opposite direction.

Sure enough, a fat biker covered with garish tattoos stepped out of the night armed with a nearly prehistoric four-shot multiple grenade launcher.

"Vaya con dios, puta," the fat biker snarled, aiming the weapon at Cinco.

"Not today," Bolan whispered, stroking the trigger of the Desert Eagle.

A huge chunk of the biker's skull was ripped away, bones, brains and blood spattering a nearby wall. Already dead, the corpse took a single step—when one of the dancers from the Coyote stepped out of the shadows to grab the MGL.

Bolan and the woman fired in unison.

As she fell, gushing blood, the incendiary charge lanced from the MGL like a controlled volcano and streaked past Cinco to head for the stars. Pivoting fast, Cinco sent back an answer from the M60, and the dying woman triggered the second barrel, the charge impacting on the side of a fuel depot for the abandoned mine. The explosion rocketed the street, but there was no secondary fireball because the huge reserve tanks of gasoline and diesel had been drained years ago by the departing crew.

As a light rain of burning debris sprinkled down from above, Bolan charged across the street to grab the MGL, and put the last two incendiary rounds into the buildings on either side of the entrenched bikers.

Now bracketed by fire, they aimed for a water tower on a nearby roof. The wooden slats splintered from the furious assault, and broke apart to release only a gurgling trickle of scummy green water.

Firing with every step, Cinco advanced to the extreme edge of the roof, the street below filled with hot lead ricocheting off the street and redbrick buildings.

Dropping the multiple grenade launcher, Bolan started moving up the street, targeting the black silhouettes of the bikers as they foolishly stepped in front of the burning Max to offer a perfect target.

Less than a minute later, Bolan and Cinco were alone with the dead.

Looking up, Bolan nodded at the man, and just for a split second he thought that the agent would turn the M60 on him, and started to swing up the Desert Eagle. Then Cinco winced and dropped the bulky weapon to grab his bloody shoulder, and shuffled away.

Reloading his weapons, Bolan got a med kit from the RV and met Cinco just as he came out of the alley.

"Get that shirt off," Bolan commanded, opening the kit.

Nodding, Cinco slumped against the wall and tried to unbutton the shirt. Looking at the amount of blood already soaked into the cloth, Bolan produced a combat knife and sliced off the garment. He then started battlefield repairs, cleaning the wound, checking for any deadly spurts that told of a nicked artery, then packing the hole with sterilized gauze, taping it and giving the man a fast injection.

"No painkillers," Cinco growled. "We're not out of this yet."

"Antibiotics only," Bolan stated, bending the needle against the wall before casting away the syringe.

Assisting the wounded man to a stand, Bolan helped Cinco to the RV and then climbed inside.

"Very nice," Cinco said, relaxing in the passenger seat. Then he went motionless and glanced sideways at Bolan holding the Desert Eagle to his temple.

"You know the drill," the soldier said, tapping a couple of buttons on the complex dashboard.

As a square plate glowed into life, Cinco pressed his hand against the plastic and waited until it chimed. A few seconds later, a side monitor flickered into life showing the flag of Mexico on top, and the CISEN agency profile and photographs of Special Agent Willard Cinco.

"Sorry, had to check," Bolan said, holstering the weapon.

"You would have been a fool not to," Cinco said with a shrug, then frowned and gingerly touched the bandaged shoulder. "Can I do you now?"

"Even if you had the Homeland Security access codes, it wouldn't help any," Bolan said honestly, getting behind the steering wheel. "I've been officially dead for a while."

In the distance, something inside the wreckage of the Max loudly exploded, spraying out a wild corona of white sparks.

"Deep cover, eh? Most interesting," Cinco muttered.

"My training says I shouldn't trust you, but my gut instinct says differently."

Bolan made no reply, letting the man decide the situation for himself.

"These people killed a great many police and soldiers," Cinco said with great deliberation. "I want them dead very badly."

"Me, too," Bolan agreed, resting his hands on the wheel. "Especially their boss."

"Does he, or she, have a name?"

"He. Dalton Greene."

Cinco frowned. "The Aussie billionaire? I know he's a Nazi, or at least wants to be, but…is he planning on attacking my homeland or yours?"

"Unknown," Bolan stated, turning on the engine. The gauges on the dashboard flickered into life, showing the fuel and ammunition levels. He was dangerously low on both.

"Do you have any idea what Greene is after?"

"None whatsoever," Bolan said, shifting into gear and driving away. "But from his attack on the police, and then the military base—"

"He's doing a stepladder," Cinco growled, brushing back his matted hair. His fingers came away streaked with red. "Escalating each attack, stealing supplies for the next, until he finally…"

Turning down a side street, Bolan knocked aside a group of parked motorcycles. Then he accelerated into the desert, the one remaining headlight bobbing across the vast barren scrubland.

"Why are you telling me this?" Cinco asked, fully reclining in the seat.

"You have a stake in the matter," Bolan said with a shrug. "And a second gun might come in useful."

"I see. If we do this, Homeland, I want him dead, not in jail. That is not negotiable."

"Wasn't planning on taking him alive," Bolan said gruffly, shifting gears again.

"The constitution of Mexico doesn't endorse these types of illicit operations."

"The same with America."

"But we both know that sometimes, breaking the law is the only way to protect innocent lives."

"Agreed."

The big Mexican looked hard at the tall American for a long time, then slowly smiled. "What's our first move, partner?" he asked.

"Intel," said Bolan, pulling out his smartphone and punching in the phone number for Hal Brognola.

CHAPTER TEN

Cárdenas, Cuba

The shimmering expanse of the vast ocean flowed endlessly below the racing Apache gunships, with the Cobras and Black Hawks close behind in a tight formation.
Their assorted collection of stolen radar defusers were
constantly alternating the size and type of electromagnetic patterns around the airships, making the Daylight
armada virtually invisible to anything but direct sight.

The sunlight dancing on the waves was mesmeriz-
ing, almost hypnotic, and Dalton Greene found himself
starting to relax in spite of the dire circumstances. If
he had been lied to, or sold false information by anybody, the results would be disastrous for the white race.

In his opinion, it was painfully clear to anybody with
a brain where humanity was going, a slow, but steady
mongrelization with the lower races, which would naturally lead to increased violence, the abandonment of
traditional morals, new diseases, earthquakes, forest
fires… The list of the Divine Retribution went on forever. Soon enough, the white race would vanish completely, the pure blood of God's own chosen people
diluted until it was indistinguishable from that of the
other lower races. Angels reduced to hyenas, feeding
on the garbage of the dead and lost in the sea of blood.

Privately, Greene admitted that he fully understood the allure of the other races, the children of Lot, so to speak. Back in Johannesburg he once had slipped and indulged in the only real sin that existed.

Her name had been Cassandra, and she had been beautiful, a dusky desert jewel, sex personified! The memory of her touch still sent shivers down his spine.

Personally, Greene knew that he had gone a little insane that terrible night, but he was all better now and could see the world for what it was, a huge melting pot whose stream of mixed races was flowing steadily downhill and straight into hell. The United States and democracy were the cause of the disease, and both had to be eradicated if humanity was to survive. But Daylight would do that, and more. It was quite literally the last desperate hope for a dying world.

"Farewell, Cassandra," Greene whispered, touching the cool window of the military gunship.

"Sir?" the pilot asked from the elevated cockpit just behind the gunner's seat.

"Nothing," Greene said hastily, then turned on the encoded radio and touched the throat mike. "Zed Commander to Goliath, how is our guest?"

"Goliath to Zed," Layne replied. "She's very unhappy, but has stopped trying to escape."

"You should have turned the bitch over to me, sir," LoMonaco declared roughly. "I could have made her see reason!"

"Of that, I am sure!" Greene laughed. "But her broken fingers wouldn't have been able to reprogram the new Skyhooks—" Abruptly, he stopped as something big flashed past the Apache, and the armored gunship rocked from the turbulence.

"That…that's a MiG-29!" the pilot gasped, and activated the master radio link. "Alert all ships! We have incoming fighters. Activate all weapons systems, fire at will! Repeat, fire at will!"

"Abort, abort, abort!" Greene loudly countermanded into a throat mike. "These are friendlies. Repeat, there is no danger! These jets are our escort!"

"Escort?"

"Confirm. We are in no danger!"

"Are you sure about that, sir?" Layne asked over the earbud.

"Absolutely," Greene said, smiling widely as two more MiG fighters streaked past. "We are now in Cuban airspace and finally free from any possible pursuit by other governments."

"Fidel Castro is an ally?" LoMonaco asked, scorn in her voice.

"Oswaldo Figuero is in charge now," Greene answered curtly as land appeared on the horizon. "And I paid him a tidy sum to allow us to land here for refueling."

"Fighting fire with fire, eh?" Layne chuckled over the radio. "Brilliant move, sir."

"Are you sure that we can trust these animals?" LoMonaco muttered, her words distorted by a brief crackle of static.

"Repeat, please?"

"Are you sure that we can trust the communists?" LoMonaco asked once more. "They aren't famous for their honesty."

"True. But their thirst for revenge is well-documented," Greene replied with a chuckle. "My father did Castro a favor once, and the price was that my family could seek asylum here sometime in the future. I have called in that debt."

"How is that revenge?"

"It will massively annoy the American government."

"What was the favor?" Layne asked.

"My father warned Castro about the American attempt to invade Cuba fifty years ago."

"Your father was the reason the Bay of Pigs failed?"

"Let's just say that he was an integral element in the event."

"I'm surprised Castro didn't name a holiday after your family, sir," Layne exhaled, clearly impressed.

"Anonymity was part of the deal."

"Your father didn't miss a trick, did he, sir?" LoMonaco laughed, as a full squadron of MiG-29 jet fighters began to circle protectively around the armada of helicopters.

"Neither do I," Greene stated, watching the beautiful white sands of the coastline come into view. "All right, all ships maintain this course! We should reach the town of Cárdenas in about an hour."

"Fuel reserves are dangerously low, sir," the pilot stated,

"We'll make it. Just keep a watch out for a giant stone crab, and—"

"What was that, sir?" LoMonaco asked sounding confused. "Please repeat!"

"Look for a giant stone crab," Greene said again slowly. "It's about thirty feet wide, and twenty high! That's your marker for Cárdenas. Land in the field alongside! Fuel trucks should be waiting for us."

"Why a giant crab?" Layne asked skeptically. "Is it a mascot for a sports team, or—"

"Just a local delicacy harvested in the warm coastal waters. Nothing special."

"Sir, what if Figuero has no intention of honoring the deal?" Layne asked bluntly. "What if he plans to sell us to the Americans at Gitmo?"

"He hates them more than he worships money," Greene stated confidently. "But just in case he has a temporary lapse of judgment, I took out some insurance."

"Insurance?" LoMonaco asked, a touch of eagerness in her voice.

By God, that woman loves bloodshed, he thought.

"Just keep a watch on the locals," Greene said, lifting a small radio detonator from a pocket. "I'll take care of the Cubans."

The flight across the island nation was swift and uneventful. The MiG jet fighters stayed close during the entire journey, only leaving once for some unknown reason, then coming right back, but with several of their wing-mounted missiles now missing. The obvious conclusion was that there had been a brief confrontation with the US military, and the Cubans had managed to hold them off again.

Probably more from political pressure at the United Nations than military might, Greene noted privately.

Like most underdeveloped nations, the Cubans foolishly thought that advanced weapons made a country strong. But a patriot with a rock would always win over a mercenary with a bazooka, Greene thought. It briefly occurred to him that the same thing could be said about Daylight. They were going to throw rocks at the world, and bring down civilization to save the white race. Thanks to Skyhook.

Swiftly the long miles passed as the Daylight armada skimmed low over farmland, rivers, swamps and forests. They passed over numerous small villages composed of ramshackle huts made of little more than wooden boards with tarpaper roofs. Families walked barefoot along dirt roads while modern electric trolleys rolled past them, and flashy new cars filled the few concrete highways crisscrossing the lush island nation. Squads of armed police roamed everywhere. Tourists never saw this part of Cuba, just the white-sand beaches, posh casinos and other such social terrariums.

Scowling darkly, Greene was utterly disgusted by the display of communism in action. It was nothing more than another form of fiefdom. There were the elite aristocrats, lowly slaves and the dead, but nobody else. Communism was an abomination against God. Early the next afternoon, Greene planned on burning this island clean of the works of Man, and making it a tropical paradise again. The stolen electrical components in the holds of the Black Hawks would make that possible, and no man alive could stop him.

At the top of the hour, Greene switched to a new scrambled frequency and tapped in a different access code.

"Samantha, any word of us on the internet?" Greene asked without any preamble.

"Checking…" LoMonaco replied over the sound of a tapping keyboard. "Negative, sir. According to the web news and pop blogs, Cancun was in a drunken brawl, that military base was hit by a splinter group of the Bolivian drug cartel, and nothing whatsoever has happened at NASA."

Greene was astonished. The ability of the American

government to control the news was truly incredible. "What about the social media?"

"If there were any survivors, nobody has posted anything yet, and I've been disseminating counterintelligence under a dozen different names."

"Such as?"

"Hmm… Aliens have landed from outer space and are slaughtering everybody across the world, an asteroid crashed into Florida and there's more coming, Mexico is in the middle of a military junta, the Chinese bombed NASA just like the Japanese did Pearl Harbor in the last century, al Qaeda detonated a nuclear device over America, and a radioactive death cloud is coming, that sort of stuff."

"This nonsense is believed?"

"Only by the lunatic fringe. But then they repost claiming to have personally seen it all happen, and spread the information farther, where more lunatics…" She ended with a laugh.

Greene snorted in amusement. "Excellent work. Keep it up! The more confusion we can generate, the faster we can get this dirty job done."

"On it, sir!"

Just then, a soft beeping started.

"Sir, we're down to the emergency tanks," the pilot announced. "We have less than twenty-nine minutes of flight time remaining."

"More than enough," Greene stated, trying to keep the excitement out of his voice. "Because there's our landing field!"

Spreading out before the gunship was a rolling plain of dark green grass that went all the way to the rugged eastern coastline. Perched dramatically on a low hill where it could be easily seen by everybody passing on the local highway was a huge stone crab.

Off to the side, a crude landing field had been established in a small dell, sizzling road flares and a row of tanker trucks set along the boundary.

Gathered loosely around the dell were several Hummers and a dozen men in bright orange jumpsuits that marked them as aviation technicians. Only one man was dressed differently. He was wearing the full formal uniform of a general in the Cuban army, a holstered pistol at his side, mirrored sunglasses hiding most of his face.

"Any other troops in sight?" Greene asked over the radio.

"North is clear," Layne reported.

"South is, too, sir," LoMonaco added.

Once more, Greene switched radio frequencies. "Romeo, tango, alpha, bravo," he said slowly.

The general lifted a radio handset to his face.

"Zulu, mike, delta, sierra, foxtrot," a new voice replied over the ceiling speakers of the gunship.

"Okay, everybody land near a tanker and get ready to take on fuel," Greene broadcast to the other gunships. "But stay alert, and keep your weapons primed! I don't like this. There should have been more troops."

Maintaining a combat formation, the Daylight helicopters and gunships landed in a series of gentle bounces, but kept their blades slowly rotating in case of trouble.

Throwing open the Apache's hatch, Greene jumped to the ground and waited.

Lurching forward, the general walked swiftly over, but the technicians stayed in place, their faces shiny with nervous sweat.

"General Ramon Ortega at your service, Mr. White," the officer said with a salute. "Now, if you have the rest of the money, we can get these ships back into the air in just a couple of minutes."

"There is no more money," Greene said, tightening his grip on the other man's hand. "Everything was paid for in advance through Swiss intermediaries."

"With my predecessor, yes." General Ortega smiled, resting his free hand on the holstered pistol. "But I am in charge now, and there is an additional, shall we say, service fee?"

"My good friend Oswaldo Figuero would not approve."

"Perhaps that is true, but what the man does not know, eh?" The general flashed a smile.

"This is a private enterprise?"

"Yes, as you say, very private, indeed."

"I see." Greene sighed, releasing the grip. "Well, then…" He extended his arm and a small derringer slapped into his palm. Greene fired.

At point-blank range, the twin .44 rounds punched a pair of holes in the general's face, and blew out the back of his head in a pink geyser. Weaving slightly as if only drunk, the corpse turned once, before dropping to the grass.

"Now, who's in charge of this fucking operation?" Greene bellowed, sweeping the smoking derringer along the ranks of technicians.

Exchanging nervous glances, none of the frightened men spoke.

"Okay, kill them all," Greene commanded, turning away.

"No, wait!" a man shouted, raising a gloved hand. "We help!"

"No, I don't think so," Greene said as the Gatling guns of the helicopters spun into operation.

Stuttering streams of fire lanced out to tear the technicians' bodies apart, blood splattering everywhere as arms and legs went flying from the savage assault of the armor-piercing rounds.

Still begging for his life, one of the technicians took refuge under a tanker. Laughing in contempt, LoMonaco unlimbered her Neostead shotgun and put a booming stun bag into the man's chest. Slammed aside, he hit the ground rolling and came out the other side. The technician stopped to see the lovely woman smiling down at him, her eyes bright with excitement.

"Oh, Pedro, you should never go back on a deal," LoMonaco said sweetly, thumbing the selector switch to the second magazine and pulling the trigger.

The 12-gauge blast of stainless-steel fléchettes ripped the technician into crimson hamburger, his death scream mixing with the booming echo of the South African weapon.

A wing of MiG jet fighters streaked overhead, still on protective patrol.

"Think they know?" Layne asked, twisting his hands on the XM-25 grenade rifle.

"If they did, we'd be dead by now," Greene said calmly. "But they're much too high and moving way too fast to see any details."

LoMonaco sneered. "Thank God for small favors."

"Amen!"

"Okay, fill the tanks," Layne commanded, resting the rifle on a shoulder. "I want us airborne in fifteen minutes."

Swarming into action, the terrorists started pulling

out insulated hoses from the tankers and running them to the waiting aircraft.

Turning on the pump at a tanker, Layne scowled as pale pink fuel trickled into an inspection tube. Pink? That should be a deep amber in color!

"Hold it!" he ordered, raising a hand.

Everybody stopped as Layne rummaged in a toolbox for a wrench and opened an exhaust pipe. He let some of the aviation fuel puddle on the ground, lit a match and dropped it into the pink fluid. It ignited, but very weakly, and soon died way.

"Sir, this fuel has been watered down!" Layne snarled, then hawked and spat at the puddle. "This shit wouldn't run a lawnmower, much less a helicopter!"

"Check the others!" Greene commanded, a faint touch of fear tickling the back of his mind. "Everybody else, get those bodies out of sight! Put them under the tankers!"

As the corpses were dragged away, Layne and LoMonaco ran fast tests on the contents of the other tankers.

"The end tankers are fine!" LoMonaco reported. "But the others are worthless!"

"Okay, I ran the numbers," Layne announced, looking up from a smartphone. "We can fill half the tanks completely, or give everybody half a tank. What are your orders, sir?"

"Half tanks!" Greene snapped. "I prepared for betrayal, and established a secondary refueling area roughly three hundred miles east of here!"

"Can we make it there on half tanks?" LoMonaco asked, licking dry lips. She intensely disliked flying, but there was no way around it for this mission.

"Easily," Greene stated, going back to the Apache

and retrieving the hand radio. "White Team to Sky-Master! We've just been informed that the Americans know we're here and are on the way. Can you fly south and intercept? Over."

There was a crackle of static. "Confirm that, White Team. Will comply. Best of luck, comrades. Long live the president! Long live the revolution!"

"Long live the revolution," Greene said, his face a mask of hatred.

In rumbling majesty, the wing of MiG jet fighters broke formation overhead and streaked away at full speed directly toward the south.

"The Americans will go ballistic when they arrive," Layne said with a humorless grin. "Quite possibly literally."

"I couldn't care less," Greene said, watching the refueling production start once more. "By the time these idiots figure out I was lying, we'll be safely far away, and the president would rather eat his own gun than publicly admit that he was tricked."

"And privately?" LoMonaco asked pointedly.

Greene shrugged. "He'll want to send assassins to capture us alive and torture us to death very slowly.

"But by then, all of our little Skyhooks will be activated, and the Cubans will have much more serious matters to occupy their attention than petty retribution."

The Gulf of Mexico

LISTENING TO A RECORDED report on the radio, Bolan and Cinco said nothing, their faces grim, as Hal Brognola described the massive destruction of the NASA launch facility. The report had been assembled for the President, so it was complete, with every bloody detail confirmed twice before being added, especially the staggering death toll.

When it was finished, Bolan turned off the radio, and the men sat in silence for a few minutes, digesting the deluge of information.

"My friend, these people have to die immediately," Cinco stated, a muscle twitching in his throat. "If Greene and Daylight should decide to attack a city..." He left the sentence unfinished.

"Agreed," Bolan stated.

The flight deck of the C-130 Hercules was large and comfortable, with well-cushioned seats for the crew. Warm air blew up from the floor vents, carrying a faint smell of disinfectant, and the four massive engines of the C-130 maintained a low background hum that made talking difficult on the flight deck, but not impossible.

The span of oversize windows offered an excellent view of the empty sky around the military transport, and on the control board in front of the pilot, a glowing radar screen showed that the huge plane was alone in the air except for a few puffy clouds, a commercial 767 high overhead and a distant flock of condors heading toward South America.

Situated behind the men was a doorway leading to the cargo deck and a closed cabinet containing various items of survival gear, parachutes, life rafts, flares and several 9 mm MP-5 machine guns perfect for close-quarters combat.

"Why would they destroy the entire launch facility?" Cinco asked slowly, smearing medical-grade epoxy over the stitches in his shoulder. "Do you think it was a diversion to hide the theft of something? What was the point? Was it merely advertising to show what they are capable of doing for potential customers?"

"Maybe. We'll know more after Air Force Intelligence is done searching through the rubble," Bolan replied. He sat in the copilot's seat, next to Levi Sorenson, the blacksuit pilot. "Are you sure that is safe, amigo?"

Cinco laughed. "If this was common household epoxy, no, of course not. It would cause the wound to fester and rot," he said, smoothing out the shiny edges. "But the medical version allows oxygen to pass and keeps the flesh alive. You've never used this before?"

"Only the commercial stuff," Bolan said.

Cinco arched an eyebrow. "And you survived?"

"Chalk it up to clean living."

"And what does that have to do with you, eh?" Cinco chuckled, capping the tiny tube and tucking it safely away in a shirt pocket.

"Not much," Bolan admitted with a smile. "Why are you keeping the tube?"

"You know that sometimes stitches burst free in battle, even with epoxy added," Cinco replied, rolling down his sleeve. "I prefer to do my bleeding at home like a proper gentleman."

Bolan tried not to laugh, and failed. The agent seemed to joke about everything, even when in a firefight. He liked that.

"I like your pilot and this plane," Cinco said, adjusting the headrest to a more comfortable position. "Even if it does seem like a waste for only the two of us to be flying in this apartment building with wings."

"Well, there's also the RV," Bolan corrected, tilting his head toward the rear of the plane.

"A most remarkable vehicle," Cinco said, clearly impressed. "Is it standard-issue for Homeland Security?"

"No. She's something that I…acquired personally."

"*Acquired* is a very vague word."

"It's a vague world."

"That it most certainly is, my friend," Cinco said with a wide grin.

Just then the radio speaker crackled with static, and out came an inhuman voice that sounded oddly like a turkey gobbling. Bolan flipped a series of switches, and tapped the descrambler code into the keypad.

"Repeat, Cooper, this is Anchor, come in, Cooper! Over," Brognola said over the speaker.

"Anchor, this is Cooper. Over," Bolan said into a hand mike.

"Our mutual friend just took out a loan at a bank in the Cayman Islands," Brognola said curtly. "Dozens are dead, the building is torched, but no money taken."

"The police got there in time to stop the robbery?" Cinco asked loudly. "Is Greene in custody?"

There was a long pause in which there only was the crackle of the natural radiation of the planet.

"Adam, Baker, Charlie," Brognola said in a deceptively calm voice. "Repeat, Adam, Baker, Charlie!"

"Charlie here," Bolan said. "Everything is fine, Anchor. I picked up a friend in Cancun."

There was a pause. "Is he intelligent?"

By that, Bolan guessed Brognola wanted to know if the newcomer was an intelligence agent. "Absolutely. In fact he's quite…bullish…even if he doesn't like alphabet soup."

"Checking," Brognola replied. "Okay, I have a conformation. The Bull of Cancun, big man, scar on his right hand…" There was a short pause. "It says here that he looks like…is this right?"

"Yes, I actually do look a little bit like the British actor Alfred Molina," glancing at the tiny screen Cinco chuckled. "With the world population at seven billion, statistically there are six people who look exactly like you, too, Anchor."

"Please confirm, Cooper."

"Well, I haven't meet all seven billion, Anchor, but the math sounds solid," Bolan said with a smile.

"Sitrep, now!" Brognola demanded.

Tolerantly, Bolan rattled off a long series of code phrases. "Happy now, Anchor? I'm not a prisoner, or being forced in any way."

"Didn't really think you could be," Brognola said grudgingly. "But the day I don't check—"

"—is the day it comes true. Roger that, Anchor. Now what was this about Greene?"

"He used a suicide bomber as a can-opener at the bank, then sent in a hot squad," Brognola continued. "They didn't hit the vault, or take anything, except a hostage, Amanda Toulane, the bank's CIO."

"The chief information officer, eh?" Cinco repeated, thoughtfully tapping a finger alongside his nose. "Anchor, did Greene use the bank's computers for anything?"

"Good guess, Cancun. He forced the hackers to alter the software in some microchips," Brognola said. "Or so we think. Very few of the blast-proof video cameras survived the suicide bomber, so we're going pretty much on guesswork here."

"Anchor, was there anything new at NASA?" Bolan

asked, a terrible suspicion starting to grow. "Maybe a prototype of some kind?"

"Unfortunately, yes," Brognola said gruffly. "There's no confirmation yet, but Eagle One said that NASA was working on a new type of engine. Very small, extremely powerful, something called a Collier-Hayes boron plasma enginette."

"I know about those," Cinco said unexpectedly. "My government helps NASA recover some of their test missiles in the Gulf, and we were strongly advised not to look inside."

"But you did anyway?" Brognola asked suspiciously.

"Negative, Anchor, we keep our word," Cinco stated stiffly. "But we took a lot of pictures of the outside, and our scientists have made some educated guesses."

Apparently, damn good ones, Bolan noted, his respect for CISEN increasing several notches. "So, what are these boron engines used for?"

"Enginettes. They're designed to stabilize HEO orbital platforms, like a space station, or deep-space telescope. Think of them as miniature tugboats, built to shove much larger ships around," Brognola said over rustling papers. "As for what else they might be used for I have no idea."

"Hee-oh?" Cinco asked with a scowl.

"High Earth Orbit," Bolan answered succinctly, then pressed the transmit button on the hand mike again. "Any idea how many of these boron enginettes were taken?"

"We don't know for certain, but the State Department claims that NASA signed contracts to sell the enginettes to a dozen other countries, so…maybe a hundred of them? Possibly more."

"How big are they?" Cinco asked.

"Unknown."

"And there's nobody left alive at NASA to ask."

"Exactly."

Bolan started to get a bad feeling in his gut about the theft. Experimental microengines, their guidance chips altered by the supercomputer of a bank. He felt positive that it was merely another link in the chain of events, but what was the ultimate goal of Daylight?

"Anchor, if these enginettes were designed for deep-space operations," Bolan said slowly, "is there any chance they can be operated by remote control?"

"Sure. But we already tried that with zero results," Brognola replied. "And even if we could get them working, the plasma drives would be damn near invisible during the day, and nowhere near hot enough for a Keyhole, or WatchDog satellite to locate."

"Okay, what about the diagnostic subprogram? If these things were basically designed as altitude jets they would be equipped to relay information on their relative speed, height and direction. That's nowhere near as good as a GPS fix, but we should be able to find them, anyway."

"That might just work," Brognola stated. "But it's way outside my field of expertise. I'll have to get back to you on this."

"Sooner would be better than later."

"Agreed. Anchor out."

"Okay, what's our next move?" Cinco asked, running a comb through his tousled hair.

Bolan saw that the man had dark circles under his eyes, and was slurring his words slightly. Telltale signs of not enough sleep, and that could get them both killed.

"Our next move is some sack time," Bolan stated. "The bed in the RV is comfortable, and the shower works just fine."

"But—"

"We'll work in shifts," Bolan continued. "First me, then you. We need to be double sharp going up against these Australians."

"We can sleep in the grave," Cinco countered gruffly. "What about repairing the RV? Got a spare missile pod?"

"Not onboard, no."

"Damn. So what about—"

Suddenly, the radio crackled.

"Anchor to Cooper," Brognola said. "Incredibly, somebody at Houston Space Command had a similar idea, and it sort of worked."

"Care to explain that?"

"It seems that our friend from Down Under is using radar defusers from Australia, America, Mexico and now Cuba, which translates into Soviet technology. Daylight keeps switching from one to another every couple of seconds making it damn near impossible to get a lock on their position."

"Never heard of anybody doing that before," Bolan replied.

"Me, neither. It's damn smart, and a real bitch to counter. But the few microsecond bursts we managed to get make it seem like the gunships are somewhere east of Cuba."

"If they're out of Cuban airspace," Bolan started, "then why not ask Eagle One to contact Gitmo and—"

"Because there's no point," Brognola interrupted. "We can just barely find these people using the entire

NORAD surveillance grid. Unless the jet fighters from Gitmo actually collide with one of the Daylight gunships, there's as much chance of finding them as there is of locating Bigfoot.

"In addition to all of that," Brognola continued, "there's some kind of internal war going on between the Cuban army and their air force…. It's chaos down there at the moment."

"More cover for his escape," Cinco stated. "Greene is very good."

"We'll just have to be better," Bolan declared. "Check the maps."

Nodding agreement, Cinco went to the cabinet and got a map of the area. Spreading it out, he frowned in concentration. "To the east of Cuba is…Jamaica and a thousand islands, atolls and spits, some of which don't even have names."

"There's nothing in the area worth destroying," Bolan said, "so he must be picking up supplies, or maybe it's personnel."

"Possibly both," Cinco added.

"Count on it," Brognola declared. "This escalation is far from being over."

Pulling out a Swiss Army Knife, Cinco pried free a tiny magnifying glass. Squinting through the lens, he started to examine the smallest landmass that could hold roughly a dozen helicopters.

"Okay, the Hercules is considerably faster than any of his helicopters," Bolan stated, listening to the engines. "But Greene has a tremendous lead, and we have to fly around Cuba. If we try to go through their airspace, the air force will launch enough surface-to-air missiles from their hidden batteries to blow a hole in the moon."

"On top of which, we don't know exactly where he's going," Cinco said, running a finger through the clusters of island nations.

"That doesn't matter," Bolan countered. "We go wherever NORAD points. Anchor, have them keep running checks every fifteen minutes."

"Sorry. The best they can do is an hour."

Bolan tried to not let the annoyance show on his face. The lag was that big? Even a damaged helicopter could cover a hundred miles in that length of time.

"Accepted," Bolan muttered. "But I want constant updates, and see if you can get them to shave a couple of minutes off that sixty."

"Will do," Brognola growled. "I'll ask Eagle One to light a fire under their ass."

"Much appreciated."

"So far, we have only one small advantage," Cinco said, turning over a map to check the key. "Greene doesn't know that we can track him. That could make all of the difference."

"He *probably* doesn't know," Brognola corrected. "I have no data on how good that CIO he kidnapped is at her job. She may have already told him the enginettes are sending back status reports, and he'll figure out the rest."

"Her?" Cinco asked with a scowl.

"Amanda Toulane. I'll send you a recent picture so you know who not to shoot in the middle of a fight."

Laying aside the map, Cinco went to a window and looked down at the vast ocean. "What if he does learn the truth and turns off the machines? What happens then?"

"A lot of people die," Bolan stated grimly.

CHAPTER ELEVEN

Rum Island, Bahamas

"Come along, Amanda," LoMonaco snarled, jerking on the rope. "Time to work!"

With both hands tied behind her back, the woman calling herself Amanda Toulane pretended to obey meekly, and shuffled along after the much shorter woman. But she never stopped looking for a chance to escape from these lunatics.

Elizabeth Carrington had just been coming on shift when the real Amanda Toulane had died in the initial explosion. Not even wearing her uniform yet, much less carrying a gun, the bank guard had sought refuge in the dead woman's office, never for a moment thinking that the thieves would bypass the vault for the supercomputer. Then, when they arrived in force, Carrington did the only thing she could to stay alive, and pretended to be Toulane. Unfortunately, now it seemed that they wanted her to hack in to something. Carrington knew that she was very good at a lot of things, but computer science wasn't one of them. Which left her in a bind. If she told the truth, the terrorists would kill her on the spot, but if she refused, well, torture seemed the most likely outcome. *Damned if I do, and damned if I don't,*

Carrington raged impotently. Unless she escaped soon, her choices were going to be torture or death.

On the other hand, almost everybody she knew on the Caymans had been killed in the mad attack, and Carrington burned for some revenge. But for now, she could only wait and hope that they had a mistake. Carrington had only a vague idea where this island was located, but she had seen a score of other islands along the way, and that was her goal. *Get free, move fast, find help.* The words kept repeating in her mind until they were almost a soothing mantra.

Tugging the rope, LoMonaco led Carrington off to the side to stand near the man called Greene and the enormous fellow called Layne. Well-trained by the bank-security experts, Carrington was trying to memorize everything she could about the mass murderers to help a court of law send them away forever. Which she had to admit seemed highly unlikely at the present moment.

In ragged formation, the helicopters landed in a wide area of compacted sand, the blades only kicking up a few loose particles and not the expected sandstorm. Rubbing the toe of her shoe across the unyielding ground, Carrington guessed that it had been sprayed with some sort of an epoxy. They'd glued the entire island into place so that the wash of the helicopters wouldn't reveal their presence. Whoever these people were, Carrington was starting to get a suspicion that they were only pretending to be terrorists, and had some much darker goal in mind. Terrorists were more hit-'n-git, while this was starting to have the feel of a military operation.

As the last gunship settled onto the beach, a crowd of

people surged forward to drag camouflage netting over all of the machines, while another team began hauling cans of fuel out of a small cave.

Wrinkling her nose, Carrington could smell the sharp stink of ammonia from the bat guano inside, but didn't see any of the animals flying about, disturbed by the invasion of their domain.

That was when she spotted a bright yellow gas canister lying near the entrance to the cave that bore the biohazard symbol. They had to have used whatever was in the canister to kill the bats. But that made no sense. Bats didn't attack people!

A couple of men dragged a limp man out of the cave, slit his throat and tossed the body into the bushes. Hardly any blood flowed from the ghastly wound, showing that the man was already dead, but Carrington felt ill at the callous action. They had just been making sure that the fellow was actually deceased and not merely pretending. That made Carrington cancel most of her escape fantasies.

Stay calm, and stay alive, she mentally scolded herself. This was real life, not a movie, and these lunatics killed the way other people waved hello.

Climbing out of a helicopter that Carrington had heard the others refer to as Gunship Zed, a bald man carrying a backpack ambled over to Greene, and they talked privately for a few minutes, their voices too low for her to clearly hear anything. She only caught the occasional word, and those were enough to scare her senseless: rockets…Skyhook…billions…war.

"All right, time to test our new weapon," Greene said, slinging the Minimi across his back before heading into the trees. "Come along, Miss Toulane. You'll need to pay close attention in case the Skyhook software needs any further adjustments."

There was that word again, *Skyhook*. Shuffling along, Carrington tried not to scowl. Further adjustments? Was that why these people had attacked the bank, but hadn't stolen any money? They only wanted to use the Cray computer to help them program some kind of weapon? This was why she hadn't been killed before. She was insurance, in case the computer experts at the bank had failed to do a proper job.

"I'm not used to writing code in the middle of a jungle," Carrington said, stepping over an exposed tree root.

"Oh, no, we have all of the necessary equipment back inside the cave," Layne said, jerking a thumb in that direction. "Everything you would possibly need."

"I see," Carrington whispered, her mouth suddenly bone-dry. "And…and if I refuse?"

Lightning fast, LoMonaco slammed a fist into her stomach, and Carrington doubled over, gasping for air, tears blurring her sight.

"A lack of cooperation would only cause you a great deal of pain," Greene said calmly, pulling a cigar out of his shirt pocket and sniffing the dark tobacco. "And in the end you would still do the work we wish."

"Just minus a few body parts," LoMonaco added, pulling a knife from behind her back and turning the blade in the bright sunshine. The edge rippled from constant stropping and looked razor-sharp.

Awkwardly rising, Carrington spat some dirt from her mouth. "What do you need done, sir?" she asked in a hoarse voice.

"Nothing at the moment." Greene chuckled, lighting the cigar and puffing contentedly. "First I want to see how good a job your staff did."

The journey through the trees took much longer than Carrington would have believed possible for such a tiny island, and she began to think they were making circles for some reason. With both hands tied, her balance was off, but Carrington knew that falling would involve unwanted assistance from LoMonaco and would most likely include as much pain as possible. Carrington had seen the wild look in the other woman's eyes, and knew that she was a true sadist. LoMonaco pinched and slapped at the slightest provocation.

Carrington was already bruised over most of her body. That only increased her desperate urge to escape, but at the moment, she had no idea how to go about such a thing. She was never alone, not even when she had used the airship's toilet. Carrington burned in shame at the memory, then dismissed it with a shake. Stay alive! That was her only concern, nothing else mattered.

Finally, the trail ended in a small clearing that overlooked the sea. Bizarrely, there was a sign nearby proclaiming that the Rum Island Restoration Project was being done by the Melbourne Environmental Corporation, a division of Greene Industries.

The only other thing in sight was an old-fashioned claw-foot bathtub filled with what appeared to be concrete.

"That looks okay," Layne asked with a scowl. "How heavy is it?"

"Almost a ton," Greene replied proudly. "That bathtub is cast iron, and I lined it with lead bars before pouring in the concrete."

Draping the rope over a shoulder, LoMonaco scowled. "Is that enough for an accurate test?"

Greene nodded. "Absolutely. Almost three times more than we could ever possibly need."

Layne grunted at that, but said nothing.

Sliding off the backpack, the bald man opened it to extract a small control box that he passed to Greene, then a coil of linked metal squares. Carrington tried not to shiver. She had seen what the limpet mine could do at the bank.

But then Carrington paused. This limpet was different from the others. It was attached to a sort of shoebox-shaped device covered with small nozzles.

"What is that?" she asked curiously, then flinched, expecting a hit from LoMonaco.

But this time, the short woman only laughed contemptuously as if their prisoner had failed to recognize some common item, like a lightbulb or a doormat.

"That is the future, Miss Toulane," Greene said, lifting one of the limpets for closer inspection, then throwing it away. "Behold, Skyhook!"

While still in the air, the linked segments spread wide, and the mine abruptly changed course to slap against the smooth side of the bathtub with a pronounced clang.

Almost instantly, the nozzles on the box glowed a dull orange in color and a barely visible flame extended. With a jerk, the bathtub started to move sideways along the ground, the stubby iron legs leaving behind deep gouges in the loose sand.

Carrington couldn't believe it. How could that little box generate so much power? Then she saw the symbol of the American space agency NASA on the side. She tried to figure out what that meant and came up with nothing. Carrington realized that she was completely out of her depth here, and once more panic threatened her resolve.

Blowing smoke out of the side of his mouth, Greene worked the controls on the plastic box. Suddenly, different nozzles flared, and the tub lurched into the air. Laughing in delight, the terrorists started to applaud as the bathtub zoomed around the clearing, skimming past them by only a few inches. Then it rammed into a palm tree, smashing through the thick trunk to the sound of splintering wood.

"My God, sir, you did it!" LoMonaco yelled, grinning widely. "You actually did it!"

"Was there ever any doubt, Samantha?" Greene chuckled, returning the bathtub to its original position, then making it leap upward again.

"No, sir!" LoMonaco stated, then relented. "Well… Yes, sir, a little. But not now!"

"This is truly amazing," Carrington whispered, impressed in spite of everything. "But what's the purpose of Skyhook?"

Slowly, Layne turned. "That really does not matter now, Miss Toulane," he said in a low voice, reaching for the Glock under his windbreaker. "Because everything seems to be functioning perfectly, which means we don't need you after all."

"Are you sure about that?" Carrington asked in a surprisingly calm voice. "Have you considered—"

"Bushmasters!" a man bellowed, charging out of the jungle with an F88 assault rifle in his hands.

That confused Carrington for a moment, and she started to look for snakes, when she suddenly recalled that was also the name of the Australian army special forces. The cavalry had arrived!

As the weapon chattered, Greene and Layne both went flying backward, their shirts ripped apart from the barrage of 5.56 mm rounds showing the body armor underneath. Stitched across the chest, the bald man staggered away clutching the bloody ribbons of his shirt, attempting to hold in the river of his life.

Diving to the side, LoMonaco rolled into the bushes and came up again with her Glock 18 machine pistol spitting a stream of 9 mm rounds. The barrage missed the Aussie Bushmaster completely, and he returned fire with a short burst from the F88. But LoMonaco was already behind the splintered palm tree, and the bullets only produced a spray of splinters and loose wood chips.

Rolling over to a prone position, Greene responded with his Falcon, the big booming Magnum rounds kicking up sandy dirt in front of the Bushmaster. Greene recognized the man as Joe Davis, a new recruit who had been with Daylight only a few months.

Utterly furious, Greene vowed to make the Australian government pay dearly for this betrayal. He was trying to save the entire white race! Why couldn't those fools in Parliament understand that he was on their side?

Snarling a curse, Davis tried to wipe the sand from his eyes, when Layne swung up the XM-25 and stroked the trigger. The 25 mm grenade slammed into the shoulder of the prone soldier, audibly breaking his bones.

Quickly rolling away again, Davis produced a Glock with his undamaged arm…but then hesitated, unwilling to fire blindly and possibly kill the civilian hostage.

"Surrender or die!" he yelled, rubbing his eyes while firing a couple of rounds into the air.

"Not bloody likely!" LoMonaco snarled, swinging around her Neostead and flipping the selector switch.

As the weapon boomed, a stun bag slammed into the weeds, just missing Davis, ruffling his hair from the passage. He shot back at the noise and scored a hit. But the 9 mm rounds ricocheted off LoMonoco's body armor to zing into the gently swaying palm trees.

Snarling like an animal, LoMonaco answered with another stun bag, then switched to the second barrel, and a hellstorm of fléchettes peppered the ground alongside the rolling man, making the soil appear to boil. Retreating into the trees, Davis took refuge behind a flowering bush and hastily spat into a palm to frantically wipe his eyes.

Just then, an F88 chattered from within the bushes. Everybody moved for cover, but the barrage of rounds didn't seem to hit anything, much less anybody.

Dropping to his knees, Greene triggered the Falcon again until it cycled empty, then he dropped the gun and pulled around the Minimi machine gun.

Surrounded by a hurricane of clipped leaves, Davis had finally got his sight clear again when from behind there came the metallic sound of an arming bolt being pulled into position. Instantly, he lanced out a boot at groin level. There was a low groan, and a man collapsed to the ground, his F88 assault rifle falling into the bushes.

Clawing the weapon free from the prickly branches, Davis briefly gave it a fast glance to ascertain the condition, then rose to start firing single rounds at anybody carrying a weapon. He hit both Greene and LoMonaco on the run this time, but with no appreciable results, their body armor effectively stopping even trauma damage from the brutal impact of the 5.56 mm rounds.

"Stinking race traitor!" Layne yelled, firing a 25 mm shell into the trees.

Traveling just enough distance to harm, the warhead violently exploded behind Davis, spraying him with shrapnel and splinters.

Bleeding from a dozen small wounds, Davis staggered away from the destroyed tree. Dropping out of sight once more, he once more futilely tried to send off a radio message from the transceiver disguised as a cheap watch on his wrist. But the terrorists never stopped jamming the airwaves wherever they went. His last report had been from Cancun just before the deadly party. Nobody at headquarters had any idea where he was right now. This had been one of the first lessons Davis learned in counterintelligence—insane didn't always mean stupid. Sad, but true.

Spreading out in a combat formation, Layne and LoMonaco converged on the area from different directions, their weapons constantly firing.

As Davis popped up from behind a fallen tree, Greene snapped out an arm to trigger both barrels of the .44 Remington derringer. One round missed, but the other slammed into the man's assault rifle, and it went spinning away. Grunting from the pain, Davis stumbled backward several of his fingers bent at impossible angles.

"Now you're mine!" Layne growled, lowering the grenade launcher.

As the fat man advanced, Davis drew his knife and flipped it forward underhand. Moving fast, Layne jerked aside, and the blade thudded into a palm tree carrying with it a piece of his shirt collar.

No longer trying to capture the traitor alive, Greene raked the bushes with his assault rifle, and was rewarded with the crimson spray of a hit.

Snarling a curse, Davis vanished again.

Victoriously thumbing fresh cartridges into the shotgun, LoMonaco froze at the telltale sound of somebody yanking out the arming pin from a grenade. But nobody was carrying any explosives except…

"Fire in the hole!" she bellowed, spinning behind a palm tree.

Half a heartbeat later, the lush foliage erupted in a fiery blast, smoking body parts spreading outward in a gory corona.

Quickly advancing on the smoky bushes, Greene raged at the sight of the ragged human corpse spread on the ground, organs hanging from the shaking greenery like demonic holiday decorations. He was furious at not being able to question the traitor, but a small part of Greene had to admire the man's courage at taking his own life rather than being tortured to death. Most civilians would do anything for a few precious moments of life. But a real soldier would rather die than betray his brothers-in-arms.

"Think he was alone?" Layne asked, scanning the jungle for anything suspicious.

"There's no way of knowing for sure," Greene said, sliding the derringer back up his sleeve. "You better execute anybody we don't trust implicitly."

"That'll kill morale," Layne said, resting the hot barrel of the grenade launcher on a shoulder.

"Tell the others you're organizing a special mission

to another island," Greene said, touching a bloody graze on his cheek. "Then when you're alone with them…" He didn't finish the sentence.

"On it," Layne grunted, and headed deeper into the trees.

"Think he'll need any help?" LoMonaco asked eagerly.

"Tend to your business," Greene began, then stopped. "Where is she, anyway?"

Turning around fast, LoMonaco looked across the war-torn clearing half expecting to see the corpse of the other woman. Instead, she only spotted a pile of loose ropes and some footprints heading for the nearby beach.

Charging out of the bushes, LoMonaco raced around the softly humming bathtub to stop on the edge of a short bluff overlooking the western side of the atoll. Down on the shore, Carrington was sprinting for the beach like a marathon runner approaching the finish line.

Grinning in savage delight, LoMonaco fired the Neostead twice.

Traveling at half the speed of sound, the first stun bag slammed Carrington in the back, and she dropped to her knees. The next impacted directly between her shoulders, and the woman pitched forward to hit the sand limply, the fingers of an outstretched hand just barely touching the clear blue water of the Atlantic Ocean.

THE C-130 HERCULES was rapidly approaching San Salvador in the Bahamas.

The coffee and sandwiches long gone, Willard Cinco

was thinking of Lucia when there came a brief squeal from the radio.

"I'll get that," he said to the blacksuit pilot. Flipping on the small monitor, he watched as the latest report from NORAD scrolled across the bottom of the screen.

"Son of a bitch," he muttered softly, then turned in the copilot's chair and thumped a fist on the wall intercom. "We found them, amigo!"

Cinco couldn't hear any reactions over the powerful hum of the engines until running feet pounded up the stairs from the cargo deck, and Bolan burst into the flight deck.

"Talk!" Bolan commanded, dropping into the navigator seat.

"See for yourself," Cinco said with a gesture. "We've gone past them! The last signal from the NASA enginette is static, and on the directional heading of south by southwest."

"Behind us," Bolan said, a smile coming and going at lightning speed. "And it's a static heading. Relative speed of…zero point zero. They've landed somewhere!"

"So it would seem. Anything on that heading?" Cinco asked.

Pulling down some maps, Bolan got busy with a compass and ruler. "Five…no, six islands. Two of them too small for anything to land on, one is an active volcano."

"Active!"

"Just rumbles and steam, no lava."

"Thank God for small favors."

"But the other three…just a moment…"

Straightening out the yoke, the Stony Man pilot

checked their heading on the magnetic compass and then on the GPS. "Well?" Cinco demanded impatiently.

"All three could serve as a base for Greene and his people," Bolan stated, leaning back in the chair.

"Better and better! Any radio dead zones, or radar anomalies?"

"Bull, this is the heart of the Bermuda Triangle," Bolan said, resting an elbow on the map. "We're surrounded by electromagnetic anomalies and dead zones."

"Excellent," Cinco whispered. "Then we've got him by the balls, my friend!"

"Not yet," Bolan countered, going back to the maps. "But with any luck… Yes, here we go. There's a small spit only a few miles away from the first of the three possible base locations. The Hercules can land there, and we cross the water in a raft."

"Two miles of open water in an inflatable raft?" Cinco asked, glancing sideways. "What's wrong with using the RV? I thought you said it could float."

"Normally, yes. But not after tangling with that Stinger. Now the rear doors wouldn't keep out a heavy fog, much less the Atlantic Ocean."

"Then row we must."

"And it's six miles, not two," Bolan amended, shifting the map around. The spit had no name, but the first possible landing site was a tiny atoll called Rum Island.

"Bah, two, six, ten miles, are not a problem." Cinco grinned. "Any CISEN agent can swim that far in full combat gear."

"Very impressive," Bolan replied. "However, in Homeland Security we're smart enough to use a raft in shark-infested waters."

"Sharks?"

"Lots of them, mostly great whites."

"Well, if the senior agent insists upon using a raft—" Cinco sighed, pretending to be disappointed "—then I must acquiesce. Age before beauty!"

"Which of us is which?"

"Damned if I know." Cinco shrugged.

CHAPTER TWELVE

Rising slowly from the cresting waves, Bolan and Cinco paused halfway out of the shallows to carefully study the sandy beach. Each man was wearing full-body armor, their web harnesses covered with ordnance, and each was carrying an M16/M203 combination assault rifle.

Their inflatable raft was gone, courtesy of a great white shark they had encountered along the way to Rum Island. The deadly man-eater had been truly enormous, but a full magazine of 9 mm rounds, delivered directly to the head, from the silenced Beretta machine pistol had discouraged the legendary killer shark.

Swaying to the gentle push of the cresting waves, Bolan and Cinco saw nothing, except for a large sign proclaiming the recent start of an island-rejuvenation project.

Cinco grunted at the name of the company on the sign, then Bolan nudged him with an elbow. Only a few yards down the beach, the sand had been irregularly smoothed, exactly as if somebody had been trying to erase footprints.

Slipping off their swim fins, the pair crawled out of the water, and along the beach. Gaining the relative safety of the trees, they stood and eased off their backpacks to hide them in the bushes. This would be their fallback position in case of serious trouble.

Retrieving the throat mike and transceivers from inside sealed plastic bags, the men put them in place and did a brief check. As expected, every radio frequency was presently being jammed.

Moving slowly through the tangle of exposed roots and leafy vines, Bolan and Cinco could hear the murmur of distant voices coming from their right, along with the clatter of metal on metal.

"Sounds like they're refueling the gunships," Cinco whispered, the M16 combo assault rifle held tight in his callused hands.

Sniffing at the air, Bolan nodded in agreement. "Good. Then it'll be harder for them to hear us," he stated, studying the treetops for any video cameras or proximity sensors. But the thick foliage seemed clear. There weren't even any animals about, which was quite odd.

There was a winding trail going through the bushes, but they avoided that, and stayed in the thick foliage. The going was a lot slower, but safer.

Reaching a small clearing, they paused at the bizarre sight of a bathtub filled with concrete. The ground nearby was littered with spent shells and splashes of dried blood, along with a lot of odd burn marks that resembled the blast marks left by a fired rocket launcher. Proceeding farther, they discovered a grenade crater in some bushes, the remains of a corpse scattered about, bones and organs exposed to the hot tropical sun.

Bolan and Cinco exchanged puzzled looks, then moved onward. They had no idea what had happened at this place, except that somebody had obviously died hard.

Keeping the thickets between them and the gunships, the two men circled around the island on a soft reconnaissance. Until they knew for certain that Greene and his people were here, their fingers would stay off the triggers of their weapons. Civilians often acted stupidly when faced with armed men, and the last thing either Bolan or Cinco wanted was an innocent life on their hands from a would-be hero trying to protect his family from armed invaders.

Catching the stink of guano, they headed north and soon located a rock mound fronted with the entrance to a limestone cave. Stationed in front of the cave was a pair of men armed with F88 assault rifles. One of them was playing a video game on his cell phone, while the other was sitting on a fallen log and drinking a beer.

Cinco grunted at the name on the giant can, and Bolan agreed. Foster's was the most popular beer in Australia. These men had to be part of Daylight.

Suddenly, the piercing scream of a woman sounded from deep inside the cave.

Without hesitation, Bolan and Cinco surged into action. Slinging their assault rifles, the two big men drew combat knives and circled around the guards to approach from behind.

Coming out of the shadows, they each grabbed the jaw of a guard and jerked it upward to prevent them from crying out, then coldly rammed a blade deep into the guard's head just behind the ear. There was a slim opening in the skull at that point that the Green Berets called Death's Doorway.

As the knife plunged in deep, each guard went rigid

from shock, then quietly died, turned off like a light switch.

Dragging the corpses into the bushes, Bolan and Cinco returned to head directly into the cave. Wooden planks offered a clean path though the reeking piles of guano. However, both men noticed a familiar chemical taint to the ammonia-soaked feces. The bats had been killed by VX nerve gas. The only possible reason for that was to prevent the animals from flying away and revealing that somebody was on the tiny island.

At the rear of the cave, the wooden boards ended at a natural passageway through the limestone. A heavy sheet of ballistic cloth had been hung to disguise the entrance. The men paused to sling their assault rifles and draw silenced weapons. Bolan had the Beretta 93R, and Cinco was now equipped with a Heckler & Koch 9 mm pistol, a sound suppressor attached to the end of the barrel.

Alert for more guards, they eased past the curtain. The rocky floor was clean and dry, battery-powered lights attached to the rough walls offering more than enough illumination to safely see where they were walking.

Just then, the woman screamed again, even louder.

Separating fast, each man stayed close to opposite walls, their weapons level and ready.

Reaching a fork in the tunnel, they paused to listen for the woman, when a guard stepped into view, popping the tab on a fresh can of beer.

As he took a drink, Bolan fired twice, the silenced rounds from the Beretta barely louder than a hard cough. Slammed against the limestone wall, the guard folded, and Cinco grabbed the can to prevent it from making noise.

Laying the guard down along the base of the wall, Cinco soaked his clothing with beer to try to make it seem as though he was drunk on duty, then Bolan pulled the pin on a grenade, and stuffed the primed explosive charge under the corpse. If anybody disturbed the body, they would know about it six seconds later.

The left passageway proved to be a dead end, so the men started down the right. Almost immediately, they passed another sheet of ballistic cloth. Several people with Australian accents were talking on the other side, their words indistinct.

Swinging up their assault rifles, Bolan and Cinco got ready to enter, when the woman screamed again, lower this time, followed by a racking sob.

Hesitating for only a moment, both men walked away from the curtain and headed down the tunnel. Greene might have been on the other side of that curtain, but first they had to find out what was happening to that woman.

Reaching another fork in the tunnel they paused. Rough voices could be dimly heard, and guttural laughter.

"Four," Bolan said, estimating the volume.

"Seven," Cinco stated.

Quickly going down that branch of the fork, they encountered a man sitting behind a row of sandbags, reading an ebook player. As he looked up in surprise, Bolan and Cinco fired their silenced weapons in unison, and the man staggered backward with a pair of black holes in the middle of his forehead.

Placing the corpse out of sight behind the sandbags,

the men renewed their pace down the tunnel. The voices were slightly louder now, and it was painfully clear that the woman was being tortured to reveal who she worked for.

"Th-the bank!" she gasped. "I work for the Cayman Island bank!"

"Then how did you escape so easily?" a man demanded. "Did you know Davis was a Bushmaster?"

"There was a fight! Nobody was looking, so I—"

She was interrupted by several hard slaps and there was the sound of ripping cloth. The woman wildly screamed with raw terror in her voice.

Taking another fork, Bolan and Cinco paused at the sight of a group of armed people standing outside another ballistic curtain. Some of them were frowning, but most were laughing.

"Sounds like they're giving it to her good," a burly man said with a chuckle, hitching up his belt. "Should have sent me in there. I know how to treat a woman!"

"Just because a lot of women have told you so," a busty redhead replied, sneeringly, "doesn't mean—"

Softly, the Beretta and HK coughed, and two of the members of the group grabbed their throats, blood gushing between their fingers. While the others frantically clawed for weapons, Bolan and Cinco kept firing until they were alone with the dead and the dying.

As the men started to reload, unexpectedly a pair of terrorists came out from behind the ballistic curtain, Glock pistols tight in their fists. Spinning fast, Bolan kicked the gun out of the hand of one man, while Cinco smashed the other across the wrist with the sound suppressor on his HK pistol. Both weapons went flying, then the terrorists were shot in their faces at point-blank range. The soft lead slugs went in deep, and came out messy.

Stepping past the curtain, Bolan and Cinco saw another man coming their way, toting an Atchisson autoshotgun. They started to shoot when they saw a woman tied to a wooden table directly behind the terrorist.

With no other choice, Bolan shot the man in the wrist, severing the tendon so that he couldn't pull the trigger, and Cinco buried a knife into his throat.

Staggering away, blind from the pain, with blood pumping from the ghastly wounds, the reeling terrorist stupidly yanked out the knife, and a torrent of blood gushed free in a crimson arc. Gurgling horribly, the man collapsed to the ground and went still in a puddle of his own wasted life.

"Idiot," Cinco muttered, retrieving his knife and wiping the blade clean on the pants of the dead man.

Heading for the table, Bolan saw that the woman was spread-eagled, her clothing completely cut away to leave her stark naked, her skin covered with shallow cuts. Her eyes were wide with horror, but they had arrived just before she'd been raped.

As Cinco approached, the woman on the table went berserk, thrashing about so hard that Bolan wasn't sure which would break first, her bones or the table.

"Stop that! We're here to rescue you," Cinco said in a soothing voice.

But the tactic had the exact opposite effect, and the woman only struggled harder.

Knowing that she was endangering their lives, Bolan flipped the Beretta in the air, caught it by the hot barrel, and expertly used the checkered grip of the gun to rap the terrified woman across the left temple.

With a sigh, she slipped into unconsciousness.

"Cruel, but necessary," Cinco said, slashing the ropes with his knife.

"Get her dressed. I'll guard the entrance," Bolan said, moving in that direction.

A few minutes later, Cinco approached with the woman slung across his shoulder in a fireman's carry. She was wearing items of clothing taken from the dead men, but at least she was fully dressed.

"Anything in sight?" Cinco asked, trying not to shift the woman around. Her underwear had been in tatters, so she was going commando under the clothing, and her unbound breasts kept brushing against his face if he moved too fast. That was extremely distracting, something that could easily get them both killed.

"No movement yet. I think they expected to hear a lot of noise, and were giving these bastards some privacy," Bolan said. "She doesn't look like Toulane. So the question is, was this a punishment for one of their own who failed at something big? Or is she a local who accidentally wandered into the wrong party?"

"Neither."

"What?"

"See for yourself," Cinco said, awkwardly proffering a wallet. "I checked the pile of her clothing and found this. Only took a glance."

Inside the wallet was a driver's license for the Cayman Islands, a speedboat license and bank identification for Elizabeth Carrington, Security Chief, Cayman Island banking consortium.

"She pretended to be the CIO to keep from being shot," Bolan observed. "But when they wanted her to hack something, she had to refuse, no matter what they did, or they'd have killed her on the spot."

"Tough lady," Cinco said, glancing at her face. "These creeps were probably going to report that to their boss... afterward."

Bolan scowled. "Yeah, afterward."

"You know, a bank officer would only be dead-weight," Cinco noted. "But a security chief must have been studying these people closely and can probably use a gun."

"Agreed. Better bring her around," Bolan said, taking a position in front of the curtain.

"We'll move faster with her awake, anyway."

"Just be careful."

"Not born yesterday, Matt."

Finding a chair, Cinco eased the woman down gently. Tying a loose gag across her mouth, he broke open a med kit and gave her half of a NATO Hot Shot. Almost instantly, Carrington started to awaken and rub her eyes.

"Easy now, easy," Cinco said softly, keeping his distance. "You're safe now. We're the police."

At those words, she came fully conscious and started to scream only to find the gag in her mouth. Her hands rose to touch it, and Carrington abruptly stopped at the realization that she could reach the gag.

Watching Bolan and Cinco carefully, she removed and gag and tossed it aside, only to flinch at the sight of the dead men on the floor. Carrington breathed heavily for a long minute, then hawked and spat on the corpses.

"Couldn't have said it better myself," Bolan said, glancing over a shoulder.

That almost made her smile, then Carrington shuddered, closing her eyes tightly as tears flowed freely.

"Dead, all dead," Bolan said, sitting down, and crossing his legs. A sitting person was far less threatening than a standing man, especially when he was armed.

"We're not completely out of danger yet, Miss Carrington," Cinco said, tucking away the medical kit, then offering his canteen.

She hesitated, so he twisted off the cap and took a long swallow before offering it again.

Gratefully, she took a drink, then poured some into a palm and wiped her face.

"Better?"

"Better," Carrington replied, returning the canteen. "Okay, what's the situation?"

"First, we need you armed," Bolan said, turning away from the curtain and going to the nearest corpse.

As Carrington watched intently, Bolan took a gunbelt from one of the dead men, checked the magazine in the Glock, then holstered the gun again and gave it to her.

Saying nothing, Carrington stood and strapped on the gunbelt, cinching it tightly around her loose shirt.

"Okay, how many more of you are there?" Carrington asked, drawing the gun and working the slide to eject a round. She caught it in the air and tucked it into a pocket.

"There's only us," Cinco said truthfully.

"Are you insane?" she demanded, still holding the Glock. "Do you have any idea who these people are, what they did at my bank?"

"Yes, and, yes," Bolan said. "Speaking of which, you're supposed to be getting raped at the moment, and there's no door, only that curtain."

Scowling in confusion for a moment, Carrington nodded, and cut loose with a full-throated scream that echoed inside the confines of the empty room.

"Shut up, bitch!" Bolan snarled loudly, then slapped his hands against each other.

They heard a guttural laugh, and footsteps receded into the distance. "Enjoy Thanksgiving," someone called.

"That only bought us a few minutes," Bolan stated. "So talk fast. Where's Greene?"

"Who?"

"The man in charge. Big, not fat, almost a giant, Australian accent—"

"He already left," Carrington said. "Something about maintaining a lunch schedule."

"Do you know where he went?" Cinco asked. "Did he mention any place at all?"

"Sorry, no."

"Lunch," Bolan repeatedly. "Could Greene have said launch, instead?"

"Maybe," she said, massaging her chafed wrists. "What did that man mean by Thanksgiving?"

"It's an American holiday where they eat roast turkey," Cinco growled. "It's also slang for having sex with a woman of color."

She blinked in confusion.

"These men are white supremacists."

Still nothing.

"White meat or dark?" Bolan explained.

Her face brightened in understanding, then darkened. "Just who are these assholes?" she muttered.

"Terrorists who have already killed a lot more people than just those at your bank," Bolan said quickly. "It's our job to make damn sure that they don't hurt any-body else." He pulled the chair closer. "What did they want you to do?"

"Aside from…" Cinco started, then stopped and ges-tured at the table.

"That was a punishment for refusing to assist them," Carrington said, holstering the gun. "They needed a samurai…." She paused. "An expert computer hacker. Somebody who could write code on the fly in case something goes wrong. They've got these things, I don't know what they're called…"

"Describe them," Bolan asked, keeping a watch on the curtain.

Briefly, Carrington described the scene at the clear-ing, and both men scowled.

"What in the world does Greene plan to use those for?" Cinco asked, thoughtfully stroking his mustache.

"I know," Bolan growled, and started to say more when he heard footsteps again on the other side of the curtain.

Immediately, all three people began to make guttural noises, but this time the steps came closer and the bal-listic curtain was pulled aside.

"Sounds like a real party!" A man laughed, stepping into the room. "Mind if I—"

Bolan fired the Beretta, answering the question with a double dose of eternity.

In response, somebody snarled from the other side of the ballistic curtain, then an F88 assault rifle poked through, blindly spraying 5.56 mm rounds across the little room.

CHAPTER THIRTEEN

Washington, DC

In the rotunda of the White House, the door to the Diplomatic Reception area slammed open and the President of the United States stormed inside. His face a mask of controlled emotions, the man was flanked by several members of the Cabinet and a cadre of Secret Service agents.

As the President took a chair, the agents spread out around the room, taking up strategic positions in a standard five-on-five formation to guard the two doors, the fireplace and all of the big bay windows. To the uninitiated, the windows would have seemed like the weakest point in the room, but in fact they were made from three layers of military plastic that not even an antitank rocket would effectively penetrate.

Already sitting on the chairs and couches of the room were representatives from the CIA, FBI, DEA, NSA, Homeland Security, the State Department, DOD and the Pentagon.

Normally, such high-level meetings would be held in the Oval Office, but at the moment that was being "painted" by the Secret Service. There were tarpaulins, cans, rollers, brushes, ladders, and afterward the office would indeed have a new coat of fresh paint. It would also have additional ceramic armor in the walls, doors and ceiling, as well as dozens of new antisurveillance devices literally buried inside the doorjambs, wainscoting and brickwork.

"Report!" the President ordered, stopping at a wheeled tray to pour himself a cup of black coffee.

In spite of the early hour of the day, breakfast felt like a million years ago to the politician. Lunch wasn't even on his schedule, and dinner was only a dimly remembered hope for the future. Food would be anything edible the President saw in passing and managed to successfully grab: apples, cookies, stale pastry. It was painfully obviously that this was just going to be one of those days that never seemed to end.

"Unfortunately, there's nothing new to report as of yet, sir," said Dorothy Poole from the NSA. A remarkably young woman for such a responsible post in the intelligence community, Poole was barely thirty-five, but with somber eyes that had seen way too much and remembered everything.

"Nothing? Please explain, Dorothy."

"Everything is in chaos on the Gulf," Poole replied, obviously fully aware that she was walking through a political minefield. "Mexico doesn't want to publicly admit that they lost a base. They're afraid that would only encourage others to try something similar."

"Such as the narco-terrorists from South America?" the President asked, sitting down and balancing a cup and saucer on a knee.

Poole nodded. "Exactly, sir. Both the Colombian and Bolivian cartels would jump at the chance to establish a permanent base in Central America."

"Not gonna happen," the head of the DEA growled.

"Not soon, anyway," Poole agreed with a shrug. "As for the Cayman Islands, they're pretending that the bank was deserted and had been scheduled for demolition weeks ago for similar reasons. They're afraid it'll hurt their reputation and kill profits."

"Lives are more important," the President stated, finishing off the coffee.

"To regular people, yes, sir. But not to corporations."

"Be that as it may, we have more pressing matters," the President stated gruffly. "Has anybody run the numbers from NASA yet?"

"It's still too early for anything but a rough estimation, sir," said Alex Crane from Homeland Security. The man had a steel briefcase handcuffed to his wrist, and a pair of Beretta pistols holstered under his suit jacket. He was one of the very few people in the world who were allowed to carry a weapon anywhere near the President.

"An estimation," the President repeated.

Crane nodded. "Yes, sir. However, at the present we're talking about one hundred dead, and roughly a billion dollars in damage."

"How soon can NASA get replacement personnel down there?" the President asked, rising again to return to the food cart.

"Already on the way."

"Excellent." The President sighed. "How is the story playing with the media?"

"It's not, sir. I have a full lid on everything involving the attack on NASA," his press secretary stated. "The explosions were just a new type of methane engine backfiring, and smoke came from a forest fire."

"But if somebody checks…"

"We set the forest on fire, sir."

"Very good. Continue."

Sanders shrugged. "That's it, sir. Anybody who knows anything isn't talking, and anybody who's talking doesn't know anything of importance."

"Didn't some cell-phone pictures get posted on the internet?" he asked.

"The pictures were briefly on social media, yes," Sanders replied. "But the NSA burned them out of existence with duplicate copies that were clearly fakes, and loaded with several new viruses, one from China and the other from North Korea."

"How long before the truth gets out?" the Man asked bluntly.

"Approximately ten to fifteen hours, sir."

"Any way we can stretch that window?"

"Not without repealing the First Amendment."

Frowning deeply, Alex Crane opened his mouth to speak, then decided against it. Homeland Security had already been granted almost unlimited powers, if they pushed for more, the backlash would probably trim them down to the level of the FBI, shackled hand and foot with rules and regulations.

"Jimmy, what's happening overseas?" the President asked.

"Our agencies have covertly spread the word to reliable sources," said James Llewellyn of the State Department. "All of the major players are tightening the security at their launch sites. Dozens of scheduled launches have been canceled across the world."

"But not all?" the President asked with a scowl.

"Sadly, no. Many of the launches are to corporate clients, who really don't care about any political situations. They just want their satellite in space, and the sooner the better."

The damn corporations, the President thought, were going to get everybody killed because of their greed. He would have to do something about them one of these days.

"The Cubans are going ballistic, sir," Llewellyn added. "Our Tomcats from Gitmo and their MiGs from Havana have been engaged in a furious dogfight of Lock and Forget for hours. When one runs low on fuel, another takes its place."

"Anybody fire a missile yet?"

"Good God, no! The Marine aviators would be court-martialed if they did, and Cuban pilots would suffer dire consequences if they broke the cease-fire and started a war. Everybody is flying around and growling at each other, but nothing more."

"Glad to hear it," the President said. "If the situation changes, inform me immediately no matter where I am."

"Absolutely, sir!"

"Now, what the hell was the real target at NASA?" the President demanded.

Just then, the Secret Service agents standing guard on the hallway door stepped aside, and a middle-aged man entered the Diplomatic Reception room. He desperately needed a shave, his suit was badly rumpled, and it was obvious that he was carrying a handgun under his jacket.

Politely, the others nodded at the newcomer as he hurried closer, and he replied with a curt nod to each.

"Mr. President, we need to talk in private," Hal Brognola announced.

Rum Island

Firing while they moved, Bolan and Cinco hammered the ballistic curtain with hot lead from their M16 assault rifles. The heavy cloth jerked under the arrival of the rounds, but no holes appeared in the resilient material. However, the man on the other side cried out as the chattering F88 was slammed from his grip.

As a boot came into view, Carrington fired. The leather exploded and toes went flying. Shrieking in pain, the man hastily retreated, then, oddly, paused to moan much louder than before.

Suspecting a trap, Bolan pulled the pin on a grenade and released the safety. Slowly counting to four, he then rolled it across the floor and under the curtain. A split second later there came a resounding explosion, the curtain billowing outward as chunks of flesh smacked into the limestone walls.

Checking outside, Bolan saw that the tunnel was littered with tattered bodies and smashed weapons. Off to the side, a human head sat staring at them in silent accusation, and Carrington fired a round into the temple to make it roll away and disappear, bouncing down the sloping tunnel.

"Mind your rounds," Cinco said. "You've got seventeen rounds left in that magazine, plus two magazines of thirty. Don't get trigger-happy."

Without comment, Carrington bent to pick up an F88 assault rifle whose barrel was visibly bent. Dropping the magazine, she tucked it into a pocket and tossed the useless rifle away.

"Never mind." Cinco chuckled. "Check the Metal-Storm!"

"Empty."

"Damn."

The sound of running boots was heard coming from up the tunnel. Sinking to a kneeling position, Carrington got ready to shoot, while Bolan and Cinco dropped to the ground and went still.

Flashing a grin, Carrington followed their lead.

As the terrorists came into view, the men and woman paused for a vital second at the terrible sight of the human bodies strewn about the bloody corridor. Instantly, Bolan, Cinco and Carrington cut loose with their assault rifles, riddling the terrorists with a triple stream of 5.56 mm rounds from the two bulky M16 assault rifles and the slim F88. The hardball ammo threw the enemy's blood onto the stone walls, and before they finished shuddering in death, Bolan and the others converged to scavenge for ammunition and grenades.

"Radio!" Carrington cried out, lifting one into view.

"Useless," Bolan countered, stuffing magazines into his pockets. "They're jamming every frequency."

Experimentally, Carrington thumbed the transmit switch and heard a loud high-pitched screech.

Muttering under her breath, she released the button, but still clipped the radio to the rear of her leather belt.

"Time to leave, amigo," Cinco said. "Greene already knows something is up, and we want out of here before they use more VX."

"What's that?" Carrington asked with a frown. "I'm a bank guard, not military like you two."

"VX is a type of nerve gas," Bolan replied, starting forward at an easy lope. "If you hear anything start to hiss, exhale as hard as you can to empty your lungs, then run for your life!"

"Will that help?" Carrington asked with a worried expression.

"Probably not," Cinco answered truthfully. "But, hey, it can't hurt!"

Her reply consisted mainly of four-letter words.

Charging back along the forking tunnels, Bolan and Cinco stopped at the ballistic curtain where they had heard voices earlier. Leaning against the limestone wall, Carrington wheezed as she tried to catch her breath.

Listening for any more talking, Bolan glanced at Cinco and he shook his head. Going flat to the wall, Bolan gently eased aside the ballistic curtain with the fluted barrel of his assault rifle. A wooden door blocked the entrance.

While Cinco and Carrington stood guard, Bolan drew a knife and tried to trick the lock. Without his keywire gun, this would have to be done old-school, and if necessary, they'd just kick the damn thing down. The numbers were falling, but he had to see inside this room. If it actually was the command center, all of the answers he needed could be only inches away.

Saying nothing, Cinco watched Carrington and noted that she held the assault rifle correctly, her fingers and thumbs safely out of danger.

"Bank guard?" he said.

"It was a very big bank," she replied.

Just then the lock clicked, and Bolan stood to throw open the door, his M16 ready to fire.

However, the large room was empty, or rather, the large cave was, the ceiling and walls much cruder than the smoothed tunnels, and there were no wooden planks on the ground as a makeshift floor.

At the front of the cave, several folding chairs sat

before a large blackboard, the smeared surface wiped
clean of whatever had been there. On a nearby table
was an open soup can with a plastic spoon sticking out
of it. Several huge crates were marked with transmit
numbers, and on the far wall a wooden rack was packed
with F88 assault rifles and stacks of ammunition clips.

"Now we're talking!" Carrington said, heading that
way.

But Cinco grabbed her roughly by the arm. "Trap,"
he said, gesturing at the rest of the cave with his assault rifle.

"Bullshit," she said.

Shooting from the hip, Bolan peppered the wooden
rack with a brief burst from his M16. The hail of bullets chewed into the wood, gouging out splinters, and
making the chained weapons rattle and jump about.

In response, the gunrack exploded, spraying pieces
of the weapons everywhere. The concussion rocked
them hard, Bolan and Cinco staggering backward,
while Carrington hit the wall and dropped her weapon
to cover her ears.

"Mother of God!" Carrington gasped. "That would
have… I was just going to… I mean…"

"Stay alert and trust nothing until we're far away
from here," Cinco stated, then frowned to spin fast.

Bolan started to ask a question when he heard an
odd revving noise coming from the crate. "Retreat!" he
snarled, turning for the exit. Bolan cursed himself for
a fool. There was a reason why this was the only room
with a door…to seal invaders inside.

Unfortunately, before he could reach the door, it
slammed shut and several unsuspected bolts rammed
into place, locking it tight.

"Whoever you are…goodbye!" a man said from inside one of the packing crates.

"Fuck you, Greene!" Carrington snarled in open hatred.

Whirling, Bolan started to fire the 40 mm grenade launcher at the door, when he realized the range was too short to arm the warhead. Starting to race away, he reached only a short distance when the crate burst apart and out rolled a squat machine covered in ugly guns, the smooth armor plating decorated with the emblem of the Mexican army.

"That's a Gladiator!" Cinco cursed, spraying the robotic killer with a long burst from the assault rifle.

The 5.56 mm rounds harmlessly ricocheted off the thick armor, and the machine responded with a burst of 9 mm rounds from its twin Uzi machine pistols. The Parabellum rounds missed Cinco, already in motion, completely, but stitched a line of holes across the blackboard, the slate cracking into jagged pieces.

Switching targets, Bolan aimed the 40 mm grenade launcher and fired into the machine, but the big shell merely hit and dented the rear armor before ricocheting away to hit the distant wall and burst open.

"Surrender, and you can live!" Greene ordered from within the complex workings of the war machine.

"Fuck you!" Carrington screamed, her F88 chattering nonstop.

"Ignore it, that's a recording!" Cinco shouted, kicking over a table.

"How do you know?" she demanded, ducking behind one of the other crates.

"The radio is jammed!" Bolan snarled, putting a full clip of 9 mm rounds into the machine. The bullets hit the floor under the Gladiator and bounced upward, but the machine neither paused nor slowed.

"But there's a wire or something," Carrington offered hesitantly.

Snatching a piece of chain off the floor, Bolan threw it across the cave. It hit the far wall with a clanging rattle.

"Surrender, and you can live!" the machine repeated exactly as before, the shotgun booming.

Convinced, Carrington aimed at the door and cut loose with her assault rifle. The wood paneling was torn away, only to reveal riveted steel underneath.

Taking cover, Cinco fired the S&W .357 Magnum revolver around the edge. The steel-jacketed rounds slammed into the robot, denting the side armor, but then flattening on the front panels.

Instantly, the Gladiator responded with a blast from a hidden 12-gauge shotgun, the barrage of fléchettes hammering the table so hard that a leg fell off to roll away.

Flipping over another table, Bolan scored several more hits onto the squat machine, but the 5.56 mm rounds had little effect, so he switched to the Desert Eagle. Those bullets seriously dented the side armor, and there came a brief spray of electric sparks.

Instantly, the twin Uzi machine pistols chattered into operation again, the 9 mm rounds stitching across the limestone walls in opposite directions.

"Surrender, and you can live!" the Gladiator boomed even louder than before.

Pulling out a grenade, Cinco started to yank the pin, then paused and shoved it away again. The cave was too small. The concussion from the blast would knock all of them unconscious, if not worse.

Firing every weapon, the Gladiator made a fast circle in the middle of the room, rolling over the folding chairs and pieces of the exploded gunrack.

Grabbing the soup can, Carrington emptied it onto the floor, refilled it with water from the canteen, then gently tossed it at the Gladiator. The can hit, and splashed water across a humming airvent. But there was no reaction from the machine, aside from a shotgun blast in her direction.

On a hunch, Bolan rolled an unprimed grenade toward the machine, and it immediately stopped firing and charged away from the clattering sphere. Okay, the computer-operated machine was smart, but not clever enough to recognize a diversion. Maybe he could use that somehow.

The lights went out.

Half expecting that move, Bolan whipped out a couple of chemical glow sticks, shook them hard to activate the chemicals, then tossed the tubes toward the sound of the electric machine.

In an eerie nimbus of blue light, the tubes bounced on the floor, and the Gladiator rolled forward, crunching them under its armored treads. The soft tubes burst open like water balloons, gushing their contents across the machine.

Now splattered with the glowing compound, the Gladiator was silhouetted in the darkness, any possible advantages completely lost. As if somehow aware of that, a searchlight cycled up from inside the machine and flashed into operation, the blinding halogen beam sweeping for targets.

Carefully aiming the M230, Cinco put a 40 mm grenade into the searchlight. The protective grille dented, the glass shattered, and the beam winked out of existence. The shotgun fired, and he was thrown backward, his shirt reduced to shreds, but the body armor underneath completely undamaged. But as he stood, the man favored his previously wounded shoulder, a fresh well of blood spreading across the ripped fabric.

Seeing that, Bolan got an idea. Grabbing a folding chair, he threw it at the Gladiator, using the distraction to cover the sound of his movements to the door. Drawing a knife, he slashed the ballistic curtain free, and then dove forward to wrap the resilient material over the military robot.

Instantly, the Gladiator cut loose with every weapon, then began to rock back and forth trying to dislodge the obstruction.

"Surrender, and you can live!" it repeated, the heavy curtain jumping from the rattling discharge of the machine pistols.

Bolan grunted from the savage pounding, it was like trying to contain a bulldozer in a bedsheet, but he knew that to let go, even for an instant, meant death.

Suddenly understanding the goal of the attack, Cinco rushed forward to ram the M16 under the robot and heave. As it began to tilt, Carrington arrived to do the same thing. The barrels of the two assault rifles started to bend alarmingly, then the struggling Gladiator tilted slightly, and Bolan scrambled off just as the machine flipped over to hit the floor in a resounding crash.

However, no parts broke off from the impact, and the Gladiator began spinning both treads, swiveling rapidly back and forth, then firing every weapon in a desperate effort to right itself.

While Cinco and Carrington dragged over the tables to try to hold the machine in place, Bolan went to the farthest part of the cave, aimed and fired.

The 40 mm grenade slammed into the locked door, blowing it off the hinges. The concussion almost overwhelmed the men and woman, but they gamely staggered into the blast and made it into the tunnel gasping. Before anybody could speak, there came a soft hissing from somewhere.

Clamping a hand over his mouth, Bolan charged through the stygian darkness of the underground tunnel, retracing his steps purely by memory. The others stayed close behind, and only a few minutes later they all stumbled out of the cave and into the bright sunlight.

As they gasped for air, Bolan noticed a subtle movement in the sky, and squinted. A Black Hawk rose from behind the trees and quickly departed to join the rest of the Daylight armada already high in the sky.

In a wordless snarl, Carrington raised her weapon in a two-handed grip, and Cinco smacked it down with the barrel of his S&W revolver.

"You can't hurt them with this," he stated, "and it will only tell Greene that we're still alive!"

As she nodded in agreement, a pair of Apache gunships turned in the air and lowered their prows to point toward the tiny atoll.

"Head for the beach!" Bolan shouted, breaking into a full sprint.

Running for their lives, the trio had barely reached the trees before the two gunships launched a full salvo of missiles. Spiraling downward, the six Hellfire missiles converged on the cave, and a thundering series of explosions shook the entire atoll.

Safe in the jungle, the three of them paused for a moment, as additional detonations erupted from different locations all across the tiny atoll.

"The bastards mined the entire atoll!" Cinco snarled, holding a handkerchief to the bloody shoulder. "After this firestorm, there won't be enough forensic evidence to stuff into a thimble!"

"Not completely accurate," Carrington said, displaying a jagged chunk of the blackboard. "I have a friend who once told me about a way to—"

With a curt hand gesture, Bolan cut her off. At first, all he could hear was only the crackling blaze and waves cresting on the shore. Then there came the distant sound of approaching helicopters.

Surging into action, Bolan led the way as they raced back to the beach. Holding their breath, they dove into the shallows and swam for the deep water.

A few moments later, ten Daylight gunships descended from the clouds and started to unleash salvo after salvo of assorted missiles and rockets until the entire atoll was awash in flames.

CHAPTER FOURTEEN

The Bermuda Triangle

Bolan and Cinco were exhausted by the time they managed to swim back to the Hercules. Carrington had passed out during the long journey, and so they had each taken turns hauling her along.

The Stony Man pilot had waited until they were close before starting his preliminary check on the engines, while Bolan and Cinco entered the aircraft and got their sleeping cargo stashed safely away in a jump seat bolted to the wall of the cargo deck. The bed in the RV would have been a lot more comfortable, but there was no way to lash the unconscious woman into place. Aerial combat could easily get her killed. She was much safer strapped into a jump seat. The Hercules had only a few hardpoints that were bulletproof, and the jump seats were among those.

"Something wrong?" Bolan asked Sorenson, as he and Cinco stepped into the flight deck. "Why aren't we moving?"

"Can't," the blacksuit pilot replied. "The headwind is against us this time, and there isn't enough distance to get off the ground again."

"We could dump the RV," Cinco suggested.

"Or we could use the JATO units," Bolan said.

Cinco gave a low whistle. Yeah, he knew what those were. JATO, or jet-assisted-take-off units, were small but incredibly powerful solid-state rockets. They had been originally designed by the US during the Second World War to help an overloaded bomber packed with fuel and ordnance get off the ground. There were no controls; once the JATO units were activated they burned at full power until they ran out of fuel. By necessity, a JATO didn't last for very long, but the raw thrust it generated had to be seen to be believed.

"Do we have any onboard?" Cinco asked, cracking his knuckles.

"Sure, down on the cargo deck," Bolan said. "Any chance you might know how to…" But Cinco was already out the door.

A few moments later, the intercom crackled. "Okay, where are they?" Cinco asked, his words echoing slightly inside the cargo bay.

"Port-side locker," Bolan said into a hand mike. "Past the fire extinguisher, near the winch."

"Found 'em!"

"Do you know where they attach?"

"No, but there's a diagram on each of them. Pretty basic stuff. I can figure out the rest. This isn't exactly rocket science… No, wait, yes, it is!" Cinco laughed. "Just give me a couple of minutes, okay?"

Helping with the preflight checks, Bolan said nothing in reply. They were already far behind the Daylight gunships, and falling farther behind with every tick of the clock. He had missed the last update from NORAD, and it would be another—Bolan checked his watch—thirty-seven minutes until the next. By then Greene and his people could have easily disappeared forever. Until the next slaughter.

There came the sound of boots banging up the metal stairs, and Cinco burst onto the flight deck again.

"We're all set," he declared, taking the navigator seat and strapping on a safety harness.

"How many did you use?" Bolan asked, as Sorenson started the four engines. Three of them smoothly started, the fourth backfired twice before finally settling into a steady roar.

"All of them," Cinco said, glancing out the side window at the stubby JATO units now attached to the wing. "I figured if there was a recess for them, then the Herc could take the combined thrust."

"Only one way to find out," the pilot said, releasing the brakes and trimming the airfoils. "Hold on to your socks."

"Atomic batteries to power, turbines to speed," Cinco muttered, tightening his safety harness.

Pulling back on the yoke, Sorenson almost smiled at the obscure reference as the big plane started to roll slowly forward, the strong wind buffeting it about.

Then, in a strident hiss, all of the JATO units loudly ignited and the plane jerked forward as if kicked in the rear by a giant. Quickly, the rumble of the units rose to a controlled roar, and the massive Hercules streaked forward with ever-increasing speed. Revving the engines to maximum, the pilot pulled back on the yoke, as the JATO units continued to build in power and volume. Concentrating on steering, he had no idea what their speed was, it was taking all of his concentration to keep the Hercules traveling into the wind, and not veering aside to crash.

With a lurch, the big plane lifted off the ground less than a yard before the shoreline. Cresting waves slapped against their wheels as they were cycled up, then the aircraft settled in to climbing high, steadily rising until the ocean dropped out of the front windows.

"Well, that was fun," Cinco said, craning his neck to pop the joints. "I'd bet that a dozen of those things could lift a dead whale into orbit!"

"Easily," Bolan agreed as the Hercules angled due south, the last known direction of the enemy gunships. Everything was reading in the green on the instrument panel, the Hercules was undamaged from the brief hell-ride and the big engines were smoothly purring.

"Anything on radar?" Bolan asked Cinco.

"Nothing yet," he replied, checking the glowing screen. Taking a hand mike, he turned on the radio. As he did, a high-pitched squeal came from the wall speakers. Changing frequencies, Cinco only heard the annoying squeal.

"Okay, we're still in their jamming field," he said, returning the mike to its clip. "Which is bad, because we can't tell Anchor where we're going, or get another update."

"But also good because it means we're close to the gunships," Bolan finished.

"Gunships which can, by the way, blow this lumbering behemoth out of the sky easier than a clay pigeon at a skeet-shooting range," Cinco stated bluntly. "The Black Hawks are no real danger, but those Cobras and Apaches will eat us for lunch. Any ideas on what to do about them yet?"

"Don't get shot?"

Cinco snorted. "Brilliant plan. I can see why you're in charge."

"Also, I own the plane."

"That, too."

Stretching ahead of the Hercules was a vast expanse of puffy white clouds. Rising through them, Bolan blinked as brilliant sunshine bathed the rocketing airplane, and their speed steadily increased until the Hercules was nearing the absolute limit of both the air-speed, and ground-speed, indicators.

"Five hundred miles per hour?" Cinco gasped. "I thought this crate could only reach four hundred!"

"Me, too."

"Matt, we might flash past Greene at this rate!"

Just then, the JATO units cut out, and a deep silence filled the Hercules as their speed began to drastically reduce to normal levels.

"Or maybe not," Cinco said with a grin. "By the way, what is the plan if we find these sons of bitches again?"

"Do nothing and stay low," Bolan said. "Find out where their base is located, then leave and call in an air strike."

"Good plan. Unless, they spot us and start launching missiles. Do we have any weapons to defend ourselves, or will I be leaning out the cargo ramp and shouting harsh words?"

"We have Angel flares, and two sets of Bofors 40 mm cannons," Bolan said, pressing his palm to a black section of the instrument panel. There came a low hum, and a part of the board flipped over to reveal a fire-control panel.

"That will do the job," Cinco told him, checking the ammunition reserves and weapons status. He had a thousand rounds for each set of cannons, and enough Angel flares to stop any missile attack. Excellent! One of the many benefits of using a Hercules was that there was lots of room for supplies.

"Some heatseekers of our own would have been nice," Cinco muttered, testing the arming circuits.

"Good idea. Mind popping out and getting some for us?"

"Maybe later." Both of the Bofors cannons were mounted at the front of the plane, and while there was no radar guidance or laser aiming, they were linked to a heads-up display—HUD.

Sliding on a combat helmet, Cinco attached a coaxial cable and flipped a switch. The helmet purred into life, and a hexagonal piece of plastic swung out from the side of the helmet to cover his right eye.

Closing his left, Cinco noted the monocle was scored in graduated circles, and along the bottom, a laser hologram scrolled distance to target, air speed and ammunition reserves. God bless America! he thought.

At least now they had a fighting chance against those Apache and Cobra gunships. Unless the gunships had rearmed on Rum Island they would be low on ammo, while the Hercules was carrying literally tons of high-explosive shells.

"Hmm, I'm not getting a reading from the starboard cannon," Cinco muttered, releasing the safety harness. "Something probably just shook loose from the JATO jitterbug, but I'd better check."

"Also make sure that Elizabeth is okay," Bolan said. "We took quite a shaking."

"Thanks for the concern, but I'm undamaged," Carrington said from the doorway. She was holding a steaming thermos from which there came the tantalizing aroma of fresh coffee.

"Glad to hear it," Bolan said, eyeing the container. "Any chance that's for us?"

"Thought you'd like something to help stay awake," she said, filling the cap like a mug and passing it over. "You two must be exhausted from the long swim."

"Not really." Breathing in the rich smell, Bolan was suddenly ravenous and drained the cap. "Thank you, Miss…Ms…?"

She took it back. "Just call me Liz."

"Matt."

"Bull," Cinco said, swinging aside the combat monocle. With a sigh, the tactical readings on the weapons board went dark.

Refilling the cup, Carrington started to smile, then paused. "Bull Cinco? Are you that crazy Mexican cop I keep hearing about on the cable news? The guy who smashed that drug cartel and rescued all those people?"

"Sorry, but I've never been to Chihuahua," he said draining the cap, and passing it back.

Not having mentioned where the incident happened, Carrington nodded in understanding as she screwed the cap back onto the thermos. Whether Cinco was exercising reticence or modesty, she had already guessed that these men weren't ordinary street cops. Her best guess was Interpol agents. Either that, or some sort of multinational task force.

Just then, one of the engines began to sputter, and the pilot quickly switched to the next fuel tank.

As the engine smoothed out again, Bolan checked the fuel levels from the copilot's seat. They needed all four of the engines going at full power to have even a chance at catching up to the smaller, and much faster, gunships. However, at this rate they'd be out of fuel before even reaching Venezuela, and, unable to contact Brognola, there was no chance of a midair refueling.

"Any chance of some food?" Bolan asked over his growling stomach.

"There are some MRE packs in the aft locker," the pilot said. "They're almost food."

"Anything would be appreciated," Cinco said, removing the helmet to set it on a wall hook. "I'll check on those connections, and be right back!"

"There's a tool kit in the RV," Bolan shouted as the man disappeared out the door.

"Is he always in a hurry?" Carrington asked, taking the empty seat.

"So far," Bolan said as the flowing clouds parted for a moment, offering a clear view for miles.

"Uh-oh," the pilot said.

That was when Bolan noticed something moving on the horizon. It was too big for a bird, even a condor, but way too small for a commercial jetliner. Automatically, Bolan went to check the radar. The machine seemed to be working, but the screen was clear of any possible targets. Taking a pair of military binoculars from a ceiling stanchion, he dialed for computer augmentation.

"Something wrong?" Carrington asked, squinting in the same direction.

"Bogey," the pilot said.

As the telescopic view cleared, Bolan cursed at the sight of a pair of angular helicopters coming their way. Apaches!

"Bull, fix that Bofors and get your ass back up here!"

Bolan snapped, thumping the intercom switch. "We have incoming birds."

The speaker crackled. "Missiles?"

"Worse. Apaches."

The man muttered something in Spanish. "How many?"

"Only two...so far."

"Two? They might be sentries set to fly behind the main body of helicopters to watch for any pursuit."

"That's my read," Bolan said gruffly. "But if they spot us, they'll come for the kill."

"Bet your ass they will. Okay, on my way!"

"Apaches," Carrington said, tasting the word. "That's a military helicopter, right?"

"One of the best in the world. Better get down to the RV and make a couple of survival packs!" Bolan ordered. "Life raft, weapons, food, parachutes, anything useful you can find!"

"On it!" she said, leaving the flight deck.

As the pilot lowered the speed of the Hercules to buy a few minutes, Bolan activated all of its defensive systems, then he activated the onboard radar jammer and radio scrambler. The task he'd sent Carrington on had been busywork. Those packs were already made. But inside the armored RV she would be safe from incoming rounds and shrapnel.

As much as Bolan would like to inform Brognola about this, it was more important that Greene never know they had survived the destruction of the island base. It also meant the Apaches couldn't turn off the radar jammer, launch a couple of long-range missiles, blow the Hercules apart and then switch the jammer back on. For better, or for worse, this was now a fair fight.

A few minutes later, Cinco appeared with a soldering iron in his grip. "Just a broken relay," he said, tossing the tool onto the floor and quickly donning the helmet. "Any chance we can get behind the Apaches and try to cripple one?"

Just then, something small and fast streaked past the Hercules, the powerful wash rocking the airplane hard.

"Not anymore!" Bolan snarled, releasing a spread of Angel flares.

From both sides and the bottom of the Hercules a hundred different types of flares dropped free. Some of the sizzling charges floated away on tiny parachutes, while others plummeted rapidly toward the world below. Mixed in with the flares were bundles of metallic chaff that reflected light, dazzling like a million miniature mirrors. Combined they resembled celebratory fireworks, but the umbrella coverage of the Angel flares stopped almost every known type of heatseeker and radar-guided missiles.

Circling back, the heatseeker abruptly switched targets and went for the burning waterfall of flares. As it dove inside, a powerful explosion filled the sky, just behind the speeding plane.

"A miss is as good as a mile," Bolan said, checking for damage. But the Hercules was fine.

"Horseshoes and hand grenades," Cinco said in agreement, cutting loose with a long burst of 40 mm shells from both of the Bofors.

A dotted line of tracers extended across the sky, sweeping across one of the Apaches. The maelstrom of shells detonated harmlessly on the armored hull of the deadly aircraft, then the side-mounted weapons pod was torn apart, and the entire load of eighteen mini-rockets detonated.

The fireball swamped the Apache, ripping off chunks of armor, and shattering the armored blades spinning overhead. Thrown sideways by the blast, the battered Apache flipped over and over, completely out of control as it tumbled from the sky, leaving behind a thick contrail of oily black smoke.

"A lucky shot," Bolan said with a half smile. "Ten bucks says you can't do it again."

"Double or nothing?" Cinco asked, triggering short bursts from the Bofors to let the barrels cool.

In a burst of speed, the second Apache angled upward, trying to get above the Hercules.

"Done!"

Savagely banking, the pilot tried to get behind the gunship.

Bending in to the grim task, Cinco unleashed another long burst from the Bofors, missing the Apache completely. Swooping down from on high, the Daylight gunship retaliated with a dozen minirockets, and several bursts from a 33 mm chain gun. The two lines of burning tracers crossed, and the barrage of 40 mm shells exploded in midair. Hot shrapnel filled the sky, and both crafts got rattled, but suffered no serious damage.

Now the minirockets arrived, flashing harmlessly past the Hercules, but one of them came so close all three men instinctively attempted to dodge out of the way.

"I think we lost a coat of paint that time," the pilot said, trying to coax more speed from the laboring engines.

Switching to fresh ammunition hoppers, Cinco merely grunted in reply. Both of the crafts were hindered by the loss of radar, and unless he was mistaken, it looked as if the Apache had only one missile left, a Hellfire antitank. If that hit the Hercules, there would only be greasy smoke left in the sky. The logical attack would be for the terrorists to get in close and fire at point-blank range.

The Hercules sharply veered to the left, and there came the sound of a chattering assault rifle.

With a snarl, Bolan desperately fought against the unexpected drag, the speed dropping. A blinking light on the instrument panel informed him that the side hatch was open. He admired Carrington's guts, but the act might just have gotten them all killed.

Blindly firing a Bofors with one hand, Cinco grabbed the hand mike. "Close that damn door!" he bellowed.

Suddenly the Hercules straightened.

"At least she didn't cycle down the cargo ramp and try to fire a Stinger."

"Yeah, she's pretty, but dangerous," Cinco agreed, triggering both cannons again. "Pretty dangerous!"

Incredibly, the Apache pivoted about in the sky and charged straight for the Hercules with every weapon blazing.

"Son of a bitch! Her mistake made him think we're damaged!" Cinco said in surprise.

"Short bursts!" Bolan commanded. "Lure him in closer!"

Nodding, Cinco did as suggested, then stopped firing the left Bofors completely.

Instantly, the Apache swung around to their left, trying to attack from their defenseless side.

"Easy now… Wait for it…" Cinco said, sending off single rounds from the cannon as if they were running out of ammunition.

Suddenly, the Hercules shook at the arrival of the 33 mm rounds, the depleted uranium slugs punching through the fuselage.

With a grim expression, the pilot dropped every airfoil, sharply brought up the nose of the Hercules to expose their belly, then unleashed another Angel.

The exploding flares and chaff sprayed across the Apache, engulfing it completely, making the windshield crack and a blade snap off.

As the pilot struggled to regain control, the Hercules dropped its nose. Cinco ruthlessly hammered the enemy gunship with both of the yammering Bofors.

Dozens of small explosions covered the armored Apache, cracking the windshield until it shattered completely, and the gunship went into a wild spin.

"Should I finish him off, or do we want to talk?" Cinco asked, using the monocle to track the descent of the damaged gunship.

"We need him alive," Bolan said. "That is, if he manages to land intact."

Below the Hercules was open water, along with several wide coral reefs visible under the surface. However, less than a mile away was a small sandbar. The top barely rose above the waves, but it was the only thing in sight not completely submerged.

"Come on, you can do it," Cinco muttered, his hands tight on the fire controls of the deadly Bofors. The ruptured fuselage of the Apache was spewing gas and oil, the off-balance blades jerking so hard he was amazed they didn't break off completely.

As the Hercules slowly circled the area, on Bolan's advice the pilot turned off two of the engines, slowing the aircraft as far as he dared.

Dropping out of control, the Apache hit the ocean and sank below the surface, only to stop less than a yard underwater.

Releasing the fire control, Cinco snorted in disbelief. "The lucky son of a bitch landed on a reef!"

"Good thing, too, because we're flying on fumes at the moment," Bolan stated, starting to angle lower. "Better suit up, guys. Looks like we're going swimming."

Fair enough, Cinco supposed. Greene and his people had successfully escaped again. The dying pilot below was probably their best chance of finding out what the Australian billionaire had planned, and maybe even to get ahead of him somewhere.

"By the way, how do we get back into the air again?" Sorenson asked.

"This plane will never taste blue again," Bolan stated, taking the hand mike, and checking the radio. The airwaves were still jammed, so he tried his cell phone. Amazingly, he got three bars. The submerged Apache was still trying to block the EM spectrum, but the equipment was starting to fail. However, there was sure to be a backup unit. Bolan knew that he had better make this quick, there was no way of knowing when he might get knocked off the air again.

Turning in his seat, Cinco hit the intercom. "Brace yourself, Liz! We're going in for a water landing, and it's going to be rough!"

"A water landing?" Carrington asked over the wall speaker. "Why in the world are we doing that?"

"I'll explain later. Now, strap in tight!"

Tapping in a memorized number, Bolan waited impatiently. "Anchor here, Cooper," Brognola said. "I have some important news that—"

"This is an emergency!" Bolan interrupted. "The Mighty Hero has splashed! We need an immediate Air Force evac at these coordinates." Glancing at the instrument panel, he rattled off the latitude and longitude.

"Roger! But...don't you mean the Navy?" Brognola asked over the soft clacking of a computer keyboard.

"Negative! Air Force only. Repeat, Air Force only! Cooper out," Bolan said, tucking away the phone.

"You clever bastard." Cinco chuckled. "The Air Force, eh?"

"That's the fastest way I know to get some air transport here," Bolan said as Sorenson dropped the airfoils and the wheels and the Hercules headed for the tiny sandbar. "Hold on to your socks, guys, we're going in!" the pilot announced.

CHAPTER FIFTEEN

Margarita, Venezuela

By the time Greene and his team reached land again, the sun was low in the sky, and the deep purple of twilight was starting to blanket the world.

"Be nice to feel dirt under my boots again," a woman said, working the arming bolt of her assault rifle.

"Cut the chatter," Greene commanded over a shoulder, then took the hand mike for the Gertrude off the wall stanchion and thumbed the transmit switch. "Get hard, people! This is a hit-'n-git operation. A blitzkrieg! Kill anybody who see us, but aside from that, stop for nothing. Timing is essential!"

"And I will personally kill anybody who fucks up, or stops to steal souvenirs," Layne added over the ceiling speaker.

"Hit-'n-git!" LoMonaco added, over the speaker. "Fast in, fast out…just like my second husband."

All of the terrorists chuckled at the joke, and the tension in the gunships noticeably eased. Everybody had planned and trained for years to do this mission, but the pressure of actually trying to save the world from itself was starting to wear them down. Thankfully, there was only a few hours to go, and then it would all be over. The end was in sight.

Just off the northern shore of South America were hundreds of small islands as different in size as they were in nationality. Some belonged to Colombia, Venezuela or Guyana, others were fiercely independent, several were in dispute and a couple of them were deserted.

The vacation resort of Margarita Island was located just off the coast of Venezuela. It was world-famous for its excellent fishing, superior scuba diving and the incredibly high alcoholic content of their justifiably famous tropical cocktails.

The homes were small, but well constructed of a redbrick locally made across the bay on the mainland. There were twice as many hotels as anything else on the lush island, and the dark sand beaches were lined with tourists lying on oversize towels, relaxing in the bright sunlight.

On the western side of the island was a small airfield just barely large enough to handle cargo planes and private jets. Commercial jetliners had to land at Caracas, and the passengers took a state-of-the-art hovercraft to Margarita.

Looking down upon the island, Layne had been amused to learn that many of the people in North America didn't seem to know that Venezuela was a major oil producer, and sold most of its crude to the United States. This brought the equatorial nation unbelievable wealth, and exceptionally lenient deals with the US military for advanced weapons systems. Which was why the capital city of Caracas was being studiously avoided by Daylight. Instead, the helicopters and gunships moved low and fast toward the virtually undefended island of Margarita.

"Masks on!" Greene ordered. "Pilots, positive air flow to the engines on my mark. Ready...and...mark!"

Immediately, the men and women flying the gunships flipped switches on their control boards and pressurized tanks of oxygen-rich air started feeding into the massive engines. It was only a precaution, but a single mistake now could mean the end of everything they had all worked so hard for all these years.

"Disengage safeties," LoMonaco commanded, leaning forward in her seat. "Activate pumps...and go-go-go!"

Strafing the airfield, the Black Hawks released their cargo of deadly VX gas. Baggage handlers, police, mechanics, pilots, tourists and everybody else simply dropped where they were, and went into violent convulsions before finally succumbing to the sweet release of death.

Minutes later, the rest of the Daylight armada arrived to hover over the field, the wash of their spinning blades dispersing any lingering traces of the lethal gas.

Landing a Black Hawk near the fuel depot, Greene scowled at the hundreds of dead bodies, then dismissed the matter with a shrug. His ships needed fuel, and after discovering that there were hidden GPS dots on the Skyhooks, all of his carefully laid plans had to be radically altered. The dots had been disabled, but Greene was going nowhere near any of his previously established supply points in Barbados. Greene had planned on using this airfield upon leaving Venezuela. Now, other arrangements would have to be made.

"Excuse me, sir," a man asked, wearing a headset. "But we seem to have lost contact with Linus and Delbart in the Apaches."

"Both of them?" Greene asked, arching an eyebrow.

"Yes, sir," the man said awkwardly. "Should we send another Apache to hunt for them?"

"No, we can't spare any more loses." Greene sighed, massaging his temples. "Please let me know if you hear from them again, but don't attempt to contact them directly."

"Because the Americans might be listening?"

"As you say," Greene replied, turning back to watch the refueling procedure.

A ring of armed men stood guard, alert for any sign of the police or the military. But nobody came, and the process was finished without interruption.

Lifting into the air once more, the Daylight armada swung deep into the jungle interior, following whitewater rivers and cutting through rocky mountain valleys. Passing close by a massive hydroelectric dam, the Daylight helicopters were challenged by a Venezuelan air-force Huey to show their transit papers. Greene had his people reply with a concentrated barrage from the 33 mm cannons, and the Huey was blown out of the sky and disappeared into the jungle canopy below.

Reaching the savannah, the armada headed down the top of the colossal mesa that more closely resembled a truncated mountain range. Almost a mile high, the Chimanita Massif was edged with huge waterfalls that thundered over rugged cliffs to descend to the savannah below and become the Orinoco River, meandering away to feed the complex array of farms and cropland extending to the distant horizon.

Landing in a relatively smooth area, the Daylight armada immediately draped camouflage netting over the helicopters once more to mask their location.

"Hell of a view," LoMonaco said, gazing over the edge of a cliff and down into the misty lands below.

"I heard that some old English author used this mesa as the location for a novel about dinosaurs," Layne said, checking over his XM-25 grenade rifle.

"I remember reading that as a kid," LoMonaco replied.

"Any good?"

Spotting a black scorpion, she crushed it under the heel of a boot. "*The Lost World*. The book was certainly better than the movie," LoMonaco said with a shrug.

"They almost always are." Layne chuckled, slinging the weapon across his shoulders.

Just then a sharp whistle cut the air, and everybody gathered around Greene. The big man was arranging rocks on the dirt.

"Okay, final prep," he announced, standing and dusting off his hands. "This red stone is Chimanita Massif… this small brown stone is the local village. Pay it no attention. There is no danger, and the villagers have nothing that we want.

"However, over here," Greene said, walking to a small collection of rocks and stones, "is the Luepa military base. Stay far away from them. Our gunships are better armed, but their air force has two Harrier jump jets that could be real trouble. They use them to strafe jungle convoys smuggling contraband."

Greene walked over to a large rock surrounded by several smaller stones. "This is our target for today, the brand-new Luepa Space Command. The Venezuelans hired the Chinese to build it a few years ago, but it was only finished last month."

"That was lucky," said a bald man, sliding on a pair of tinted sunglasses.

"Luck had nothing to do with it." Greene smiled coldly. "My conglomerate helped with the construction, and I arranged for countless small delays in concrete shipments and electrical fixtures until we were ready to move."

"You don't miss a trick, do you?" Layne asked.

Greene allowed himself a small smile. "Not yet, old friend." He paused as a jaguar screamed in the distance, only to be answered by another much closer on the mesa. Instantly, everybody drew a weapon and thumbed off the safeties.

"Anyway," Greene continued, slowly holstering his 10 mm Falcon pistol. "The Bolivar telecommunications satellite will be located on the top floor of the main building. All of their security is on the ground floor. The roof is too cluttered with exhaust fans, air-conditioners, power lines and water tanks for anybody to safely parachute onto, much less to land a helicopter. The Venezuelan military is absolutely positive that the building is completely secure on the roof." He grinned. "But we know better, eh?"

That made everybody laugh.

"If all goes well, Alpha Team should be in and back out again, in twenty minutes," Greene said, pulling out a cigar and biting off the end. "We'll stay here to guard their flanks in case of trouble. Anybody gets cut off from the others, head toward Colombia."

"But, sir, what about the drug lords in the mountains?" a man asked nervously.

"You'll be taken captive, of course, that's a given," Greene stated. "But use my name, and you'll be safely

released in Cartegena. I have a deal with the cartel for
your safe passage."

"Can they be trusted?" a woman asked anxiously.

"As much as any of these inbred primitives can be,"
Greene said, lighting the cigar and drawing in the dark
smoke with obvious satisfaction. "Now, if you can't get
a flight to Australia in time, find someplace safe to hide
far away from the city until the armageddon is over.
We'll come looking for you in the aftermath."

Shifting about in the weedy grass, everybody softly
muttered about that, their faces excited, frightened and
hopeful all at the same time.

"Okay, let's move with a purpose, people!" Layne
announced loudly, slapping his hands together. "The
Brazilians will pick up the satellite around dawn. Alpha
Team, get your gear assembled. Beta Team, stand guard,
one-hour shifts. Everybody else, get some food and
sleep, two-hour rotations."

"We gotta be sharp, people!" LoMonaco added,
hands on hips. "Tonight is when we change the world!"

Murmuring agreement, everybody broke into groups.

Going to a Black Hawk, the five members of Alpha
Team slid back the hatch and started hauling out wooden
crates marked with the logo of the Martin Corporation
of New Zealand.

The Martin Jetpack was an invention of the New
Zealand company. It actually wasn't a jet pack. They
just called it that to promote sales. In reality, the Martin
was a set of extremely powerful turbofans.

Even out of the crate, the Martin was huge, and oddly
resembled a refrigerator with wings. The main assembly
stood five feet high, and the two wing-engines extended
an additional five feet. The curved cowling covered the

complex internal machinery. There was a fairly standard safety harness in the front, along with two cushioned horns to go under the pilot's arms and help him stay in place during operation. To the left was a small control panel showing direction, speed, height. On the right was another panel showing electrical power, fuel level and engine temperature.

The members of Alpha Team said very little as they strapped themselves into the machines, then hung lumpy python bags across their chests. They each knew that the contents of the bags were more important than their lives.

"Everything depends on you now," Greene said. "If you fail, we lose."

"We won't let you down, sir," said the team commander, working the slide on a Glock .22 pistol to chamber a round. The pistol was tipped with an acoustical silencer. Combined with the small-caliber bullets, the Glock was barely louder than a whisper.

"You have the floor plans? Access codes? Schematics?"

"All systems are go, sir!" said a man, sliding a key-wire gun into a holster.

"Your tools are all coated in rubber to leave no scratches? They must never know that you were ever there. A single slip…"

"We'll be ghosts in the wind," a woman stated proudly, sliding on a helmet and flipping down the visor. The helmet gave a soft hum as its night vision activated.

Bowing his head, Greene said a brief prayer for their success, then stepped back and threw his arms wide. "Alpha Team, steal me the stars!"

In unison, the five terrorists turned on their Jetpacks and lifted off the ground in a rush of warm air. Hovering in the air for a moment, they nodded respectfully at the billionaire, then angled away and disappeared into the darkness heading for the launch facility with their precious cargo of Skyhooks.

The Gulf of Mexico

HITTING THE BUTTON on the cargo-deck wall, Bolan cycled down the aft ramp of the Hercules. It splashed into the waves and went half underwater.

Roughly a thousand feet away, he could see the submerged Apache, the surrounded water tinged with a greasy rainbow from the leaking aviation fuel and oil. Flotsam sprinkled the water, slowly expanding away from the crash site. Bubbles were still rising from the hot engine, and the blades were sloshing back and forth, moving at the mercy of the ocean currents.

"Any sign of the pilot?" Cinco asked, quickly inflating a rubber raft.

As if in response, an F88 assault rifle chattered, and bullets ricocheted off the ramp and walls.

Dropping to the deck, Bolan rolled into a kneeling position and fired back with the Beretta in automatic mode. The three-round burst of 9 mm rounds smacked into the oily water in front of the submerged Apache, but the pilot floating behind the blades didn't flinch. He answered back with another burst from the assault rifle, then changed his grip.

"Incoming!" Bolan yelled, diving out of the plane and into the ocean.

He knifed in deep, his belly scraping across the lip

of the sunken cargo ramp, then he twisted aside just as a powerful explosion erupted inside the plane, throwing out loose tools, packing straps and other assorted debris.

The mound of sand that the Hercules rested on was surprisingly huge, spreading out for dozens of yards in a gradual incline, and Bolan swam as fast as possible to try to get around to the other side. There were schools of colorful fish darting about, along with the lurking tangle of a deep-water squid, but no sign of any sharks. Bolan was thankful for that. This late in the year, great whites were sometimes seen in the Gulf, and there was always the menace of makos. They were nowhere near as large as a great white, only reaching about fifteen feet long, but they were just as savage and had the disturbing trait of swallowing their wounded prey alive.

Following the natural curve of the land, Bolan moved away quickly as bullets continued to smack into the water. However, his boots and weapons seemed to become heavier by the moment, and by the time he reached the penumbra of the Hercules, it felt as if his lungs were on fire, and his vision was starting to turn reddish.

Finally breaching the surface, Bolan hungrily drank in fresh air until his vision cleared, and his laboring heart slowed to normal. From the other side of the plane, he heard the hard chatter of an M16, closely followed by the slightly slower response of an F88.

Bolan cursed himself for a fool. He should have expected the downed pilot to have an F88 assault rifle, and most of those came with a MetalStorm version of an M203 grenade launcher. It carried three 40 mm rounds sealed into the same barrel, so that was probably all the pilot had available. But if the man was a good shot, it might be enough to shift the Hercules off the sandbar and sink it into the Gulf. Then Bolan and the others would be at the mercy of the currents, and predator sharks.

Rising and falling with the swell of the gentle waves, Bolan swam around the prow of the military transport and reached the side door. It was open, but about a yard above the ocean. However, Cinco was there with his S&W Magnum revolver in one hand and a coiled rope in the other.

"I'm alone, no sharks," Bolan said coming closer.

"Never hurts to be safe," Cinco replied, tossing out the rope.

Snagging it in the air, Bolan pulled himself out of the water and into the plane once more.

"You okay?" Carrington asked, fumbling to insert a fresh clip into the F88.

"Not dead yet," Bolan answered, draping the rope over a wall hook. "Try tilting it slightly, then push."

She did, and the clip locked into place.

"Okay, since we didn't blow this guy away while safe in the air, I'll assume that you want him alive for questioning," Carrington said, working the arming bolt.

"That was the plan," Cinco replied, tossing aside the tattered remains of the lifeboat. "But it might be smarter just to ace this guy, then search the wreck for any clues to the whereabouts of Greene."

"He *is* a pretty good shot," Carrington said, angrily hefting the assault rifle.

"That's our last resort," Bolan countered. "We can't unkill him if we don't find anything."

Just then, there came a bright flash of light and a sizzling signal flare shot into the open end of the Hercules. Bouncing off the wall, it hit the RV, and shot up to the ceiling, only to come down again and skitter across the tiled deck to splash into the ocean.

"Okay, this guy is really starting to piss me off," Cinco growled, taking down his M16 from a wall hook. Briefly, he checked the weapon over. "Your call, Matt. Kill or capture?"

"There's a third option," Bolan said, going to the RV.

His footing was a little unsure from the awkward angle and his wet boots kept slipping on the floor tiles, but the man finally made it to the kitchenette and pulled open a wall panel to expose a long sniper rifle.

The Yugoslavian-made Zastava Black Arrow was a .50-caliber monster very similar to the Barrett sniper rifle, but Bolan preferred the smoother action of the hand-tooled bolt action.

Checking the scope, Bolan worked the bolt to chamber a massive .50-caliber cartridge. Resting the rifle on top of the kitchen table, he aimed toward the distant Apache and stroked the trigger. The Zastava boomed like chained thunder, and a small geyser formed alongside the submerged gunship.

"Missed me!" the pilot said, laughing in contempt.

"No, I didn't!" Bolan shouted down the cargo deck, as he worked in a fresh cartridge. The old one jumped out to hit the floor with a musical ring. "That was a warning shot. The next time won't be so pleasant!"

"Prove it!" the pilot yelled, then added a vulgar racial slur that made no sense whatsoever.

"I'm Mexican, you idiot, not African!" Cinco bellowed.

The reply consisted almost entirely of four-letter words and additional slurs.

Ignoring those, Bolan aimed carefully and put two more booming rounds into the water close to the gunship, not willing to risk killing the pilot. The first caused a sudden surge of oil, and the second caused the already weakened windshield to shatter. As the water flooded into the gunship, it slightly shifted position, and the pilot came briefly into view.

Setting the crosshairs on a foot, Bolan fired, and the pilot screamed as his boot exploded, blood spraying out the hole in the bottom.

Cursing nonstop, the pilot thrashed about, the water swirling with blood. Holding on to the central support for the blades with one hand, and keeping the assault rifle out of the water with the other, there was nothing the man could do about his gaping wound except suffer.

"That salt water must burn like acid," Carrington said, scowling. "Why doesn't he just surrender?"

"He's either a fanatic, or else help is on the way," Bolan said, levering in a fresh round.

"He was positioned as a rear guard, so my bet would be for fanatic."

"Unfortunately, I agree," Cinco grunted, flexing his bandaged shoulder. "However, that doesn't mean help isn't also on the way to save his dumb ass."

Carrington scowled in thought, then gasped.

"Oh, my God, you're deliberately keeping him alive as bait in a trap," she said in sudden understanding. "To lure in another gunship!"

"If you have a better plan, now is the time to start talking," Cinco stated, triggering a couple of short bursts from the assault rifle.

The greasy water near the Apache boiled from the arrival of the 5.56 mm hardball rounds, and the pilot replied with the grenade launcher. The shell slammed onto the aft ramp again, the blast shaking the entire aircraft.

Just then, the Hercules gave a low groan as it shifted to a new position on the tiny sandbar. Bolan and the others braced themselves for a fast dash to the side door, then the noise faded away.

"Okay, say this works," Carrington said. "How are we going to take out helicopters with assault rifles?"

"I've got a Carl Gustav inside the RV," Bolan answered. "Including some AA rockets. Those will take out anything short of a battleship."

"AA?"

"Antiaircraft," Cinco said, lying on the sloping deck to launch a 40 mm grenade. It skipped across the surface of the water, going right past the Apache.

"Who are you guys, really?" Carrington demanded softly. "Honestly, I've got to know!"

"Mossad," Bolan said with a straight face.

"Interpol," Cinco added, yanking out the spent casing.

Bolan fired again. "Now, I thought you were KGB?"

"And I thought you were NATO," Cinco said, thumbing in a fresh shell.

"Great," Carrington muttered. "Two assholes."

Spotting a fin moving toward the downed gunship, Bolan narrowed his gaze. Blue top, white belly, that was a mako! Adrenaline pumping, he quickly aimed at the dorsal fin and fired. The big bore .50-caliber round punched a clean hole through the fin, and the shark abruptly turned and headed away.

"Next time, I won't stop it!" Bolan shouted. "Now, do you want to cut a deal, or do I let the sharks eat you alive!"

"What kind of a deal?" the pilot yelled weakly, a tremor marring the words.

"Tell us where Greene will strike next, and you live," Bolan stated, letting go of the rifle to scratch at his bandaged ribs. "It's as simple as that."

"Paris! No, wait, it was Rome!" The pilot laughed, waving the F88 about like a garden hose, the 5.56 mm rounds ricocheting wildly about inside the Hercules. Bolan and Cinco responded in kind, with Carrington watching them from the sides, wondering exactly who had rescued her.

Suddenly, an infallible raft bobbed to the surface of the water with the pilot already sitting inside, and bailing like crazy. They heard the hum of a drill, or some kind of an electric motor, and the raft began to skim quickly away from the Apache, the water churning in its wake.

"He's getting away!" Carrington yelled, firing her F88 in a long discharge.

"Is there another raft?" Cinco asked, casting a brief glance at the pile of tattered rubber strips on the deck.

"No," Sorenson said gruffly.

"Will that thing float?" Carrington asked, jerking a thumb at the RV. "Some of the richer tourists arrive riding in those things."

"Seals are shot," Bolan said, coming out of the RV. "She'd sink after only a few yards."

"Then there is no choice," Cinco said, walking to the edge of the ramp, his boots just touching the water.

"Afraid so," Bolan said, going alongside the CISEN agent.

As Bolan knelt to aim, Cinco hung the M16 on a

wall hook, then dove into the water. He hit it clean, knifing in deep.

Aiming at the rapidly dwindling raft, Bolan adjusted his aim for speed and wind distance, then stroked the trigger one more time.

The Zastava boomed, and the Daylight pilot was thrown forward, crimson spewing from his ruined neck. Grabbing his neck with both hands, the terrorist weaved drunkenly, then went over the side with a splash. Freed from his weight, the raft streaked onward faster than ever.

"That was murder," Carrington said, an uneasy tone in her words.

"No, it was an execution," Bolan said, closely watching Cinco swim toward the Apache. As the man reached the submerged gunship, he drew in a deep breath, and went underwater.

Staying alert, Bolan scanned the surface of the ocean for anything suspicious. As expected, the shark rushed back at the scent of fresh blood. It went out of sight near where the pilot had gone in, and there came a great welling of blood in the water. Seconds later, the mako surfaced with a human leg in its mouth. The boot had a hole in the rubber sole.

As the shark swam away with its meal, Cinco surfaced gasping for air, then went right back down.

Cradling the F88, Carrington stepped closer to Bolan until she could feel the heat from her body.

"If I were to shoot you right here and now," she said in a tight whisper, "would anybody care or come looking for me?"

"Maybe Cinco," Bolan said honestly, staying perfectly still. "Sorenson might have something to say about it. Might shoot you on the spot."

Bolan knew the woman had gone through a lot lately, and he had been waiting for some sort of an emotional break. To be honest, he had expected her to burst into tears and hide in the RV's washroom, or possibly attempt to take her own life. This reaction was completely unforeseen.

"I like Cinco," Carrington said in a monotone.

"Me, too."

"He's good man."

"And a good cop."

She scowled. "What about you?"

Instead of replying, Bolan slowly turned to face her. Carrington had the F88 pointed to one side of him.

"If you're going to do this, better step back a few paces," Bolan said. "Or else when my skull explodes, you'll get splattered."

A long minute passed, then another.

Closing her eyes, Carrington started to cry, then turned and walked away.

Bolan had seen a similar reaction from newbies during their first time in combat. Some people could take the killing, others couldn't. There was no pride, or shame, involved with either. That was just how they were hardwired inside.

Erupting from the water, Cinco whooped in victory, and started swimming back toward the Hercules using only one arm, the other held high to keep a water-soaked map out of the ocean.

Rising, Bolan held out a hand to assist the man up the wet ramp. "Find something?"

"Bet your ass!" Cinco grinned, proffering the map.

Then he frowned at the sight of the soggy wad, the colors all running together into an indecipherable smear.

"Goddamnit, I was afraid it wouldn't last out of the water!" Cinco muttered, crumpling the soggy mess in a fist. "Good thing I memorized as much as possible."

"Was it a map of the Gulf?" Bolan guessed, resting the Zastava on his shoulder.

"Yeah, and all of the places Greene has hit were marked with either a square, or a triangle. Except for one, that was circled in red."

"Think it might be his base of operations?"

"Highly unlikely," Cinco said, bending to wash his hand clean in the waves. "I've heard of the place before. Compose Island. That's the main launch facility for the Brazilian space agency."

"Used to be," Bolan said. "They abandoned the island years ago and transferred everything to a new facility on the mainland."

"Easier to defend?" Sorenson asked as he joined them.

"Easier everything."

"Greene attacked NASA, reprogrammed these enginette things, and now has gone to an abandoned space base," Cinco said thoughtfully, massaging his shoulder. "Think he's going to try to send something into space?"

"Can't be done," Bolan stated. "Everything of value is long gone—fuel pumps, generators, computers.... Greene would have to bring in a million tons of supplies and machinery to reactivate the facility."

"Then why would he go there?" Sorenson asked curiously.

"Hiding in plain sight?" Carrington asked from one of the wall-mounted jump seats. "What better location to vanish than someplace that everybody knows has absolutely nothing you want?"

Bolan and Cinco looked at the woman, then nodded. The idea made sense. Sort of like an escaped convict hiding in the ruins of an old prison. It was quite literally the last place in the world that anybody would hunt for him.

"There certainly would be enough places on the island to hide all of those gunships," Bolan noted, leaning against the curved wall. "And the laboratories would be on top of a maze of service tunnels, offering dozens of escape routes to the sea if discovered."

"In addition, Brazil doesn't have an extradition treaty with either America or Mexico," Sorenson added. "Legally, there's not a cop in the world who could touch him there."

Bolan almost smiled. "Then it's a good thing we're not police officers."

"Okay, I want in," Carrington said, rising from the jump seat.

"There's going to be bloodshed," Bolan said, studying the grim woman. "I guarantee it."

"Still want in," she repeated, cradling the F88 assault rifle.

Saying nothing, Bolan looked at Cinco.

It was clear to the Mexican agent that something serious had happened between the two of them while he was gone. He could also tell from Carrington's demeanor the bank guard was in earnest. She had changed in those brief few minutes, and was no longer scared.

"Willard Cinco, CISEN, Mexican Intelligence," he said, tossing her a salute.

"Special Agent Matt Cooper, Homeland Security,"

Bolan added, resting the stock of the Zastava on a hip. "Welcome to the team, Liz."

With that, there came the sound of a powerful engine somewhere outside the Hercules.

Instantly, Carrington dashed up the stairs for the flight deck, while Bolan and Cinco rushed to the doors on opposite sides of the plane.

"Incoming!" Cinco reported, scanning the sky and water with a pair of binoculars. "It's okay, our ride is here! I see a USAF Super Stallion heading our way."

"Plus, a US Navy Rescue Hawk helicopter, and an Albatross seaplane," Bolan announced, dialing for computer enhancement on an Army monocular. "Along with a Marine Corp Sea Knight helicopter, and a C-130 Hercules fitted with pontoons."

"They make those for that?"

"Guess so."

"Is it Navy, or Air Force?" Sorenson asked.

"There are no markings," Bolan replied.

"Ah, the CIA has arrived. Impressive." Cinco laughed, closing the door. "Anchor doesn't follow instructions very well."

"Me, neither." In spite of everything, Bolan tried not to smile. Hal Brognola was amazing.

"Who's Anchor?" Carrington said from the upper landing. Behind her, the Sea Stallion moved slowly past the cracked windshield, temporarily blocking out the sun.

"Just a friend," Bolan said, winking at Sorenson.

"A damn good friend, I'd say," Carrington snorted, starting down the stairs.

"None better."

The water outside the cargo ramp started to flatten,

then shimmy and whip into a froth. A moment later, a Harrier Jump Jet descended into view, and paused to hover a few yards above the turbulent ocean. Oddly, the fuselage was painted a flat black, and there was no insignia or identifying marks, of any kind.

Something softly buzzed in his pocket, and Bolan pulled out his smartphone. It was dripping wet, but seemed functional. However, when he flipped it open, the screen remained blank, and only static crackled from the tiny speakers. Bolan tucked it away again. He'd send a coded message over the radio once they were in transit to Compose Island.

"Okay, dealer's choice," Cinco said, climbing into the RV and grabbing his python bag. "Which do we take?"

"The fastest," Carrington said resolutely. "Wait, make that the best armed."

"We take all of them," Bolan stated, going to the side door and waving the Sea Stallion closer.

CHAPTER SIXTEEN

Luepa Base, Venezuela

Night had fallen across the savannah, and the tiny launch facility blazed with brilliant electric lights that could be seen for a hundred miles. In the far distance, some of the more primitive hill folk gasped at the marvel, then quickly retreated into their huts.

Trucks and Hummers scurried frantically about performing last-minute chores, while a massive Soyez rocket stood at the gantry, the cluster of after-vectors giving it a strong resemblance to a banyan tree. Wisps of steam came from the ventilation ports and thick insulated hoses were topping off the fuel tanks with liquid oxygen and liquid hydrogen.

Invented by the Soviets more than fifty years earlier, the Soyez had been the vanguard of the space age, and now was considered the workhorse of the twenty-first century. It was relatively cheap, amazingly powerful and as close to reliable as a complex piece of machinery could ever be.

These days, the Russians sold the Soyez to every technologically advanced nation on the planet, including the United States. With all of the recent budget cuts for NASA, to boldly go into the future, they need something from the past. In engineering terms, the Soyez was considered a fork, as close to perfect as it was possible to achieve.

At the top of the gantry, a team of Chinese and Venezuelan scientists were carefully closing the hatch on the payload compartment, sealing in the two huge Bolivar-class telecommunication satellites.

Finished with the installation, the scientists sealed off the hatch and took the elevator down the gantry. As they reached the ground, a loud warning siren started to sound.

"T-minus ten and counting," a voice echoed across the facility from a series of speakers. "Chavez One is ready for lift-off!"

Clambering into a waiting Hummer, the team of scientists quickly drove away from the launch site.

"On internal power!" the speakers boomed, just as the electrical cables dropped away. "Starting preflight ignition!"

In the brick-lined blast tunnel underneath the colossal rocket, a huge steel wheel began scraping across chunks of flint, throwing off a bright shower of sparks.

After several disastrous explosions, NASA had discovered that in spite of all of their precautions, sometimes a little fuel leaked out of the aft vectors of a rocket before the primary ignition began. When that happened, as the main rocket engines ignited, the spilled fuel exploded, the blast knocked the rocket off balance, and it toppled over to detonate into a fireball of biblical proportions. The simple addition of the grinders caused any minor fuel spill to burn off before it reached dangerous levels.

"We have main engine start," the voice announced calmly. The Soyez trembled slightly as there came a low rumble, and a torrent of flame blasted out of the aft vectors to thunder along the tunnels into nearby rock quarries.

"Countdown is three...two...one...release!"

Huge steel clamps broke away from the trembling Soyez as a hundred gallons of cryogenic fuel began to burn per second. Dark smoke shot into the sky, as deafening flame washed from beneath the rocket. Instantly, pressurized fuel hoses cut their flow and snapped away to be disintegrated in the fiery wash before reaching the ground. Then the Soyez began to lift majestically off the concrete launch pad, thick sheets of ice breaking away from the lower fuselage.

"Chavez One is go!" the speakers announced, and from numerous locations people cut loose with ragged cheers and mixed applause.

As the huge rocket rose higher, water began to gush across the gantry to prevent it from melting from the cluster of aft flames. Rotating slightly, the rocket steadily climbed ever higher, the entire launch facility briefly illuminated in the garish light of the four cryogenic engines.

An artificial dawn came and went as the Chavez One seemed to bend from the world rotated underneath. But the bellowing rocket continued on its original course and soon was lost from sight.

At five miles, the first section broke off and fell away. The second stage did the same thing at a hundred, and only minutes later, the rocket left Earth's atmosphere.

Approaching the 350-mile mark, the bulbous nose of Chavez One cycled open to release the pair of huge telecommunication satellites. But an instant later, the satellites burst apart disgorging hundreds of Skyhook units.

Their tiny enginettes blazing with power, the cloud of Skyhooks spread out in every direction hunting for an appropriate host.

It was common knowledge to everybody working in the field that the main problem with space travel wasn't reaching orbit, but surviving there. Over the past sixty years, humanity had been launching countless tons of experimental machines into space, almost all of them still in orbit. There was an unknown number of burned-out probes, damaged capsules, cracked nose cones, obsolete satellites, empty fuel tanks, busted heat shields, ripped spacesuits, dead monkeys, garbage, debris, frozen human waste and just about everything else imaginable.

Including an unknown number of missile platforms from a dozen countries. Sent up in pieces to be carefully assembled in orbit, some of the platforms were larger than a two-story house, and armed with enough rockets to destroy a major metropolis.

The supposedly empty space surrounding Earth was actually filled with tumbling garbage. Occasionally, a piece wandered too close, and came down in a fiery re-entry to impact in some isolated mountain range or the open sea. Many experts had argued that space needed to be cleaned, and the delegates at the United Nations debated for years over the merits of launching thermonuclear missiles into orbit, and burning space clean. But so far, nothing had been done, and the problem of the deadly litter grew worse every year.

Streaking across space, the Skyhooks ignored anything below a certain size, and only attached themselves to something large enough to survive the journey back through the dense atmosphere below. Massive steel girders were found for abandoned space stations never built, entire rockets that had failed to separate.

As each Skyhook found an appropriate target, it firmly attached itself, then sent down a coded message and patiently waited for the next command.

CLATTERING LIKE A LAWNMOWER, a lone Martin Jetpack came streaking out of the darkness to crash-land near the Daylight gunships. Rolling over onto her back, the pilot turned off the struggling turbofans and slumped in the safety harness.

Casting his tray of food into the campfire, Greene rushed over. "Well, is it done?" he asked in a tight voice.

Hesitantly, the pilot removed her dented helmet. "Dead, all dead," she mumbled, her bruised lips puffy and cracked. Her body armor was covered with flat lead bullets, her pants dark with dried blood.

Scowling, Greene slapped the woman across the face sharply to bring her back to consciousness. "Is it done!" he demanded.

"Yes…" she croaked. "We gutted both of the satellites and packed them full of the Skyhooks."

"Thank God." Greene sighed, slumping his shoulders.

"What about the rest of your team?" Layne asked, looking into the dark jungle.

"Dead, all dead," she said weakly.

"What happened?" Greene demanded with a scowl.

Kneeling alongside the woman, LoMonaco poured some water into a palm and wiped it across her lips, then allowed the woman a couple of sips. "Easy, not too much too fast or it will just come back up," she warned gently.

Nodding in thanks, the pilot did as commanded, and finally pushed the nearly empty canteen away. "Th-thank you…" she whispered.

"Okay, what happened?" Greene demanded impatiently, looking at the distant launch facility. It was an island of lights in the dark jungle, and everything seemed peaceful. There were no sirens, no searchlights, or shouting men to be seen.

"Jared hit a power line," the woman reported struggling from the Jetpack. "He burst into flames when… He must been dead before crashing into that wall…"

Slowly, a large crowd of the terrorists gathered around the last member of Alpha Team.

"Dubois got shot by a guard," she said hoarsely, then burst into hysterical laughter. "He charged the man, and they flew out a closed window together! The glass cut them to ribbons… My god, there was blood everywhere."

"He died a hero," Greene interrupted, swinging around his laptop. "And the rest?"

"D-D-Daw…" she whispered, then collapsed again, her breathing soft and regular.

Quickly, LoMonaco pressed a finger to the woman's throat. "Her pulse is strong, she just fainted. Will somebody help me carry her to the medical unit? She's been shot and hit with a lot of shrapnel in the legs—"

"The legs?" Layne asked suspiciously. "Nowhere else?"

"Well, the hands some, too."

"Son of a bitch!" Greene snarled, drawing his Falcon pistol. "That's not shrapnel damage, but dog bites!"

Even as he said the words, several large shapes serrated from the night, and raced across the field, moving incredibly fast.

As everybody scrambled for a weapon, the huge animals streaked closer to pounce on a man. Screaming, he went down under the animals, and one ripped out his throat to cast away the horrid gobbet of flesh, then moved on, blood smeared across its teeth.

"Dobermans!" Greene yelled, firing fast three times directly into the black face of a dog. The head exploded from the triphammer arrival of the 10 mm Magnum rounds, but the sheer inertia of its mass kept it going to crash into the man and send him rolling across the ground.

Now, the night became alive with sporadic gunfire, as the terrorists attempted to track the animals. But, trained as attack dogs, the Dobermans never paused for an instant. They were constantly in motion as if the long run from the launch facility had invigorated them.

Bizarrely, the dogs also never barked. They sped across the clearing, circling the terrorists, biting legs and nipping legs. But they never gave a sound aside from a low panting.

Trying to kill one of them, a man accidentally swept his F88 across another member of Daylight, and she fell backward, her belly blown open.

Aiming at a darting dog, Greene cursed as the Falcon jammed. Thrusting his hand forward, the trick derringer slapped into his palm and discharged both barrels. The animal yipped as the rounds scored bloody furrows across its flanks, then turned and charged, moving low and fast.

Greene waited until the dog leaped for his throat,

and slammed it across the face with the pistol. Bones crunched and the animal dropped, temporarily stunned.

As Greene clawed for a knife, LoMonaco fired bursts from her Glock machine pistol, and the big Doberman was reduced to hamburger before it ever had a chance to make a sound.

Nodding his thanks, Greene dropped the useless pistol and swung around his F88 assault rifle. There were a lot less dogs now than there had been a few minutes earlier.

Aiming ahead of a zigzagging animal, Greene burped the assault rifle. The dog ran into the stream of bullets, yelping loudly as blood and fur went flying.

As it fell, Greene fired the grenade launcher. The range was too short for the warhead, but the 40 mm shell slammed the Doberman in the belly, forcing blood and intestines out the mouth. Shuddering all over, the dog began thrashing about.

Ignoring its death throes, Greene quickly reloaded the F88. "Anybody need help?" he shouted, squinting into the darkness.

They heard the roar of an engine, and a LAV-25 smashed out of the jungle, its 25 mm cannon firing in short bursts. Explosions filled the night, and bodies went flying from the powerful detonations.

But then, in a rush of hot air, a Cobra lifted off the ground, deactivating the safety locks on its weapons systems. Instantly, the pilot cut loose with a stuttering stream of 35 mm minirockets from the side weapons pod.

Tipped with depleted-uranium warheads, the minirockets punched through the thick armor of the APC, and thunderously detonated inside, chunks of men and machine flying wide in a grisly corona.

In ragged formation, a dozen more gunships went airborne and angled their prows around to point at the distant launch facility.

"Incoming, sir," a pilot crisply reported over the Gertrude. "Radar shows two helicopters and a dozen vehicles, two of them very large, possibly tanks."

Somewhere in the mountains, a dog howled from the ultrasonic transmission.

"Take them out," Greene growled, keeping a hand on his wounded arm.

"Then we attack the base, sir?" another pilot asked eagerly.

"No, my friend, then we leave," Greene said, sitting cross-legged on the grass and opening the laptop. "I have something a lot worse than death in mind for these inbred savages."

CHAPTER SEVENTEEN

Soaring high above the Pacific Ocean, just past the last vestiges of atmosphere, a Skyhook activated and began firing off short bursts from the boron enginettes.

Code name, Comrade Lenin, the old Soviet nuclear reactor the Skyhook was attached to was huge, close to five metric tons of steel, lead shielding and assorted electronics. A dozen cosmonauts had perished hauling pieces of it into space, and the Kremlin had wanted the Comrade Lenin to be the heart of a massive military space station whose lasers would seize control of space for the Communist nation.

Unfortunately, those dreams of conquest had been abruptly shattered when the Soviet Union went bankrupt, and the fully functional nuclear power plant had been simply abandoned, forgotten and ignored because it was simply too expensive to send a mission into space merely to shove the hulking brute out of orbit to drift away into the stars.

However, Dalton Greene considered it the crown jewel of all the garbage floating around Mother Earth.

As the Skyhook kept pulsing, the huge Soviet reactor hesitantly began to move, slowly rotating in place, its speed gradually increasing.

When the Comrade Lenin was spinning like a top, the Skyhook changed the angle of its drivers, and began nudging the colossal reactor until it reached the assigned latitude and longitude.

Now the boron drives of the Skyhook flared with full power, feeding off the stored electricity of the reactor's solar wings to relentlessly shove the reactor away from space and down into the gravity well of the planet below. The Comrade Lenin inched along at first, its progress barely detectable, until the first tugs of gravity appeared, and it started to accelerate rapidly. Steadily moving faster under the combined efforts, the reactor was soon hurtling through the rarified atmosphere, the outer protective shield growing warm, then red hot. No consideration was given for the delicate instruments onboard, or fuel rationing. This was a carefully aimed one-way trip to the rotating planet below. And ground zero had been chosen with extreme care.

At three hundred miles of height, all external fixtures softened and were blown away by the increasing heat and atmospheric friction. A contrail of vaporized metal stretched out behind the reactor like the tail of a comet.

Reaching optimum altitude, the interior of the Comrade Lenin reached critical temperature and everything began to soften and melt, despite the insulating effect of the lithium-fiber heat shield. Stubbornly, the Skyhook fed every last volt of power to the boron drive in an effort to keep the reactor on-target. Then it also overheated and slagged to merge with the multiton sphere of red-hot metal.

The reactor was approaching Mach speed as it reached the cloud layer, then, with a sonic boom, it punched through and flashed straight down toward the coastal city of Caracas, the capital of Venezuela.

It hit the downtown shopping district like the fiery fist of God.

In a blinding flash, a hundred buildings disappeared, pulverized by the sheer force of the gargantuan concussion. Then a fireball larger than the atomic explosions at Hiroshima and Nagasaki combined thunderously and engulfed the city. Umpteen-millions of tons of concrete, cars and corpses were blown away.

Outside of the primary blast zone, the rest of the city crumpled then burst into flames, building and highways compacting into an allotropic conglomeration before exploding outward in a hellish corona.

Bombarded by the concussion and heat wave, the beleaguered ocean turned into steam, and was forced away from the melting shoreline, the reverse tidal wave racing out to sea and sweeping everything out of its monstrous path. Oil tankers, warships, cruise liners and fishing boats were carried like leaves in a maelstrom, the passengers and crew mercifully parboiled to death in under a heartbeat, dead before even hearing the boom of their own destruction.

Compose Island

MOTORS PURRING, the US Navy Albatross seaplane raced into the night. The pilots of every assigned rescue craft had jockeyed for the lead position, but the undisputed winner was the SuperStallion helicopter, its six blades reaching out so far that nobody else dared to get close out of the fear of getting clipped.

Staying in tight formation around the seaplane, the pilots and navigators maintained a strict radio silence, which proved especially difficult when they learned about the near-total destruction of Caracas.

"It must have been a nuke," stated the pilot of the Rescue Hawk. "Had to be."

"No, ma'am," the copilot stated, minutely adjusting the transceiver. "NORAD says the Keyhole satellites report no radiation."

"How can a city be hit like that, but there's no radiation?"

"God alone knows."

In the rear of the Albatross, Bolan was slumped over in a seat catching some much-needed sleep. Refreshed from short naps, Cinco and Carrington were sitting close together, holding knives and discussing techniques. Sorenson had caught a flight back to the States.

"Twist and stab?" she asked, performing the move.

The woman had changed out of her filthy clothing for a clean set of fatigues of mottled greens and browns, camouflage for a jungle insertion. Several members of the mixed crews had been women but only one was the same size as Carrington. The pilot of the Sea Stallion was working in her underwear, which oddly did not seem to bother any of the male members of her crew.

"No, more like this, stab then twist," Cinco corrected, displaying the attack on empty air. "You want deep penetration for maximum damage, then you twist the blade to increase the blood flow from the wound, and to break the natural seal living tissue makes around your blade."

"Sort of like cracking the seal on a pickle jar to make it easier to unscrew the lid," Carrington said thoughtfully, trying again.

"Oddly enough, that's exactly correct." Cinco grinned. "Liz, I think you'll do fine next time."

"Next time," Carrington repeated with a serious expression. "There's always a next time in this line of work."

"Not for you," Cinco said honestly, tucking away the blade. "Matt and I have to go after Greene, that's our job. But you can sit this one out and stay onboard the plane. This is not your battle."

"Yes, it is," she said with a grim air of finality, practicing the thrust and twist again. "If you had seen what those bastards did to my friends at the bank, all of those bodies…"

"Excuse me, Agent Cooper?" the copilot asked, glancing over a shoulder. "There's just been a report. I…"

"What's wrong?" Cinco asked with a sinking feeling in his stomach. "Has another city been attacked?"

"Yes, sir." The copilot swallowed. "Johannesburg, South Africa."

Instantly, Bolan was awake.

"Greene's hometown," Cinco said thoughtfully. "Guess he still wanted revenge for making him emigrate to Australia."

"Any radiation?" Bolan asked, placing aside the blanket.

"No, sir. Same as before."

"How many dead?" Carrington asked. Oddly, she felt calm and unaffected by the news. The woman had a thick callous on her trigger finger from spending so much time at the gun range, and now she wondered if the same thing could happen to the human heart. After a while, death stopped horrifying you.

"Thousands," the pilot said, touching his own headphones. "It's just like Caracas. Major devastation."

"Skyhook again," Bolan said softly, weighing the word in his mouth. "These almost sound like hits from a Thor. But I've never heard of a Thor that could deliver this massive a level of destruction."

"Some new version?" Cinco asked uneasily.

"What's a Thor?" Carrington asked, half expecting to be ignored.

Reaching into a pocket, Bolan took out a bullet and gently tossed it over. The round hit the woman in the chest and fell to the floor with a clatter. It rolled across the vibrating deck to disappear under a seat.

"Okay," she said hesitantly. "That proves what?"

"Speed is what makes the bullet dangerous," Bolan explained. "You must have heard the old urban legend of a piece of straw being found embedded into a telephone after a tornado strike?"

"Of course. Wait, you mean that really happened?"

"All of the time. Now, haul a steel girder into orbit, one about the size of a telephone pole, then let it simply drop. The beam accelerates back to Earth under the steady rate of thirty-two feet per second. Only this time it's going so fast that when it hits the ground and stops...all of that speed turns into pure radiant heat. The result is a massive explosion."

She swallowed hard. "And you think Greene is dropping steel girders, these Thor things on these places?"

"Not with that kind of a yield." Cinco snorted. "This is bigger. Much, much bigger..." He snapped his fingers. "The washtub! Gotta be!"

"Deadly litter?" Bolan asked with a slow scowl.

"That certainly fits the criteria."

"Damn, that's clever."

"And unstoppable."

"Theoretically unstoppable," Bolan corrected. "Nobody will ever know for sure until some lunatic tries."

"Jesus! I need to call my director, and the president!" Cinco said, reaching for a cell phone. "They'll have to start an evacuation of Mexico City, and warn the federal police and the air force and…"

His hand paused an inch away from a pocket, then slowly lowered. The mission was under radio silence. If he tried to warn his country, it might only get more people killed. The only solution was to find Greene, and send him to hell in as many small pieces as possible.

"Is there a lot of this space junk in orbit?" Carrington asked, sheathing her blade. "I mean honestly, how many failed space missions and such could there have really been?"

"Hundreds of them," Bolan retorted. "Nobody has any idea of the exact amount of dead tonnage circling the planet."

"Tons?"

"Megatons."

"But Greene could hammer the entire world with that sort of stockpile! Smash civilization back to the Stone Age!"

"Which might be his goal," Cinco replied, rubbing his hand. "Send everybody back into the caves to start all over again, with his group as the people in charge."

"Except that he would also die in the maelstrom," Bolan said, leaning forward in his seat. "Unless he's got a way to control what city gets hit."

Cinco brushed back his thick hair. "Not necessarily,"

he said. "Those Skyhook things might be on automatic. Attacking whatever city comes into range."

"If that's true, we've already lost," Bolan growled. "But I don't read him as a man who trusts anything, much less complex machinery like this. He'll have some kind of a fail-safe, some way to control the Skyhooks…." His voice trailed off in thought.

"I saw him with a laptop," Carrington said. "Weird thing, almost looked like a toy, or a movie prop."

"Describe it," Cinco snapped, leaning forward.

She did, and the men briefly conferred.

"That's a military laptop," Bolan said. "It has a built-in satellite dish and is tougher than a free steak."

"Hey, any chance you guys have a miltop onboard?" Cinco shouted at the front of the plane.

"Sorry, no," the pilot said, both hands on the yoke.

"But the Rescue Hawk probably does," the copilot stated. "I have a buddy who flies one. Miltops are standard equipment for field surgery. You know, for detailed views of internal organs, and such."

"Say what now?" Carrington asked skeptically.

"They come with wands, minicameras thinner than a roofing nail. You can push them into wounds to see how much damage was done, locate shrapnel, all sorts of stuff. Very useful."

"Also good for looking around corners in a firefight," Cinco added knowingly.

"Planning on doing a switch?" Carrington asked. "Swap his laptop for a dummy, preferably loaded with high explosives?"

"Can't hurt to have a decoy," Bolan said, rubbing his unshaved jaw. This whole thing was a carefully laid out jigsaw puzzle of pieces. Nothing seemed to make sense until it connected with the next piece. Greene was smart, maybe too smart.

An alarm buzzed on the instrument board at the front of the plane.

"Approaching the jump zone," the pilot declared, leveling out the plane in regard to the ocean below. "Sir, ma'am, do you really want to hit the silk this far away?"

"I have a strong feeling that if we were to parachute onto the island itself," Bolan said, getting to his feet, "it would be the very last thing we ever did."

"Where will the rest of you be hidden?" Cinco asked, sliding on a parachute.

"There's a small island to the north of here that's still owned by the United Kingdom," the pilot reported. "We can refuel and be waiting for you there."

"Send the word, and we can be with you in an hour," the copilot told him.

"Here are the code words," Bolan said, handing over a folded piece of paper. "If we want a rescue, we'll ask for you. If we need medical, the Rescue Hawk."

"And if we want the place leveled, that'll be the Harrier," Cinco finished, sliding on a parachute.

"They do pack quite a punch, that's for damn sure!"

"Amen to that, brother."

"Liz, ever done a high jump before?" Bolan asked, watching the woman mutter to herself as she slowly got into the rig.

"Sure, all the time," Carrington said, locking the harness into place. "This is how I beat the morning traffic jam." Then she frowned. "Where are the cup holders for my coffee?"

Smiling, Cinco looked at Bolan. "She'll do."

"Yeah, I think so," Bolan agreed, stuffing an inflatable raft into a python bag.

"Chutes at five?" Cinco asked, touching his throat mike. The transceivers had a very short range, and were deemed safe to use once they were far away from the other aircraft.

"Four," Bolan said, securing the flap over the Desert Eagle. "We must not be seen arriving."

Cinco did the same thing to his Colt Magnum. "Then let's make it three."

"Agreed, two, it is." Bolan smiled, tucking away a grenade.

"Boy," Carrington snorted, putting a wealth of emotion into the single word.

"One minute to the jump zone," the pilot announced.

Attaching a parachute to their equipment bag, Bolan went to the side door and twisted the handle. Opening it took some muscle because of the wind pressure, but Bolan locked it aside and studied the sky below. There was nothing to be seen but the vast ocean.

"Geronimo?" Carrington asked.

"Or you can simply count to five," Bolan told her.

"Okey-dokey," she muttered, reaching back to tuck her hair into her collar.

"Try this," Cinco said, handing her a used sock.

Confused, the woman stared at the piece of clothing as if it were infested with insects, then nodded and pulled it over her head, mashing her long hair flat. "Thanks."

"Got your six, sister."

"And...now," the pilot calmly announced.

Tossing the python bag out the door, Bolan waited until the parachute automatically opened, then he dove out. Immediately, he was hit in the face with a strong wind, and his belly tightened from the wonderful sensation of free-falling. The soldier curled into a ball to briefly accelerate his descent, then spread his arms wide and slipped sideways across the sky to get closer to the slowly descending equipment bag.

At two thousand feet, Bolan pulled the rip cord and the parachute exploded from his backpack in a hard jerk to blossom overhead. Then Cinco shot by, the straps of his chute hopelessly tangled. Dropping out of control, the man spiraled away...then slapped the release and the knotted chute flew off his body.

"Water!" Bolan yelled in warning.

Everybody crossed their arms across their chests to reduce the rush of water up their noses, and crossed their ankles. A long moment later, they hit the ocean, the impact jarring them hard. Disorientated for a moment, their minds were filled with chaos, then reality returned with the urge to breathe. But by now they were deep under water, and their descent was already starting to slow.

Slapping the release on the chest harnesses, they shrugged off the sodden parachutes and started for the surface, remembering the ancient sailor adage—always follow the bubbles.

Reaching the surface, Bolan and the others separated to hunt for the equipment bag. Carrington found it less than a hundred feet away. The military raft had inflated upon impact and was bobbing about in the gentle waves.

Grabbing hold of the rope lining the gunwale, she crawled onto the raft, then shook a hand to get rid of excess moisture and sharply whistled. A few moments later, Bolan and Cinco arrived.

Hooking an ankle under the rope, Carrington reached across the raft to help each man onboard in turn.

"Neat trick, where did you learn that?" Cinco asked, settling into place near the python bag.

"I live on an island," she replied, getting her ankle free.

Releasing the dragging parachute, Bolan watched it vanish into the murky depths below, then broke out the oars. He and Cinco each took one and started an easy stroke.

"More this way," Carrington said, checking a compass and pointing to the left.

Angling into the new direction, Bolan heard the distant purr of an airplane engine, then it briefly tripped. That was an old combat pilot's way of saying either hello or goodbye, whichever was more appropriate.

A slow hour passed while the men stroked the oars, and Carrington kept checking the compass to keep them on course. Ahead of them, a school of flying fish broke the surface of the ocean, their "wings" sparkling like jewels in the sun.

After a while, Carrington scanned the horizon with a compact Air Force monocular. "Nothing in sight... No, wait a moment," she reported, dialing for computer augmentation. "Okay, I see the island! Rangefinder says it's 5.23 kilometers away." Damn, this thing was accurate!

"Watch the trees for any reflections," Bolan advised, maintaining a steady rhythm. "If Greene has any snipers positioned, that's where they'll probably be hidden."

"No problem," Carrington said, reaching down to pat the tightly holstered Glock on her hip.

"Don't worry about it," Cinco said with a laugh. "You never hear the round that blows off your head."

"Very funny. Ever considered working as a stand-up comic?"

"Thanks! I'll be veal all week. Try a waitress, they're delicious!"

Both Bolan and Carrington snorted a laugh at that.

All conversation stopped as they heard the distant sound of waves cresting on the beach. Bolan and Cinco paused to free their weapons, then started rowing again, with Carrington at the front of the raft cradling an M16/M203 assault rifle, the strap wrapped around her forearm in case it went overboard.

Stopping in the shallows, they carefully surveyed the beach and the trees, watching for any sign of motorized vehicles or footprints. But the wide strip of golden sand seemed undisturbed aside from the trail of a turtle waddling out to sea, and the only activity in the trees were a few parrots and a some very tiny monkeys.

Easing over the side, Bolan took the lead, while Cinco and Carrington paddled closer to the shore until the bottom of the raft scraped sand.

Wading through the low waves, Bolan headed for the turtle tracks and got onto his belly to crawl across the open beach and into some flowering bushes. Once in position, he waved the others on, and they did the same, with Cinco dragging the raft along behind.

While Carrington stood guard, Cinco began unpacking the raft, and Bolan cut down a leafy tree branch to sweep the beach clear of their tracks. Now if anybody noticed the disturbance, they'd think it was just more turtles. Hopefully.

Donning some lightweight Navy body armor, Carrington made no complaint as she awkwardly pushed her breasts into place. It was a tight fit, but anything was better than getting shot.

"Silenced weapons only," Bolan reminded, slinging the Zastava across his back and drawing the Beretta.

Nodding, Carrington checked the sound suppressor attached to the barrel of her Glock.

"I'm surprised you had one of these tucked away in that RV," Cinco said, slinging the M16 assault file across his back and swinging up a Barnett Ghost military crossbow.

Designed for nighttime combat, the skeletal crossbow was composed entirely of reflectionless black aluminum with two crossarms, and was topped with a multispectrum monocular as a scope. A quiver bristling with black arrows hung at his side.

"I have a friend who swears by the Barnett, so I always try to keep one handy for him," Bolan said, smearing camouflage paint across his face.

"A real hard case, eh?" Cinco asked, doing the same thing.

"Oh, he's Stony Man."

Switching on their transceivers to the shortest possible range, Bolan took the lead as they proceeded into the jungle. Soon, they encountered a brick wall topped with a wire fence that was in turn topped with old barbed wire. The sides of the wall were thick with creepers, some of them partially covering a sign written in several languages that said this was a government installation and trespassers would be shot on sight.

"Shouldn't we be smelling gasoline, kerosene, whatever it is they use in rockets?" Carrington asked.

"Liquid oxygen and liquid hydrogen," Bolan replied.

"Rockets haven't used kerosene as a fuel since before you were born."

"Liquid oxygen smells like freshly fallen snow," Cinco said, inhaling deeply. The only smells he could detect were those of the jungle, green plants, flowers, fresh fruit and the rich dark earth.

"Snow?" Carrington scoffed. "Sorry, never even seen snow in real life, only in movies."

"You never went skiing on vacation?"

"Bank guards do not make much money."

"Which is something we'll discuss later," Cinco said, taking the point position, his crossbow held at the ready.

Following the base of the wall, Bolan checked for snipers, Carrington watched the wall for any video cameras, and Cinco kept a close watch on an EM scanner, but so far there were no land mines, proximity sensors or even live video cameras.

"The place feels dead," Carrington whispered, watching some monkeys scamper back and forth among the tree. The little animals didn't seem afraid of them, as if they had no idea the people were dangerous.

"Agreed, something's wrong here," Bolan said, straining to try to hear anything from the other side of the wall. But there wasn't a sound; no truck engines, hissing pressure lines, thumping compressors, music playing, nothing. If Greene was using the abandoned facility as a base, then surely there would be some small indications of his people being present.

Continuing along the wall, Bolan spotted more signs of disrepair, strands of barbed wire that had come free and were swaying in the breeze, a warning sign almost rusted through....

Turning a corner, they found their path blocked by

a large clump of flowering bushes. Edging past the obstruction, Bolan paused at the sight of the front gate.

The windows were broken in the guard kiosk. The wooden beam used to block the entrance was lying on the pavement and windblown leaves were everywhere.

Warily approaching closer, Bolan stayed in the shadows and used the monocular. The parking lot was completely empty, as was the helipad and airfield. All of the buildings were in disrepair, windows broken and the doorways full of dried leaves. Animal droppings were everywhere, and weeds were growing from every crack in the sidewalks. Down a sloping hill, Bolan could see the launch pads, the tall gantries thick with creepers, and alive with countless bird nests.

"I'm not picking up any heat signatures," Cinco said slowly, using the IR function of the monocular to scan the facility. "There's nobody here."

"Did we came to the wrong island?" Carrington asked, breathing heavily.

"No, we simply came too soon," Bolan answered, tucking away the monocular. "This must be their bolt-hole, a fall-back location."

"We lost them?"

He smiled. "No, they simply haven't gotten here yet."

"Yet," she repeated, then smiled. "Okay, so do we blow it up, or lay a trap?"

"An ambush would seem to be the wisest course," Cinco stated, turning off the monocular. "Let them come to us, and we end this clean and quick."

"We want his miltop undamaged and with the access codes entered," Bolan said, then abruptly stopped as a subtle movement in the distance caught his attention. Swinging up the Zastava, he used the powerful telescopic sights to scan in the area around what looked like an assembly building. For a moment, Bolan thought he had been mistaken. Then something stirred inside the shadowy interior of the building, briefly silhouetted by the light coming through a dirty window.

Snapping his fingers, Bolan got the attention of the others and let them see him turn off his transceiver. They did the same and waited expectantly.

"Gladiators," he whispered, raising four fingers.

Cinco nodded, Carrington scowled.

Slowly retracing their steps, Bolan and the others eased around the flowering bush and melted back into the thick jungle foliage.

CHAPTER EIGHTEEN

The stars were fading, and night was just starting to give way to the red of predawn when the Daylight armada came out of the clouds and descended toward the tropical island.

"All ships, ready all weapons," Greene directed over his throat mike, the dull pulse of the blades overhead seeming to fill his body. "Turn off the defusers on my mark. Ready…and…mark. Full radar scan!"

A minute passed in silence.

"Clear, sir," came the crisp reply from the pilot of the lead Apache. "There's nothing in the sky but us."

"Acknowledged, Apache One. Defusers back on," Greene drawled, reaching for a cigar then staying his hand. Smoke bothered the delicate instruments onboard, and this wasn't the time.

Gazing languidly out the side window, Greene saw a school of dolphins leaping madly out of the ocean, each time going higher and higher, almost as if they were trying to catch the hovering gunships.

"Any chance they can hear the Gertrude like those dogs?" Layne asked, pressing his face against a cold window to try and look directly down.

"That seems reasonable," Greene said in annoyance. "Get rid of them, please."

"No worries, mate," Layne said, lapsing into the colloquial slang of his youth.

Going to the gunnery chair, the fat man checked the feed of the ammunition belt to the Remington .50-caliber machine gun, tripped the safeties and started firing short bursts. The ocean seemed to boil from the arrival of the heavy-duty combat rounds. The terrified dolphins attempted to escape, but soon there was only bloody chum in the water, a host of other fish already eating the tattered shreds as they began to sink out of sight.

A single dolphin was racing away faster than Layne had ever imagined possible, after a moment he decided better safe than sorry, and targeted the lone runaway with another long burst.

"Clear," Layne reported casually, going to his seat to finish his cup of coffee. Damn, it was warm now. How annoying.

Casting a glance at the crimson water below, Greene pulled down a monocular from an overhead stanchion.

"How far away is the island?" he asked, thumbing the controls to activate the device, then starting to hunt for the landmass. The range finder said forty-nine and a half miles.

"Fifty miles and closing," LoMonaco reported crisply, checking the 3D map on the screen of the new miltop in her lap. It was identical in every way to the miltop carried by Greene. She considered such precautions slightly paranoid, but then sometimes paranoids actually did have enemies, so what the hell.

"No sign of any intruders, sir," reported the pilot of an Apache. He studied the island through the monocle attached to his helmet, the target acquisition and designation system hunting for any thermal discrepancies, or anomalies or cold spots. "Just the usual birds and monkeys."

"You sure they're monkeys?"

"Yes, sir, without a doubt."

Lowering the monocular, Green grunted at that. "All right, all ships prepare to fire!" he commanded into the throat mike.

"But not at the garage!" he quickly averred. "We may need our little tin soldiers…afterward."

"I'll access the Gladiators and send them down to the basement," LoMonaco said, typing away on the miltop. The screen gave an answering beep. "Done! They're out of danger."

"Excellent. All ships, fire at will," Green commanded, sliding on a pair of mirrored sunglasses.

In ragged harmony, the Apaches, Cobras and Black Hawks unleashed a full salvo of Hellfire missiles. Then the Cobra used its TOW missiles, and the Apache sent off a full salvo of Hydra rockets.

Streaking in hard and fast, the missiles and rockets slammed into random targets across the base, chewing a path of destruction through the assorted buildings. Broken bricks and loose chunks of concrete were thrown far and wide from the fiery explosions. All three of the gantries crashed to the ground, and the access bridge collapsed in a roiling geyser of cement dust.

Laboratories, offices, machine shops, fuel depot, building after building was annihilated until the facility resembled a war zone. In the jungle outside the wall, swarms of screaming monkeys fled into the hills, and flocks of parrots launched into the sky, furiously flapping for the imagined safety of the distant mainland.

"Enough," Greene commanded over the Gertrude. "We don't want the base too battered for us to live in, eh?"

The question of where Daylight should go after the nuclear world war began was a serious matter that required a great deal of deliberation. They wanted to stay out of the way of the radioactive winds but also have easy access to some sort of supplies when it was time to emerge and start their long journey back to Australia. The answer was, of course, somewhere already destroyed. When NATO, the Americans, whoever, came hunting for them, seeking revenge, nobody would expect Daylight to be hidden inside a demolished launch facility. Once more, they would hide in plain sight. So far, that had worked out very well for them.

Briefly, Greene had debated actually using a Skyhook on the base, but the slightest miscalculation on his part might result in the island getting blown out of existence. That wouldn't be particularly advantageous for Greene and his people, so they would have to do the job themselves. Better safe than sorry.

"Cobra Three, hit the crater in the parking lot again, please. It's too small," Layne directed, studying the gaping hole with a pair of binoculars.

"Confirm!"

A moment later, a pair of 70 mm rockets leaped away from the weapons pod alongside the gunship and zoomed down to slam into the ragged side of the opening. The double explosion ripped away chunks of concrete, throwing out a huge cloud of debris.

"Clear the air, please, Apache Two," Greene directed, looking through a monocular. "I need to see the diameter."

"Roger wilco!"

Breaking formation, the nimble gunship swooped down to assume a position directly above the decimated area. The powerful wash of its turbo-blades soon forced away the dust cloud to reveal an irregular hole almost a hundred feet wide. There was only smoky darkness at the bottom of the hole.

"Yes, that'll do," Greene said, removing the safety harness. "Pilot, take me down. I'll walk us in."

"Sir, you really don't need to risk your life like this," the pilot countered, turning sideways in his seat.

"On the contrary, I do," Greene corrected, attaching the miltop to his wrist with a pair of handcuffs. "The safety of Daylight is my sole responsibility."

"As you say, sir." The pilot sighed, changing the pitch of the overhead blades, and started down toward the base.

Chunks of masonry were still raining down across the jungle, when the Black Hawk slowed to a stop directly above the hole in the parking lot. Sliding back the side hatch, Greene buckled himself into a rig, while Layne checked the winch.

"All set?" Layne shouted over the roar of the blades.

Accepting a python bag from LoMonaco, the leader of Daylight gave a nod, and Layne winched the cable tight until Greene's boots left the deck. Swinging out of the helicopter, Greene gave a wave, and Layne slowly lowered the man down into the hole.

"I'm down," Greene announced. "All clear! Winch up the cable, and start sending them in one at a time."

Dropping out of the sky, the armada began to form a ragged line toward the hole when suddenly dots of green light appeared at the bottom.

"Mind the wash!" Layne said, winching up the cable and closing the hatch.

Now, the Black Hawk carefully lowered into the darkness until the chewed ruin of the floor came into view. Safely off to the side, Greene was cracking more cold light tubes and tossing them about to help dispel the dusty gloom.

Originally, this had been a vast natural cavern, but the Brazilian Space Agency had modified it to be used as a massive cistern to hold the thousands of gallons of water necessary to cool the gantries during a launch. After they departed for the new base in southern Brazil, the cavern had been abandoned.

When Greene was arranging the final details of the mission, one of the first things he had done was to drain the cistern, and make sure there was an easy way for his people to climb out of the makeshift hangar.

"Easy now, nice and slow!" Cracking a couple of more glow sticks, Greene waved the Black Hawk down, then directed it off to the side.

"How big is this?" LoMonaco asked, craning her neck about.

"Big enough to hold twice as many helicopters as we brought," Layne said with a note of pride. "S'truth!"

As the Black Hawk settled onto the flooring, LoMonaco got out and headed directly to a diesel generator sitting alongside a watertight inspection hatch. Starting the engine, she let it warm to operational temperatures, then flipped a long series of switches. Instantly, clusters of halogen lights came on to brightly illuminate the entire cavern.

"Better." Greene sighed, tucking away the last unbroken glow tube.

In spite of the electric lights, getting every helicopter safely down and parked away from the others, was a slow and tedious process. But eventually, it was accomplished. As the last Cobra descended into the hole, Bolan, Cinco and Carrington charged out of a bedraggled guard kiosk. Their clothing was thickly smeared with mud, and each of them had dead monkeys lashed to their backs in an effort to confuse the TADS sensors.

Reaching the edge of the hole, Bolan, Cinco and Carrington stopped to heave a piece of broken concrete. The first passed through the spinning blades without incident, but the second slammed directly into the intended target.

Instantly, both of the reinforced blades shattered, the shards spraying across the cistern like a shotgun blast to ricochet off the walls and rebound onto the other gunships. A dozen people cried out as they were slashed to bloody ribbons.

With both hands still on the yoke, the pilot of the damaged Cobra tried to regain control of the gunship as it plummeted the additional fifty feet to the rocky floor. It hit with a deafening crash, the people inside the Cobra screaming briefly before going silent forever.

"No…" Greene whispered, reaching out a hand for the crumpled machine. In a whoosh, both of the engines caught fire as the fuel tanks burst open wide.

"Everybody grab fire extinguishers!" LoMonaco shouted, heading back toward the Black Hawk. "We've got to help them!"

"No, run for the hatch!" Greene growled, backing away from the crash. The smell of aviation fuel was thick in the air, and he knew there was no chance of the fire-suppression system on the broken machine ever stopping the growing blaze. It was designed to counter a broken fuel line or engine leak, not the tanks themselves split open wide.

Trying to look in two directions at once, LoMonaco hesitated. "But, sir..."

"We got to get away before the flames reach the weapons pod!" Greene interrupted, breaking into a full sprint.

"The blast could start a chain reaction with the other gunships..." Layne added, not finishing the sentence.

In spite of the order to flee, everybody paused, uncertain of what to do next. Then the ammunition in the Gatling gun began to cook off from the heat, the 20 mm shells zinging about in every direction. A woman fell with blood on her face, the windshield of a Black Hawk cracked, a cluster of halogen lights exploded into darkness. A shell hit the far wall and detonated, spraying out rock chips and sending two more people in bloody pieces to the floor.

Scrambling madly, the terrorists raced around the armada of gunships and helicopters, trying to reach the inspection hatch in time. A split second later, a deafening fireball filled the cistern, the roiling flames rapidly expanding outward.

CHAPTER NINETEEN

London, United Kingdom

With the low hum of electric motors, the truncated steel door cycled open, and the prime minister strode into the hallway flanked by an armed escort of Royal Marines.

Well-known, almost famous, for his love of fashion, at this moment, the middle-aged man was unshaved, wearing patched jeans, sneakers and a T-shirt bearing the logo of the Mayo Hurlers. A pair of gardening shears was sticking out of a back pocket, and he was still wearing dirty leather gloves.

In comparison, his escorts were in full-dress uniforms, every crease was razor sharp and their shoes were polished to a mirror shine. The men and women were also carrying 9 mm Browning sidearms, L85 assault rifles. Two of them cradled Atchisson autoshotguns, bandoliers of spare cartridges draped across their chests, while everybody was wearing Threat Level Three ceramic body armor.

"Good evening, sir," said the minister of defence, stepping away from the wall to join the parade.

"Don't think it's going to be good for anybody, Bob," the prime minister said without any visible emotion. "What is the estimated death toll?"

"Only guesstimates are available," the minister replied, checking a computer tablet. "There are no bodies. Caracas is nearly destroyed, and part of Paris is on fire. The best guess is one hundred thousand dead."

"Bloody hell," the prime minister muttered in horror, then instantly regained his composure. "What about our embassy personnel?"

"Gone, sir. One of them was Skyping at the time, and we have footage. It isn't recommended viewing."

"Understood. Please have it sent to the War Room at once."

"Yes, sir. Of course."

The hallway was lined with oil portraits of former prime ministers, starting with Winston Churchill, who had first envisioned building the very military base that the current PM was now entering, codename Pindar, the supreme high command for all of the defense forces of the British Isles.

Buried below Whitehall, the fortress was protected by reinforced ferro-concrete walls, which were in turn encased by a live Faraday Cage and then sheathed with enough cadmium and lead shielding to withstand a direct nuclear explosion.

The air and water could be recycled indefinitely. There was a massive library of fireproof hardback books. The medical unit could perform any possible surgery, from brain surgery to a briss. Plus, the row of supply rooms held enough food for twenty-seven years, included beer and chips.

Self-contained and self-supporting in every way imaginable, Pindar was powered by two subterranean nuclear reactors and contained more communications equipment than the BBC and Star channel combined.

Curiously, the name of the British base came from an

ancient Greek tale of a man named Pindar whose house was the only building left standing in his village after a terrible earthquake. Over time, the name of Pindar had become synonymous with surviving any holocaust.

Passing several checkpoints and two guard stations, the prime minister finally reached the set of double doors at the end of the hallway. As he approached, a UV laser scanned his face, checked for the chip implanted under the skin of his left shoulder blade, then obediently cycled open the solid steel doors that had been expertly painted to look like ordinary wood.

Inside the War Room were a dozen men and women in various states of dress sitting around a huge cherrywood table. Everybody was drinking tea and typing furiously on miniature keyboards built into the table in front of their old leather chairs. Recessed monitors strobed with incoming data, and humming printers were endlessly disgorging classified reports.

Three of the walls were decorated with the emblems of the monarchy and topographical maps of England, Wales, Scotland and a tiny piece of northern Ireland, showing the exact location of every military base, submarine pen, gunfort, disguised airfield and secret missile silo. The remaining wall was covered with a thick curtain of ballistic cloth bearing the royal monogram.

"Sorry to disturb your evening," the prime minister said as a greeting. "Has the sighting been confirmed?"

"Not yet, no, sir," replied the Assistant Minister of Defence.

The prime minister scowled. "Where is Lady Foxworth-Durante?"

"She has a cold, sir."

"Good God, and she stayed at home for that? Get her on the phone and tell her that—"

"She has a cold, sir," the man interrupted, stressing each word. Then he tactfully coughed.

As comprehension arrived, the prime minister grunted. Ah, Susan was dead drunk again. Fair enough, all work and no play… "Then it would seem that the job is yours tonight, Mr. Wainwright. Welcome to the pitch."

"I won't throw you a googly, sir!"

"Good to know," said the prime minister, turning toward the heavy curtains.

"Red alert! Sighting is confirmed," a voice spoke calmly over a wall speaker. "Red alert, incoming at forty-three degrees. Origin space, target…London."

Quickly pressing a button on a small control panel, the prime minister impatiently waited as the curtains slowly rumbled aside to reveal a gigantic window facing a room full of scurrying people. Officers and noncoms from every branch of the service were hunched over computer consoles situated before a wall of plasma monitors.

Some of the monitors were operating independently to show local weather patterns or the ready status of a military base, while others were linked together to form a segmented vector graphic of the world and every known satellite in orbit. Along with quite a few others not publicly or officially known to exist.

Even the stalwart Americans admitted that MI-6 was one of the best intelligence agencies in the world, and all of their hard-earned information flowed directly onto these monitors. The images were filtered, but not modified, by the five IBM supercomputers locked in the armored air-conditioned room in the basement.

"Trouble with the equipment?" the prime minister demanded gruffly.

In the center of the wall display a dozen monitors were linked into a single homogenous picture of the world, with red crosshairs placed over several major cities: Caracas, Budapest, Yemen City, Tokyo, Berlin, Johannesburg... My God, how many other cities had been hit? he wondered. Then he noticed that a couple of the side monitors were blank.

In the front row, a young colonel wearing headphones rose uncertainly and saluted. "No, sir. Redundancy probes show our transmitters functioning perfectly. Secondary and tertiary circuits are in the green."

"Fair enough," the prime minister replied, returning the salute. "Do we have hard data on the incoming projectile?"

"Yes, and, no, sir," the colonel replied, removing her headset. "It has already started to melt, so our IRAS satellites cannot get a proper identification."

"What about the Greenwich telescope?"

"The same, sir. However, from our records of the debris orbiting in that area our best guess is that this is a Chinese antimatter reactor built to power a Mars probe."

"Antimatter!" the Home Secretary gasped in horror.

"Calm down, the stuff only explodes in the movies, old bean," the prime minister said soothingly. "In reality, antimatter just sort of fizzles out when it touches regular matter. MAM reactors simply don't work. End of discussion."

Vastly relieved, the Home Secretary gratefully sat down, then paused at the memory that the hulking giant boondoggle was streaking toward London at Mach speed.

"All right, one problem solved, one to go," the Assistant Minister of Defence said. "Judging from the size of the fireball, if we try to blow it up, we'll just make a dozen smaller fireballs, spreading the damage around and killing even more people."

"We could use nukes?" an adviser asked.

"And have radioactive fire rain down across the nation?" the prime minister asked. "No, we have to divert it. But where to?"

"Into the sea!" everybody chorused.

"But anywhere it goes the people on the shore will be hit by a tidal wave of unprecedented proportions!" the Home Secretary declared, waving a hand at the island nation.

"There'll be a lot more dead if the damn thing hits Picadilly!" the Lord Chancellor declared.

The Home Secretary glumly nodded. Well, that was certainly true enough.

"Excuse me, Colonel?" a burly lieutenant asked, turning away from his computer.

"Talk to me, son," the prime minister said, raising a finger.

Glancing at the colonel, then the politician, the soldier briskly saluted again for no reason. "I've just received a coded report form NORAD in the United States. They managed to launch enough Patriot missiles to divert the incoming fireball from the White House and into the New Jersey swamps! You can see the strike zone on our Skynet satellite." He tapped a button, and the side monitor flickered into an aerial view of an enormous crater in the ground.

If the area had once been a swamp it was desert now, the soil bone-dry for miles. In the center was a depression hundreds of feet deep, the sloping walls fused into a crude glass. At the bottom was a bubbling pool of red-hot liquid that strongly resembled lava.

"Did the impact trigger a volcano?" demanded the Home Secretary.

"No, sir, that's just normal thermal residue from an impact of that caliber," the lieutenant said.

"All right, if the bloody Yanks can do this, then so can we!" the prime minister stated confidently. "I want every bloody thing we have that can fly and explode shoved up that thing's arse! Triton, Harpoon, the new Soyez we rented from Russia…aim everything for the eighty-kilometer mark!"

"That's pretty close at those speeds," the Minister of Defence said.

"Any higher and not all of our missiles can reach it," the prime minister said. "Any lower, and we could miss."

"And if we do?"

"God have mercy on us all."

On the wall monitor, the fireball continued downward as reports began scrolling about the ready status of SAM bunkers, army bases, RAF jet fighters, the entire Royal Navy and a dozen submarines stationed in a cordon around the island nation.

"Colonel, you may fire when ready," the prime minister said in a deceptively calm voice.

Without comment, the officer turned and pressed a glowing red button on a console.

In a rippling effect, all of the wall monitors merged into a single vector graphic of a giant sphere hurtling straight for London. Suddenly, bright orange triangles rose from a dozen locations streaking upward almost too fast to follow. Then another dozen appeared...a hundred, multiple hundreds, until the screen was almost blocked with a death cloud of streaking metal.

The fireball streaked down as the missiles and rockets lanced upward. The three opposing forces collided at just under the eighty kilometer marker, and a white sphere rapidly expanded outward to fill the entire screen.

For several seconds, nobody spoke, moved or even dared to breath.

The prime minister cleared his throat. "Well, Colonel?"

"Checking secondaries, sir," the colonel muttered, typing at lightspeed. "Here's a preliminary report from the *HMS Black Duke*..." he spun, grinning widely. "Success, sir! Our missiles blew it into the North Atlantic!"

"Thank God for that," the Home Secretary breathed.

"Any casualties?" the prime minister demanded.

"None reported, sir!"

Miracle of miracles.

"Well, then, carry on, Colonel," the prime minister said, pressing the button to close the curtains once more. "And congratulations."

"Sir! Thank you, sir."

Turning away from the window, the prime minister sat down weakly, and somebody placed a glass of whiskey in front of him. He drained it in a gulp, then gestured for another. The man felt flush from the rush of simply still being alive. Then he thought about what might have happened to London and fought back a shiver.

The attack was stopped, but just barely. Unfortunately, there were a lot more junk satellites in orbit than Britain had missiles. Some of the unknown wrecks were larger than the one that hit Caracas. The UK could stop another two, possibly three, such attacks. But after that, the nation was in deep trouble.

"As it was, so shall it ever be," the prime minister said under his breath, activating a secure line for a telephone, and starting to dial the private line for the United Nations Security Council.

Compose Island

As a HUGE CLOUD rose from the hole in the pavement, Bolan and the others dusted off their hands, then paused as there was movement inside the undamaged garage.

Trying to stay behind the smoke, Bolan pulled out the monocular and switched to the UV function. The world went black and white, the hot cloud faded into a rippling blur, and just barely visible on the other side were the four Gladiators surrounded by the vast expanse of rubble.

"Trouble?" Carrington whispered, swinging around the assault rifle.

Bolan scowled, and Cinco moved closer to the woman and slapped a hand over her mouth. She scowled in puzzlement, then nodded in understanding, and lowered the weapon.

However, Bolan saw that she had been heard. The lead Gladiator had raised a parabolic dish from inside its armored chassis, and was swiveling a sensitive microphone back and forth to try to find the source of the whisper. Obviously, the machines were programmed to recognize keywords.

Tucking away the monocular, Bolan eased up the Zastava and set the crosshairs on the tiny opening at the base of the parabolic dish. If he could get a round inside the machine, it would ricochet about and might just take it out. Of course, then the others would instantly attack, but what other choice did they have?

Slinging the Barnett over a shoulder, Cinco swung around his assault rifle and aimed the M203 grenade launcher at another robot.

Just then, there was a low cry of pain from the burning wrecks underground.

Pushing the broken pieces of concrete out of their way, the four Gladiators rushed to the edge of the hole and began scanning the smoky darkness below.

Incredibly, one of the Gladiators called out a question in an unknown language, but the only reply was a crackle of exploding bullets.

Using that as cover, Bolan waved the others back, and they carefully retreated to the kiosk. Once it was between them and the machine, Bolan took the point again with Cinco and Carrington staying on his flanks.

Moving fast and low, they swept along the battered wall to reach the front gate and slip back into the noisy jungle. The parrots were long gone, but the little monkeys were very upset, screaming and jumping about, some of them even resorting to more base displays of their intense displeasure at all of the explosions and fiery smoke.

"Is it okay to talk now?" Carrington whispered into her throat mike. But there was no reply in her earbuds aside from the ever-present crackle of the radio jamming field.

Wordlessly, she touched Cinco on the shoulder.

Instantly, the man spun around with his crossbow leveled, then relaxed and tucked it away.

Silently, she asked a question.

Shaking his head, Cinco pressed a finger to his lips, then jerked a thumb toward Bolan.

Hopping over exposed roots, ducking under low branches and dodging snakes, the group finally reached a large stand of palm trees. Stopping on the lee side, they listened to the rustle of the palm fronds, and the gentle cresting of the waves on the nearby beach.

"Clear," Bolan stated, resting the Zastava on a shoulder.

"No sign of the droids, either," Cinco added, scanning the jungle with a monocular. "I think we lost them."

"We can take them," Carrington stated defiantly.

"Maybe we can take them, maybe not. But that's not something I want to try until absolutely necessary," Bolan said. "However, the best way to win a fight is to conduct it on your terms, not on those of the enemy."

Saying nothing, Carrington nodded as if filing the information away for later use.

"On top of which, that one back on Rum Island almost kicked our ass. Now there's four of them?" Cinco laughed wearily, easing the pressure off the taut drawstring of the crossbow. "Good thing the fire masked our presence from those *puta* machines."

"Any idea how we kill them?" Carrington asked, trying to redeem herself from the earlier blunder.

"Still working on that," Bolan said, pulling out a canteen and taking a drink. "Their ceramic armor is a real bitch to penetrate. We'd need something a lot more powerful than even my Fifty here." He patted the Zastava.

"Any chance that you're now going to tell me why we threw rocks instead of grenades?" Carrington asked, stepping over a wiggling snake.

"Grenades would have told them others were on the island," Bolan said, exuding patience. "The concrete could easily have been just some of the debris from the earlier explosions."

"Now Greene doesn't know for sure if anybody else is here, and will take all sorts of unnecessary precautions," Cinco added. "That'll weaken their position, and offer us some additional leeway to maneuver."

"But if they knew, then all of them would have gone on the hunt, and we'd be fighting a retreat instead of attacking."

"By George, I think she's got it."

"Okay, now what? The airwaves are still jammed. We can't call for help," Carrington said. "Hey! If we had ropes, we could have rappelled down the hole and attacked Greene from behind. They never would have been expecting that!"

"Sounds good," Bolan said. "Any chance you've got a thousand feet of rope in your pocket?"

"Nope."

"Then we need another plan."

"Well, at least you were right about Greene," Carrington said, resting the stock of her M16 assault rifle on a hip. "The first thing that fat bastard did is nuke the launch facility. How did you know?"

"It's what we would have done," Cinco replied instead, pouring some water into a palm to wipe down the back of his neck.

"Beg pardon?"

"Hide in plain sight, again," Cinco said. "It's a bold move. If Greene wasn't such a murdering prick, I could almost admire the son of a bitch."

Carrington tried not to laugh. "Please, Bull, don't hold back. Tell us what you really feel."

"Can't. There's a lady present."

"Damn, is she bigger than me?"

Unable to resist, Cinco looked directly at her breasts, then smiled widely. "No way in hell!"

Caught completely off-guard by the half-assed compliment, Carrington blushed bright red, unable to think of a proper retort.

"At least we took out a Cobra gunship," Bolan stated, screwing the cap back on his canteen. "Then again, from all of those secondary explosions, we might have taken out four or five gunships total."

"Still leaving around nine or ten of them," Cinco said with a lot of meaning, glancing at the clear sky. Dawn had arrived with all of its glory, and it was promising to be a beautiful day.

"Any damage done to the enemy is a point in our favor," Carrington said in a singsong voice as if she was quoting something.

"What is that from?" Cinco asked, furrowing his brow.

"Robert E. Lee."

"Really?"

"I read a lot of military novels. Sort of my hobby."

"Me, too!"

Suddenly, a thunderous explosion sounded from the

direction of the launch facility, and a huge cloud of smoke and flames erupted into the sky. A few seconds later, an Apache rose into view. It hovered amid the dissipating cloud, and slowly turned around as if searching for targets to attack.

Snapping his fingers, Bolan got the attention of the others, then closed a fist, made a slash across his throat and jerked a thumb over a shoulder.

Moving as fast as possible, the three of them took off through the dense foliage.

CHAPTER TWENTY

Beijing, China

A heavy rain was falling on the August the First Building, the headquarters for the Central Military Command for China.

Overhead, the sky was dense with rumbling black clouds. Even in the downpour, the market was still open. Under wide awnings of patched canvas, the farmers sold their produce amid a general babble of languages.

In the nearby harbor, the dark shapes of cargo ships and oil tankers loomed like metal islands on the choppy waves, along with a number of warships—destroyers, aircraft carriers, submarines and a lot of missile frigates, the hatches already open on the honeycomb launch pods in their armored decks.

Ever since the attacks the Chinese High Command had activated the national defense grid. Squadrons of MiG fighters patrolled the stormy sky above. Doppler radar, telescopes and halogen searchlights swept the heavens for the slightest hint of an orbital attack. All commercial air traffic had been shifted to Shanghai, the outraged tourists and foreign businessmen given no explanation whatsoever. Welcome to China.

Meanwhile, geosynchronus satellites above Beijing watched space with the cold scrutiny of computers. Everything the CMC had was on alert, Beidou, FY3, Shii-jan, Zi Yen, Cybers and a score of White Lotus–class hunter-killer satellites. If anything shifted position in space, their orders were to destroy the satellite instantly, without question or pause. Of course, it was difficult to properly track the foreign satellites amid the vast cloud of tumbling wreckage, but that was an acceptable risk.

On the ground, four battalions of Gargoyle surface-to-air missile trucks were positioned around the capital city, as well as the old K1, and brand-new K12, antisat-ellite missile trucks. Sitting inside the cabs of the trucks, Chinese soldiers carefully watched their glowing radar screens, praying and hoping that they would remain blank. Nobody was expecting trouble, but just in case, the president and his executive staff had long since fled to an undisclosed location in the distant mountains.

Parked on the busy streets of the metropolis were dozens of old Soviet MRL trunks, the chassis repainted with the Chinese flag, and the huge launch pods already aimed at the sky in preparation for battle. Everything the nation had was primed and ready.

Slowly, the long hours passed, and the elite high command was still arguing over how they should po-litically respond to the threat of a falling satellite, when the White Lotus satellites in orbit blinked off-line, and every radar station in China went crazy as something unbelievably huge began to descend from orbit.

Built by the India Space Agency twenty years ear-lier, the *Lady Durga* was designed to be part of a per-manent base on the moon. The cylindrical cargo pod weighed almost seventy tons and was packed solid with steel beams and curved sheets of boronated plastic to use both as insulation and protection from the deadly solar winds. However, the United Nations had blocked the final step of India landing on the moon under the rules of a multinational treaty. Military bases weren't allowed on the moon under any circumstances. The strategic advantage was overwhelming. Whoever controlled the moon, controlled Earth. Thus, nobody was allowed to build an armed base there.

Of course, India claimed the weapons were purely for self-defense. However there were far too many long missiles fully capable of reaching Earth than could have ever been justified with that argument. Nobody sane thought that India was planning to try to conquer the world, but the possibility of the Indians attempting to remove their hated enemy Pakistan from the map was more than credible. So the colony had been blocked and stalled and delayed until the money ran out, and India abandoned the materials for some future project.

As the *Lady Durga* plummeted almost straight down, every MiG jet fighter near Beijing sharply angled upward to unleash salvo after salvo of advanced medium-range air-to-air missiles. Dozens of Gargoyles were launched from their MRL pods on the back of trucks, along with everything else. K12 antisatellite missiles rose on fiery columns from the vertical launch tubes in the frigates and submarines. Swarms of J10 jet fighters were thrown skyward from the aircraft carriers, and in the far distance Red Dragon antimissile lasers stabbed into the stormy heavens. The lights dimmed from the power drain, but the people on the rainy streets cheered.

Unfortunately, the counterattack was disorganized, missiles colliding with rockets that were then burned by lasers, long before reaching their assigned target.

The technologically superior Red Army was brutally hobbled by a severe lack of properly trained soldiers.

The suddenly hot rain sparkled with the high-altitude explosions, then there came a sonic boom and the molten sphere that had once been the *Lady Durga* slammed into the ground, vaporizing city blocks.

Compose Island

FINALLY REACHING the trees lining the beach, Bolan paused to check the sky, while Cinco scanned the ocean with the monocular.

"Clear?"

"Clear! Now what?"

"Fire tunnels," Bolan stated, heading due south.

The tunnels were a standard design element of every launch facility in existence. Built of ferro-concrete and usually lined with fireproof bricks, the tunnels acted like channels to safely vent out to see the thundering exhaust of a launching rocket. Bolan couldn't imagine any bombardment that might have damaged those unless the island got hit by a tactical nuke. They should be safe there from being overheard, and even better, the tunnel would give them a direct access to the old launch pads, which were less than a mile away from the destroyed buildings and the subterranean cistern.

Staying in the trees, the team easily located one of the fire tunnels. Actually, it was hard to miss. The beach in front of it was melted into a rippling glass field, and the water offshore was bare of any life.

Using the EM scanner, Cinco checked the entrance for any traps or sensors, while Bolan and Carrington stood guard, their weapons at the ready.

"We're good," Cinco announced, tucking away the device.

They assumed a combat formation and put on night-vision goggles before slipping into the dark tunnel. There were no infrared heat sources inside the brick-lined passage to illuminate their way, so they switched to ultraviolet, and then to Starlite. That did the job. Once amplified by the goggles, the weak sunlight streaming in from the mouth of the tunnel was more than enough to brightly illuminate it for hundreds of feet.

Everybody froze as they heard the sound of rotor blades. Suddenly, the loose sand on the beach began to form a whirlwind across the rippled glass, and a shadow darkened the mouth of the tunnel... Then it brightened again as the helicopter moved onward.

There was no talking as they proceeded along the tunnel. The floor was sprinkled with only a few leaves blown in from the mouth of the tunnel, along with the occasional banana peel from a feasting monkey, and the usual reeking organic aftereffects. However, there were no colonies of bats, which was a great relief to everybody.

Staying alert for hidden video cameras, Bolan was pleased that his theory had been correct. The fire tunnel had clearly proved more than strong enough to resist the aerial bombardment of the parking lot. There was no noticeable damage down here, although it might just be hidden from sight by the inner layer of bricks. He would try to keep an ear out for any telltale groaning that might indicate a forthcoming cave-in. Being buried alive was a bad way to go.

The long tunnel was as straight as a superhighway. Bolan could soon see the light at the other end, which meant this was about the middle. Catching sight of an old dirty cloth hung on the wall, Bolan had almost passed it by when he recognized the material as ballistic cloth.

Quickly stopping Cinco and Carrington, the man jerked his head toward the cloth, then pointed at Cinco. Pulling out the EM scanner, Cinco took a reading.

Gesturing for the others to stay put, Cinco laid down his crossbow and assault rifle, then began divesting himself of everything made of metal. Wearing only his skivvies, and carrying a few plastic tools, Cinco padded barefoot to the cloth, working the delicate controls of the scanner.

It took several minutes, but he finally got a green light and checked under the cloth. As expected, it was a steel door lined with Claymore mines.

Pulling aside the cloth to let the others see, Cinco then got busy disarming the antipersonnel mines, moving slowly, as if he were underwater.

"And…we're clear," Cinco said, tucking away the scanner.

"Wonder what's on the other side?" Carrington whispered, studiously ignoring the man. "Think that's their headquarters?"

"Might be," Bolan admitted, hefting the Zastava. "Or we might find all four of those Gladiators, and down here in this tunnel we'd have no place to maneuver."

She looked hard at the door. "Now why would you think that? Oh…because that's what you would have done. Right?"

"Right," Bolan said, going to the keypad. "Bull, have you touched this with a bare hand?"

"Not born yesterday, amigo," Cinco said, pulling on his pants.

Bolan smiled. "Thanks, that's good to know." Ejecting a round from the Desert Eagle, Bolan used a knife to pry off the lead bullet, then he poured the silvery powder inside onto a palm. Very carefully, he blew the propellant across the keypad and it stuck to four numbers.

"Birthday?" Cinco asked, arranging his weapons once more. "Or the date he left South Africa?"

Bolan thought back to the dossier on the billionaire. "The former," he said, tapping in the numbers.

But just before putting in the last digit, Bolan recalled that Australians, just like Europeans, put the day first, then the month, not the other way around as did Americans.

Switching the digits about, Bolan tapped in the date. The door gave a low hum, a soft click, and then silently swung aside to reveal a small room almost completely filled with a machine of some sort.

"What is it?" Carrington asked, arching an eyebrow. "Some sort of an airboat?"

"Terraquad," Bolan replied, making sure there were no video cameras in the room. But it was clean. There was only the Terraquad, and another door on the opposite side of the room.

"A Terraquad?"

As Cinco headed for the second door, Bolan briefly explained. The Gibbs Terraquad was the last addition to the Australian military. Essentially, the machine was a boat with four-wheel drive, and could drive through just about any type of terrain from desert to the ocean. This Terraquad was painted in irregular blue-and-white patches, camouflage for the open sea, and art-fully painted across the bow was the name *Cassandra*.

Inspecting the second door, Cinco discovered that it was also lined with Claymores, but this time they were all pointing out of the room. Curious.

Pulling out his tools again, Cinco got busy. Working from the rear of the AP charges, they were easy to dis-arm, and the door itself opened without incident. But on the other side was only a solid rock wall.

"That looks like granite," Carrington muttered. "But that's not possible on an island this size."

"That's not granite, it's gunnite," Cinco stated, pull-ing out a knife. "An industrial form of ferro-concrete that could be sprayed into place like a thick paint. The material is tougher than stone, but not as resilient." Pressing the knife point into the gunnite, he started twisting the blade back and forth trying to make a tiny hole.

"There's only room for two in this thing," Carrington said, looking at the mounds of supplies inside the strange-looking vehicle. There was a lot of military ordnance, and a large canvas lump in the rear cargo area. "This must be his private escape route, reserved just for him and his assistant."

"Or a hostage," Bolan said, using the tip of the Za-stava to look under the canvas. Snorting in surprise, he flipped the canvas aside to reveal a pair of Mar-tin Jetpacks. Before Carrington could even ask, Bolan snapped off the attached instruction manual and passed it over for her to read.

Carefully withdrawing the knife, Cinco peeked through the tiny opening, but saw only darkness. Pulling on the night-vision goggles, he tried again, and gave a low whistle.

"This isn't a bolt hole, it's his main base," the man reported, shifting position slightly. "The next room is full of supplies, crates, pallets, trunks, drums...enough supplies to last a hundred people for fifty years!"

"Any guards?" Bolan asked, coming closer.

"Not that I can see," Cinco said slowly. "No, the place is clear. The lights are out, and the doors are sealed with plastic sheeting to keep out the external air."

"Any weapons?"

"Matt, most of it is weapons. There's enough guns and ammo here for Greene to take over the world!"

"Or build a new one," Bolan corrected grimly.

The soldier had encountered similar lunatic plans long ago in Seattle and years later in Argentina. Every now and then, some disgruntled lunatic decided it was time to reshape civilization into something where they would be on top. No thought or consideration was ever given for anybody else. They would make flowery speeches about freedom, but in the end it was all just plain, old-fashioned greed, and an unquenchable thirst for power.

"Can these really fly?" Carrington said in delight, lowering the manual. "Great! Then let's fly the fuck out of here and call the Marines!"

Glancing at the Terraquad and the gunnite wall, Bolan smiled. "I've got another idea," he said, and briefly explained.

"No, I don't like it," Carrington stated, vigorously shaking her head. "I want to help kill these assholes."

"Sorry, but you'll only be a liability in this kind of a battle," Bolan stated honestly. "We're going to be doing a blitz, a full-power charge right through the very heart of the bastards, killing everybody we see without question, or pause."

"There'll be no quarter given, and anybody who surrenders will get shot anyway," Cinco added grimly. "We can't take prisoners, and we can't leave them alive to attack us from behind."

"Bull and I have done this sort of thing many times before," Bolan continued. "It's a nightmare, and we don't want to do it. Nobody sane would. But there's no other way to get that miltop."

"God alone knows how many more people have died since that last report," Cinco said.

Breathing in deeply, Carrington let it out slowly, then nodded. "All right. I'll be the cheese. But when you blow that piece of shit away, be sure to say hello for me."

"That's a promise," Bolan stated in a grave tone.

"Okay, let's get to work!" Cinco said, slapping his hands together.

Moving in unison, the three of them removed all of the Claymores from the outer door, and attached them to the mines lining the hidden doorway. Then Bolan and Cinco removed the Jetpacks and carefully stacked them against the opposite wall.

"Are you sure that's enough C-4 to set off the other stockpile of munitions?" Carrington asked, placing her assault rifle in the passenger seat before sliding behind the steering wheel of the Terraquad.

"More than enough." Bolan smiled without a trace of humor. "It'll completely collapse this fire tunnel, and send up a mushroom cloud large enough to see in Miami."

"Good to know." Starting the engine, Carrington

listened to the powerful purr for a moment. Then she glanced sideways at Cinco and motioned him closer.

"Something wrong?" he asked, sauntering over.

"This," she said, handing him the miltop they had brought along. "Just in case."

"Thanks."

Reaching out, Carrington then grabbed him by the shirt and hauled the man down for a long kiss. Cinco seemed surprised at first, then participated as much as she did, but his hands never left her shoulders.

"Just for luck, amigo," Carrington said, letting him go and shifting into gear.

"Much appreciated, my beauty," Cinco said, trying not to smile and failing.

With a cheery wave, Carrington drove away, and turned left in the tunnel toward the beach. "See you in hell, boys!" she shouted, disappearing into the darkness.

"Hey, Matt. I noticed that you didn't get a lucky kiss," Cinco said proudly, brushing back his thick black hair.

"I'm naturally lucky." Bolan chuckled, going to the Jetpacks and tucking the miltop into a small cargo crease.

While Bolan ran through the preflight procedures, Cinco rigged a series of detonators to the double ring of Claymore mines. He had lied to Carrington when he'd said this was enough to set off the stockpiles of munitions. It was only *probably* enough, but this was the best chance they had at a diversion. If the explosion was loud enough, Greene and all of his people would come charging down here, leaving the gaping hole in the parking lot unguarded. Aside from those four Gladiators. But the Jetpacks should get him and Bolan safely past the robots. If not, well… Damn, that had been an amazing kiss! he thought.

"Ready?" Bolan asked, screwing the gas cap back on the fuel tank of a Jetpack.

"Ready," Cinco answered, pressing the button on the detonator.

There were no blinking lights, revving noises or any other indication that it was operational. But now the two men moved fast. Checking their weapons one last time, they strapped on the Jetpacks and turned on the engines. Rapidly building power, the low murmur of the four turbofans sounded oddly like a helicopter in the confines of the small room.

Twisting the hand controls, they gently lifted off the brick floor in a rush of hot air.

"Rather like flying a motorcycle," Cinco said, shifting his weight to try and to stay away from the wall.

"Just don't bump the ceiling!" Bolan warned. "Those bricks will remove the top of your skull like blowing the foam off a beer."

"Tell me something I don't know," Cinco said, awkwardly wobbling out of the room and into the more spacious tunnel.

Separating to a safe distance, the men started toward the right, slowly increasing their speed until the bricks were only a reddish blur.

"When we reach the end, I'll go left, you go right," Bolan commanded. "We rendezvous at the parking lot and dive in as fast as we can!"

Cinco started to reply when he noticed the time on his wristwatch. "Showtime," he announced calmly.

A split second later, there was a powerful explosion

far behind them, and the tunnel became harshly illuminated with orange and red light.

But then…a secondary explosion even louder than the first, closely followed by a third, fourth fifth, sixth…

The entire island seemed to be shaking from the triphammer detonations, the fire tunnel was cracking along the walls, hundreds of loose bricks were falling free.

Momentarily losing control of the Jetpacks, the men struggled to stay away from the walls as the tunnel started to break apart, wide cracks lancing along the interior, making countless bricks fall.

Desperately dodging out of the way, Cinco flew too low and scraped a boot heel across the floor, then Bolan went sideways to carom off the shuddering wall, sparks spraying off the housing as it rubbed the shattering bricks.

Suddenly, a painfully bright light filled the long tunnel. Glancing into a cracked rearview mirror, Bolan saw a monstrous fireball expanding along the tunnel like the exhaust charge of a firing cannon.

"Fly or die!" Bolan shouted, twisting the controls to maximum.

Side by side, the two men streaked along the collapsing tunnel, the steadily rising heat wave prickling their skin, and threatening to steal the very air from their lungs. A turbofan faltered, then another, and their control panels started to flash a warning signal as the speed of the Jetpacks began gradually to slow.

CHAPTER TWENTY-ONE

Every alarm the Brazilian space facility still possessed was going at full volume. The combination sounded almost as loud as the mind-numbing detonation that had ripped up through the concrete apron like a volcano, throwing dead men and broken machines high into the crystal-clear sky.

Stumbling through the swirling smoke, Dalton Greene had a wet cloth wrapped around his face to keep out the acidic fumes. There was a great deal of blood on his shirt, making it stick to his body armor, but none of it had come from his veins.

Only minutes ago, Greene had been in the makeshift kitchen getting a cup of coffee with some of the young recruits from New South Wales. They had been talking about the prostitutes of Adelaide at the Crazy Horse Saloon, telling lies and swapping jokes, reaffirming their love of life as soldiers always did after a successful mission. Then the world seemed to explode. Everybody was thrown off the floor, several of the terrorists smashing their heads against the bare concrete ceiling to come back down as decapitated corpses.

The window near Greene had violently shattered, spraying him with glass shards, cutting his clothing to pieces, but never reaching his flesh. Then a second explosion blew in the front door, and it slammed into a recruit, crushing him flat against the far wall. His blood and organs gushed out from the sides as if he were a squashed bug, and Greene got covered with the sticky life fluids.

Shuffling out of the assembly building, Greene saw that most of the facility had been damaged. Tilted buildings were on fire, smoldering debris was strewn everywhere, and bodies, or rather pieces of bodies, were sprinkled about, most of them still oozing blood.

"Shut off those damn alarms!" Greene commanded into his throat mike.

A moment later blessed silence returned, along with a pronounced ringing in both of his ears. Having fought in combat before, Greene knew that would soon pass. The effect was a minor annoyance, nothing more.

Searching for his Minimi machine gun, Greene staggered from the kitchen and down the hallway toward the front offices. The dead and the dying were everywhere, the smoky air foul with the stink of freshly spilled blood and soiled clothing.

Heading directly for the garage, Greene paused for a moment to allow the Gladiators to allow him entry, then he rushed inside. The ground floor was bustling with activity. He was pleased to see that the place was already being used as a field hospital. Wounded people were lying on the floor in neat rows while other members of Daylight hastily tied tourniquets, applied CPR or quietly used sharp knives to end unbearable pain.

Layne rushed in carrying an armload of medical supplies from the Rescue Hawk in the cistern. Gratefully, others converged on the man and began gathering sterile gauze or painkillers.

Seeing that everything was under control at the

moment, Greene went upstairs and found LoMonaco standing guard at a window, the Neostead shotgun lying across her lap, the fake miltop sitting on the floor by her boots.

"Sam!" Greene shouted, heading that way. But the woman never moved, or answered back, until he tapped her on the shoulder.

Abruptly looking up in surprise, she beamed a wide grin displaying a couple of broken teeth, then touched the side of her head and shrugged.

Tightening his grip on her shoulder, Greene scowled at the sight of the pinkish fluids trickling out of her ears. Concussion damage. Unless the woman received immediate medical attention, she would be permanently deaf. Unfortunately, the closest hospital was in Rio de Janeiro, about six hours away by a fast plane.

"Am I dying?" LoMonaco asked in a surprisingly normal voice, her hands going knuckle-white around the shotgun.

"No, you will live," Greene said, looking her directly in the face and pronouncing each word distinctly. "But you're deaf. Never will hear again."

Inhaling sharply, LoMonaco nodded at the dire pronouncement. "Are you okay?" she asked, reaching out to touch his gore-covered clothing.

"Not mine. Undamaged."

Briefly she smiled. "Good. What happened?" she slurred, fresh blood appearing on her lips.

Greene didn't react to that. Damn, she had massive internal damage. Samantha was already dead.

"I do not know what happened," he shouted. "Stay here! I will find out!"

"I have your six," LoMonaco said, trying to stand.

Greene pushed her back down. "Stay here! Here! Understand? You see anybody, shoot them. Guard that miltop!"

LoMonaco glanced down at the military laptop on the floor as if she had never seen the thing before. Then she turned around with renewed determination on her face. "I'll guard it with my life!" she stated, then she shuddered all over, nearly dropping the Neostead.

Patiently, Greene waited until the seizure passed, then stepped back to throw her a salute, turned and quickly left the crumbling building.

Killing LoMonaco would have been a kindness, but bad tactics. Now the crippled woman would serve as a burglar alarm. She would go down hard, of that Greene was sure, and the sound of her dying would give the rest of Daylight exact knowledge of where the enemy was at that moment. NATO, Mossad, CIA, British Intelligence, Greene had no idea who had attacked the island. But when he found out, there would be retribution on a scale unheard of in the history of the world. He would have the Skyhooks throw everything toward that one nation until it was burned out of existence!

Following the blast pattern of the debris on the ground, Greene became steadily more concerned as he drew closer to the launch pads and the fire tunnels. He stopped on a small slope designed to control fuel spills, and scowled. Off to the side of a tunnel was a large gaping hole in the pavement, thick smoke still rising high, and there was the nonstop crackle of bullets cooking off.

Removing the mask, Greene breathed in deeply. He clearly could smell the acidic stink of C-4 in the air, and knew the horrible truth. Somebody had blown up the armory, which logically meant that the *Cassandra* was gone, either stolen or destroyed. For some reason that summoned a wellspring of mindless rage. Shaking both fists, Greene bellowed at the sky, letting out all of his frustration. How could this have happened when they were so close to victory?

Over the distant jungle, Greene saw a tiny speck moving, jungle, the treetops wildly shaking underneath. Was that one of his Jetpacks? If so, it meant that the enemy had looted his stash of supplies before attacking. Excellent! That meant there either weren't enough of them to get the job done, or else they had been seriously damaged by the earlier bombardment. Possibly both.

"Bad move, boys," Greene said.

Kneeling on the dirty pavement, he opened the miltop, and started furiously typing.

WITH HIS JETPACK rattling like a vacuum cleaner after sucking up a penny, Bolan quickly headed for a small clearing inside the wall of the base.

Turning at the strange noise, a guard gasped at the sight of the flying man, and Bolan fired the Beretta, a stream of silenced bullets tearing away his life.

Landing among the rustling bushes, Bolan looked about for any more guards, but the area seemed clear. Most of the activity was down by the relatively unharmed garage, the four Gladiators standing sentry outside in a literal ring of steel. But even as he watched, the four robots broke formation to race across the vast field of rubble toward the east.

Directly toward Cinco.

"Incoming!" Bolan snarled into his throat mike.

"Bull, droids on your nine!" But there was only the crackle of the jamming field.

Swinging up the Zastava, Bolan fired a round at the treetops in that direction, clipping off a branch. If the man was nearby, he would understand the message.

His Jetpack started rattling even louder, and Bolan killed the engine and started to divest himself of the damaged machine. In spite of their best speed, he and Cinco had just barely gotten out of the fire tunnel in time. Like the discharge from a cannon, the funneled explosion had gone right past them to extend across the launch pad annihilating everything in its path.

The fantastic shock wave had slammed both of the men aside, and the only reason they had survived was that they were already in the air. If Bolan and Cinco hadn't been wearing earbuds, he felt sure they would now both be permanently deaf.

Spinning wildly about out of control, Cinco had disappeared into the east, toward the jungle, while Bolan was sent tumbling head over heels toward the distant ocean. He barely got the Jetpack under control again before splashing into the waves. Rising high once more, Bolan kicked the excess water off his boots, and grimly flew straight back to finish the mission. Until the miltop was secured, Bolan couldn't allow himself to stop or rest for any reason. There were too many innocent lives at stake. Win or lose, live or die, he was going in.

As the Jetpack fell to the grass, Bolan stretched for a moment, then checked the perimeter of the blast zone with his monocular. Any decent commander would check on the amount of destruction done to the facility, and with any luck…

There was Dalton Greene, kneeling on the pavement, his head bowed as if in prayer.

"Sorry, but God won't save you from me," Bolan muttered, dropping the monocular and swinging up the Zastava .50-caliber sniper rifle.

As the terrorist leader came into view in the scope, Bolan realized he was typing on a miltop, instantly switched from Greene's head to the miltop and fired.

The man reared back as a chunk of asphalt was blown away by the massive .50-caliber bullet. It slammed into the miltop, sending it sliding down the sloping hill toward the smoking crater.

Spinning to spoil the aim of a sniper, Greene then dove after the runaway computer.

Bolan levered in a fresh cartridge and fired again, catching the giant man still in the air. His ceramic body armor exploded into pieces from the glancing blow, violently throwing Greene below the rise and out of sight.

Quickly looking around, Bolan saw that none of the trees nearby would support his weight, so he burst into a full sprint toward the nearest building, some sort of an electronics laboratory judging from the rusty sign still attached to the exterior.

The front door was barely hanging in place from one twisted hinge. Kicking it away, Bolan saw an armed man turn, an F88 assault rifle in his grasp. They fired in unison.

The burst of 5.56 mm rounds ricocheted off the body armor worn by Bolan, but the thunderous 700-grain hardball round from the deadly Zastava blew a hole through the terrorist and the wall behind. Even as the man sagged, moaning, to the floor, Bolan was already racing up the stairs and levering in a fresh cartridge.

Reaching the next level, he saw that the lab had been cleaned out to make space for a barracks, the floor lined with bedrolls and inflatable pillows. But the windows were gone, shards of broken glass sparkling on top of everything, and there were numerous small pools of blood.

Charging to the window, Bolan tried to find Greene once more, but the billowing smoke from the fiery crater was making it very difficult to see clearly. Taking a fast look through the monocular, Bolan switched to UV function and got a glimpse of Greene reaching for the miltop. Locking that image into his mind, Bolan switched to the Zastava, aimed and fired, then switched back to the monocular.

Spurting blood, Greene was down, holding the ruin of his left hand, and the miltop was spinning crazily along the cracked expanse of concrete. As Bolan watched, it went right over the edge of the blast crater and out of sight.

Going back to the Zastava, Bolan fired five rounds into the area as fast as he could work the arming lever. When he took a look again through the monocular, Bolan couldn't find any traces of Greene. The terrorist leader was either dead, or he had gone after the miltop.

Clambering back down to the ground, Bolan took off at a full run after Greene, when he heard a dull whooping sound from a dark shadow across the pavement. An Apache!

Diving to the side, Bolan was hit multiple times by pebbles spraying out from the hammering arrival of the 30 mm rounds from the tribarrel chain gun. However, the gunship was seriously dented in several locations, and streaked with the residue of chemical explosions.

Stopping for a long second, Bolan aimed and fired. The Zastava roared, there came the sound of a splintering plastic and a startled cry.

Spinning quickly, the Apache suddenly straightened and gracefully landed only a few yards away.

Sprinting over, Bolan saw the dead pilot slumped behind the yoke. There was a large hole where his nose had formerly been located, and the back of his head was completely missing. Inside, the ceiling was thickly coated with what looked like overcooked oatmeal, splattered human brains.

Obviously, the Apache had taken damage from the earlier explosions in the cistern. Otherwise, even the Zastava wouldn't have been able to penetrate the plastic windshield. Bolan had gambled on that possibility, but the soldier felt no surge of pleasure at the minor victory. He had transportation again, but without a windshield he was a sitting target for anybody directly in front. Even if they missed him, a ricochet could easily take him out from behind.

Suddenly, a bullet zinged off the aft rotor assemble of the Apache, closely followed by several more. Racing around the machine, Bolan climbed in through the front, slapped the release on the safety harness holding the limp corpse in place, then shoved it outside.

Ignoring the blood and brains smeared across everything, Bolan turned off the autopilot and got the Apache back into the air. He neatly pivoted just as a large group of terrorists streamed over the slope with their assault rifles chattering steadily. Then a fat man knelt to aim a Carl Gustav rocket launcher.

Flipping the safety off the firing controls, Bolan cut loose with a long burst from the chain gun, the 30 mm rounds chewing the people apart as if they had been tossed into a wood chipper.

Hit multiple times, Layne fired the launcher as he collapsed, and the rocket skipped across the pavement to slam into the garage. The building violently exploded, bricks, flames and tattered bodies forming a monstrous geyser.

Then two Gladiators rolled out of the inferno, their weapons searching the sky for a target.

Switching to a missile pod, Bolan got a negative reading. A quick glance at the instrument board revealed that the Apache was out of Sidewinder missiles, and minirockets. Only the chain gun remained.

Flying sideways, Bolan chewed up the pavement alongside the robots, until finally getting the range. With the wind in his face, it was difficult to see, so the soldier went on gut instinct, trusting his combat reflexes. Now the 30 mm rounds stitched a row of dents across their tough armor. Angling upward, both of the Gladiators answered back with Uzi machine guns, and the 9 mm rounds peppered like hail across the cracked side windows. The plastic splintered slightly.

Hovering in the air, Bolan pivoted to face the deadly machines directly, aimed and fired again.

This time he concentrated on just one robot, the 30 mm rounds smashed aside an Uzi, then tore off a piece of the armor exposing the vulnerable interior. Sparks flew from the triphammer arrival of the big-bore rounds, hydraulic fluid squirted high like inhuman blood, then the interior of the robot burst into flames.

Still firing, the Gladiator began to spin in a circle, the machine pistol chattering away at the vast and empty sky. But now, the second Gladiator fired back, the 9 mm rounds ricocheting off the nose of the gunship, crawling steadily toward the open windshield.

Taking a moment as if he was merely at the shooting range, Bolan centered the chain gun on the same location as the last robot, and pressed the button. Man and Machine faced each other, their weapons firing nonstop. Even as the armor plate buckled on the robot, Bolan was hit in the chest and the shoulder from the fusillade. A hail of 9 mm rounds ricocheted around the interior of the Apache, and Bolan felt the armored seat hit several times as he stayed the course, pouring in the 30 mm rounds. Abruptly, the Uzi stopped as black smoke rose from inside the machine, then a short-circuit crackled over the armored chassis of the Gladiator a split second before the ammunition reserves violently detonated.

Leveling out again, Bolan angled toward the garage, strafing anybody on the ground with the chain gun. A dozen of the terrorists died before Bolan decided he had delayed long enough, and slid sideways across the destroyed base returning to the hunt for Greene.

Activating the thermal sensors, Bolan began to probe deep into the smoking ruin of the blast crater, when something flashed by the Apache in a blur. *That had been a Hellfire antitank missile!*

Quickly pivoting, Bolan saw an undamaged Black Hawk helicopter coming his way. Banking fast, Bolan got only a brief look at the other pilot, but there was no doubt that it was Dalton Greene, grinning like a madman as the side-mounted Remington .50-caliber machine guns surged into deadly action.

CHAPTER TWENTY-TWO

Soaring along the battered wall surrounding the space facility, Cinco kept a close watch out for Cooper, or any of the terrorists. But this section of the base seemed to be clear of any hostiles.

Except for me, Cinco added in dark humor.

Then he noticed that the barrel on his M16 was slightly bent out of alignment. He cursed bitterly. The rifle had to have gotten hit with a flying brick during their escape from the fire tunnel! The assault rifle was now useless, an eight-pound paperweight. However, there was still the 40 mm grenade launcher.

Landing gracefully on top of a palm tree, Cinco took the weapon apart, tossing away the rifle, but keeping the M203. His old M203 would have been pretty much useless without the M16 attached. But this new launcher was actually designed to be used separately, and came with a pair of pistol-grip-style handles, along with a convenient side-port for thumbing in fresh shells. Cinco didn't have many of the long shells for the launcher, so he would use the S&W Magnum revolver first, and keep the M203 in reserve strictly for emergencies.

Suddenly, a frond was ripped away from the palm tree, and a full second later there came the rumbling echo of a high-power sniper rifle.

Instantly taking flight, Cinco whipped out a monocular and scanned the horizon. Unfortunately, the billowing smoke from the recent detonations covered the base, making it difficult to see clearly. A sniper rifle always came with an excellent scope, so either the person operating the weapon was a damn poor shot, or else Bolan had deliberately done it to get his attention. But why?

The answer arrived a few seconds later, as he heard the clanking rumble of armored treads below his position and two Gladiators rolled out of the billowing smoke.

Twisting both of the handles, Cinco rose even higher, and moved rapidly away from the robots. As he departed, they both opened fire, but the 9 mm rounds only punched holes in the empty air. Bye-bye, boys! Nice meeting you! he thought.

Streaking through the smoke, Cinco came out the other side coughing and dirty. That was when he saw a battered Apache having a dogfight with a Black Hawk, the air between them full of tracers.

It took only a second to figure out what was happening, but he paused, unsure of how to proceed. His .357 Magnum revolver and M203 wouldn't dent the armor on a Black Hawk. He would need something a lot more powerful.

Just for a moment, Cinco toyed with the idea of trying to grab a Gladiator and dropping it on the Black Hawk from above, then he saw the pile of ragged corpses near the garage. Doing a fast swing over the pile of dead terrorists, Cinco spotted a lot of F88 assault rifles, an XM-25 grenade launcher, several pistols and the Carl Gustav. Bingo! Immediately, he landed and waddled closer.

Under closer inspection, the Carl Gustav seemed intact, and searching the nearby corpse yielded Cinco two live rockets. Unfortunately, both of them were antitank. They had a decent range, but most definitely weren't designed to use on a nimble aircraft. Cinco would have to get in close, dangerously close, to make sure of a kill and not take out the Apache by accident.

The decision made, Cinco loaded the Carl Gustav, attached the other round to his web harness and lifted off again in a rush of hot air, and swept upward in a steep curve to join the aerial battle.

The pair of big helicopters were only blurs inside an artificial hurricane of smoky exhaust. Stray rounds from their weapons systems filled the sky in random bursts, and Cinco was rocked hard as the Jetpack was hit twice by shrapnel. The damage was minor, but one of the turbofans now had a high-pitched rattle, and the man knew that he had only moments left before he was heading back toward the ground, whether he wanted to be or not.

Then I seriously have to not fuck this up! Cinco thought, awkwardly hefting the launcher. The open mouth of the man-portable device was a wind trap, and the faster he moved, the more it fought to tear out of his grip. Not going to happen! he vowed.

Black and green, large and small, the Apache and Black Hawk dove, darted and spun around each other like mad insects trapped in a glass jar.

Staying carefully out of the way, Cinco loaded the launcher and coolly waited for the two combatants to break apart to allow the onboard computers to reacquire target stats and trajectories. During an aerial fight this close to the ground, it would be easy for a helicopter pilot to dart in the wrong direction and slam into a tree or the unforgiving ground. They had to break soon, or risk killing themselves! When it happened, Cinco knew that he would have only a few seconds, maybe less to get the job done, and if he missed...

Suddenly, the helicopters spiraled away from each other, and for a brief instant Cinco saw open air between them. His heart beating wildly, the man carefully aimed, paused to correct for windshear, then pulled the trigger. The rocket streaked away to slam into the side of the Black Hawk with thundering pyrotechnics that blanketed the sky!

As the roiling cloud of dark smoke cleared, Cinco was astonished to see that the Black Hawk was still flying, even though the entire left side was split wide open, numerous different-colored fluids freely gushed out from the complex machinery.

Just then, the windowless Apache swung round the Black Hawk, and ruthlessly Bolan filled the crippled helicopter with 30 mm rounds from the spinning chain gun.

The interior seemed to explode from all of the ricochets and sparks. Seats disintegrated, the other hatch was torn away, and Greene's mouth opened in a scream just as the Black Hawk burst into flames.

Entirely out of control, the burning wreck plummeted swiftly downward to crash violently on the cracked concrete, then detonate, the reserve fuel and spare munitions combining to form a fireball of gargantuan proportions.

Shouting in triumph, Cinco paused when he saw that Bolan wasn't landing the Apache. Instead, he headed away from the crippled Black Hawk to descend into the fiery abyss of the underground storeroom.

Realizing there was only one thing that could make the man undertake a suicide mission, Cinco shouldered the launcher, and streaked across the base to join his friend in finding the miltop.

Cinco got only halfway there before two squat shapes appeared out of the billowing smoke with their Uzi machine guns ablaze. Cinco cursed as hot lead painfully stitched across his chest to ricochet off his body armor and tear apart the controls.

As the turbofans died, Cinco released the launcher to try to get out of the rig. But it was too little, too late. Dropping way too fast, he hit the ground hard, and both of his legs shattered. White-hot pain filled his world, and Cinco lost all track of time.

Eventually, reality began sluggishly to return, and Cinco blearily saw that the two Gladiators were converging on the blast crater, not him. *The tin bastards were after Cooper!*

Racked with unimaginable pain, Cinco dragged himself away from the robots, leaving behind a wide trail of blood. Where was the damn thing? It had to be nearby, it had to be!

Spotting the launcher, Cinco redoubled his efforts as cold adrenaline filled his veins. Reclaiming the weapon, the agent shook the sweat from his eyes, took a deep breath, then maneuvered the second rocket from his web harness and loaded the Carl Gustav. Shaking with the intense pain, he aimed and fired.

The antitank rocket streaked away to slam into the first Gladiator, the powerful blast engulfing both of the machines and tearing them apart. Loose treads, live shells and circuit boards wildly bounced across the ground in glorious destruction.

A split second later, the Apache rose into view dripping flame from numerous locations. Landing on the edge of the crater, Bolan scrambled out of the aircraft carrying a military laptop. He hit the ground running just before the Apache toppled backward over the edge. Almost immediately it thunderously exploded, the strident blast sending the bleeding man tumbling across the littered ground.

As he came to a ragged stop, Bolan yanked open the miltop and began to type furiously....

EPILOGUE

Dappled sunlight streamed into the Oval Office through the bulletproof windows, and the French doors were open, admitting a warm refreshing breeze.

"So they're all destroyed?" the President asked, steepling his hands on top of the desk. "These Skyhooks?"

"Completely, sir," Hal Brognola reported, checking a Justice Department–issue smartphone. "Striker had them detach from whatever they had found, and simply enter into the atmosphere all by themselves. The Skyhooks completely vaporized before reaching the cloud level."

"Good to hear," the President said with a smile. "Now, will there be public trials for the members of Daylight, or did they all, how shall we say, resist arrest?"

"There were no survivors, sir."

"Honestly?"

"Yes, sir."

"Problem solved."

Outside the White House a wing of jet fighters streaked by overhead in tight formation, closely followed by two more wings.

"I see that the Air Force still has you under protection," Brognola said. "Out of curiosity, sir, will there be any fallout for you on the political front?"

"Not really." The President leaned back in his leather chair. "Our ambassador to the UN is going to strongly push for a unilateral, multinational effort to clean space of all that debris."

"After what happened to Caracas, and everywhere else, I would think that'll pretty much be a slam dunk. If not, they're idiots."

"Well, they are politicians, Hal."

Tactfully, Brognola didn't respond.

"I understand that Ms. Carrington is okay," the President said.

"Yes, sir. The Terraquad may be a true all-terrain vehicle, but it's slower than DC traffic, especially in open water. She reached the rescue team just in time to be shipped back home."

"Speaking of which…" the President began.

"Already taken care of, sir," Brognola said. "The Justice Department sent Elizabeth off to Aspen for a couple of weeks. Just a grateful nation's way of saying thanks for her assistance."

"That is one mighty tough lady," the President said, giving his highest compliment. "If we ever need a new recruit for Stony Man, I think she might do very well."

"Already under consideration, sir."

"Good to hear. Now, what about this William Cinco?"

"Willard," Brognola corrected. "He's recuperating nicely at the Mayo Clinic. Apparently, his legs were merely broken, not shattered, and after a few months of traction, he'll be back on the job."

The President's demeanor took on a sly aspect. "You

know, Hal," he said slowly, "we could really use a man like that here."

"Not a chance in hell," Brognola snorted. "Cinco is a fanatical patriot, and he can't wait to get back to Mexico."

"Pity."

"Oh, on the other hand, he has expressed interest in working again with Striker."

"They did make a good team. Speaking of which, for once I would like to thank Striker in person."

Brognola shook his head. "Sorry, sir. He's already handling another problem."

"Anything serious?" the President asked, his smile fading.

"There's always something, sir. But Striker will never let us down."

* * * * *

JAMES AXLER

DEATH LANDS

No Man's Land

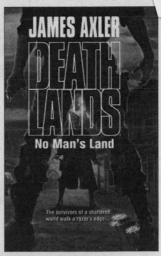

The survivors of a shattered world walk a razor line.

A civil war raging in the Des Moines River valley forces Ryan and his companions to take sides, or die—because somewhere in the middle of the generations-old conflict is a lost redoubt. But Snake Eye, the deadliest gunslinger in Deathlands, stands between them and the way out...and he won't step aside until he has Ryan's head.

Available November 2012!

TAKE 'EM FREE
2 action-packed novels plus a mystery bonus

NO RISK
NO OBLIGATION TO BUY

AleX Archer
CITY OF SWORDS

The road to hell is paved with holy relics.

Drawn to France to explore the myth of Saint Christopher and the dog-headed men, archaeologist Annja Creed finds herself targeted by mercenaries. At the source is a descendant of King Charlemagne, who thinks collecting the world's most precious swords will fulfill his ancestor's failed goal to build the City of God. Now he has his eye on a very special sword— Annja's. And he'll have to kill her to get it.

*Available **November 2012** wherever books are sold.*

GOLD EAGLE ®

www.readgoldeagle.blogspot.com

GRA39